ALSO BY D.J. BERSHAW

SISTERS IN ARMS SERIES

Other Blood

Blood's A Rover

Blood Tide

Blood Sisters

OTHER NOVELS

Saving Sophie Scholl

Guardian Angel

Eco-Freak

Seen the Elephant, Heard the Owl

ORAL WARS

by

D. J. Bershaw

For

Kenneth R. Cantwell

Published by Sucker's Junk Press
P.O. Box 85
Lafayette, OR 97127

Third Printing, March 2020

ISBN:

Cover design by Kate Mashall (kmarshallarts@gmail.com

PROLOGUE:

The first thing Byron Duncan saw when he stopped on the Wildwood Trail to take a piss was a stack of women's clothing neatly piled on a thick, rotten log lying beside the trail. He examined it carefully as he continued drenching the trailside ferns, then, everything tucked away, moved nearer the log for a closer look.

Blue and white Nike cross-trainers supported a folded pair of national blue running shorts, a white cotton short-sleeved shirt, a sports bra of indeterminate size -- but not small -- and a pair of cotton panties.

Puzzled, Byron stood up as straight as his five-and-a-half foot frame would allow and scanned the surrounding sunlit forest. No nude ladies in evidence, and the neatness of the piled clothing suggested foul play hadn't been involved.

Admittedly, Byron had women on his mind. Out of Dental School for two years, a faithful Mormon with his Temple Pass validated, his single status was the only cloud in his world. An unmarried Saint, unsealed to another in holy matrimony, had no chance of entering the Celestial Kingdom, the highest tier of Mormon Heaven, and this had come to obsess him.

He had been close right after graduation with a blonde pixie named Bethann Fretwell. But Bethann had run off with a Sears appliance salesman from Klamath Falls who'd been a good half-foot taller than poor Byron.

That had been the crux of his problem with Bethann, he firmly believed. He was short. He made a good living -- most dentists did, these days -- but he was short. He leaned toward the log and craned his neck, viewing the woman's Nikes from a different angle, then sighed with resignation. Nines or tens, he guessed, which even in a woman's size, meant this nude person was taller than Byron.

His habitual depression, somewhat alleviated by his early morning workout, descended on him like a grey cloak. The unfairness of his situation rankled him. How could a benevolent God deny his faithful servant the highest level of everlasting glory because of size?

A low, harsh growl some distance up the trail interrupted Byron's reverie. Startled, he turned to see a large cat-like creature fifty feet away, regarding him with dark brown eyes. It moved toward him, growling repeatedly, step-by-step, its long tail switching above its tawny rump.

At first, he thought the thing was a cougar, but its golden-brown fur bore stripes extending from the short muzzle, up over the round skull, and along the long, muscular back. Coarse hackles rose above its shoulders, and the wide-open mouth displayed massive saliva-wet fangs. Its growls grew louder.

Byron forgot any question of the beast's identity or probable country of origin. He turned and ran as though Satan himself pursued. Like the rest of him, however, his legs were short.

He didn't get far.

He didn't last long.

ONE

When Captain Karl Elch, Chief of Detectives for the Portland Police, arrived at the homicide scene in Forest Park, Detective Lieutenant Ron Wismer was watching his partner, Boothe Deakins, monitor the measurement and search teams.

Wismer *felt* rather than heard the tall Lincolnesque Captain approach. Elch was not a heavy man, but his big footfalls were solid, and this was not the first time the Lieutenant had literally felt the earth move under his feet.

Of course, Wismer mused, a lot of Portland's politicians, self-styled environmentalists, and business people had experienced the same thing, only figuratively. Elch was an apolitical no-nonsense man in a somewhat non-sensical town, and high-profile miscreants frequently heard the long arm of the law coming for them down the halls of power, one solid step at a time.

"Morning, Ron. Mornin' Boothe," their Captain said pleasantly, "What we got here?"

The Lieutenant looked sharply at his boss before replying. Elch occasionally sprinkled his speech with African-Americanisms, as if to remind the world that his mother was the daughter of a black Air Force sergeant who'd been stationed in Germany. Elch's own father was a *Bundesgrenzshutz* officer who'd courted the Sergeant's daughter over forty years earlier. The local press commonly referred to Elch as 'African-American,' but sometimes as 'Germano-American,' and every once in a while as 'Afro- Germano-American.' The latter always tickled the Captain, and he usually called the reporter who wrote the story to tell him or her how the attention to detail was appreciated.

"A dead dentist," Wismer said finally, going for the smart remark rather than the others he'd had on the

7

tip of his tongue. "Also a woman's running outfit, shoes and clothing." Out of the corner of his eye, he saw Boothe's lips twist briefly into a trademark Deakins' smile.

"Um," Elch replied, and lifted the tarp up from the body. "*Lieber Gott!*" he said in shocked tones, looking down at the mangled remains of Byron Duncan.

"A mess, huh?" Wismer said, his question rhetorical.

"Eviscerated the poor kid. Looks like a young teen-ager."

"Twenty-seven. Small for his age."

"Won't be getting any bigger."

The Lieutenant shook his head. "Nope."

"Some parts are..." the Captain bent down, peered around the victim's abdominal cavity "...missing."

"Our best guess is it was a cougar. They don't ordinarily kill for sport. Eat everything but the stomach and the intestines."

Elch's hazel gaze lifted to Wismer. His sizeable nose seemed to twitch for an instant. "You wouldn't be puttin' me on, would you, Ron?"

Wismer shrugged, tried to keep a smile off his face. "You grew up on the mean streets of Wiesbaden, Germany, Sir. I'm a country boy from Central Oregon. Every once in a while, we'd lose a calf to a cougar. I'm no expert, but maybe I know more than you do about 'em." Behind their boss, another grin flashed across Deakins' pale freckled features.

"So you think it's a cougar?"

"Well, yes and no. It's probably a cat, and big. Cats typically kill animals our size by biting through the spine at the back of the neck. Everything fits there, except that Cougars will try to stash their kills. Drag 'em somewhere and shove 'em under a log. Or cover 'em, at least. So they can come back later for another meal."

The captain shook his head at the thought, looked down at the body again. "Jesus. Maybe somebody scared it off?"

"Probably not. This isn't the main trail, not that many runners until the evening usually, according to the people I've talked to. The two women who found him only found him two hours ago. It's ten in the morning. He was supposed to be at work at eight. He had to be attacked sometime between six and seven, likely closer to six. He was on his way back to his car, we think, would then go home and shower before going to the office. Timeline's pretty solid."

"Cat would have had plenty of time to hide the body?"

"Oh, yeah."

"You sure it's a cat, then?"

"Every part of the death says 'cat,' Captain. The neck, the obvious claw marks, and eating the choice parts first. Dogs rip and tear, but lack the biting strength to do the neck thing. Dogs bring their prey down, then start eating, usually before the prey's dead."

"You talk to the Oregon Zoo? They're not that far away from here."

"Sure. They said everybody's home this morning."

"Exotic animal permits?"

"Ongoing, but probably no luck there. The yahoos who kept big, bad pets like lions, cougars, carnivorous swamp burros, that kind of shit, twenty years ago, aren't around anymore. Laws got tougher. People who have 'em now in urban circumstances are usually part of some exotic animal support group. Critters don't *get* out."

"Carnivorous Swamp Burros? Never heard of them."

9

"Oh, yeah. Down in Guatemala. Big suckers. Got a fierce bray. Transfixes the victim, then the burro hoofs 'em to death."

"You *are* shittin' me."

Wismer grinned at the taller man. "Yes, Sir." He couldn't look at Deakins, could practically smell her amusement.

"So, how long before it has to kill again?"

"Two, three, days. Woulda been longer if the body'd been stashed." The Lieutenant looked down at the late dentist. "Guess we could leave him here, just off the trail. Stake it out, put a couple people with night eyes and sniper rifles up on the hillside...." He let the sentence hang.

"You're a cold bastard, Lieutenant."

"Yes, Sir."

Elch turned to Wismer's partner. "I don't suppose I have to ask you if you approve of your partner's suggestion, young lady?"

"No, Sir," Boothe replied, nodding her platinum blonde head, her grey eyes serious. "I'd volunteer for the stake-out." Deakins was generally thought to be a 'shoot first, and ask questions later' sort of cop, but Wismer had never known her to ask questions. She just shot, though not recklessly, and always to good effect.

"So, two-three days then?" Elch continued.

Wismer nodded. "Think so. And Captain?"

"Yeah?"

"Goes much longer'n that, it's not a cat."

Elch studied the huge moss-laden trees around them without looking at Wismer, then looked down at his feet. "You said it was."

"Yeah, I know," Wismer agreed, with a rueful smile.

Deakins seemed to perk up at his last words. Not a good sign. She was into all that northwest weird, legendary animal shit.

10

Sighing, the Captain raised his head. His smile matched Wismer's. "As of this moment, you two are in charge of this investigation. So, let's have a look at that running gear."

TWO

Paul Tiernan firmly grasped the crown of old Mister Chen's mandibular right central incisor in the forcep's beak and turned the tooth gently to the patient's left. A bead of yellow-cream pus appeared on the crest of the gum tissue and rolled around the circumference of the tooth, briefly making the tooth appear to be set in a Cloisonne porcelain base.

Since Mister Chen gave no sign of pain, Paul rotated the incisor in the opposite direction, severing its connection to the bone around it. Another short turn to the left and the tooth was out of the mouth and on the bracket table behind the patient's head. Three more incisors soon joined the first, two sutures were placed, and Mister Chen's new partial denture shortly resided in its intended home.

When instructions and a prescription for pain meds had been given to Mister Chen's English-speaking daughter, the spry old man gave Paul a surprisingly strong hug, bathing him in fumes of stale cigarettes and some odd-smelling soap, presumably Chinese.

The two immigrants departed toward the front desk, escorted by Paul's assistant, Gina, and Paul gratefully retreated to his private office to write up the chart, his workday over.

He'd just finished the chart when the green light of his private phone line lit up. After regarding it warily for a moment, he lifted the receiver from its cradle. "Yeah," he answered, reasonably certain his family wouldn't be calling this time of day. During June, the ranch generally occupied his father and brothers until nearly sundown.

"Hey, Paulie, you goin' to the Multnomah County meeting tonight?" It was Marty Pastore, one of his less-reserved classmates in dental school.

"Thought I would," Paul replied, smiling. Hard not to, with the up-beat Marty.

"You missed the fistfight at the last one. Terry Koch rode his Harley to the meeting. Leather outfit, the works. One of the old guys -- with a skin full -- accused him of not bein' a dentist. When Terry protested, the old guy popped him one. They even rolled around the floor."

"Sounds swell," Paul agreed, laughing. The average age of dentists in Oregon was the mid-fifties, so there were plenty of old guys, most of them wealthy, and most of them still hard-chargers.

"You talk to The Creep lately?"

Paul's grin faded slightly. "This morning. She said she'd probably be there." Claire 'The Creep' McManus was generally assumed by Paul's compatriots to be his girlfriend. Paul wasn't sure that was the right term, but their relationship, begun in college, continued.

Claire was his height, and they'd both played basketball at Oregon State before dental school. She was stubborn, willful, combative, a gifted athlete, and a damned good dentist. And damned hard to put up with, Paul thought, but probably worth the effort. Sometimes he told her the only reason he tolerated her was the simple fact that no one else would.

He had scars from her reactions to those remarks.

"When you two gonna get married?" Marty asked cheerfully, bringing Paul back to the conversation. All his classmates ribbed Paul incessantly about Claire, Marty among the worst.

That was worth a guffaw. "Soon, Marty. Soon. You'll be the first to know. Hell, you could even be my best man. And did I ever mention Claire has a just-younger sister? Kathy. She's a firefighter. Claire says she's a real handful. We'd be glad to fix you up."

13

Now Marty sounded worried. "No, I don't think so. I'll stick with the nice Italian Catholic girls my family finds for me." His laugh returned. "At least they can cook. All The Creep can do is eat like a horse."

Paul tried to put as much innuendo as possible into his response. "I will respectfully decline to comment on what Doctor McManus can or cannot do, Doctor Pastore. I'll see you tonight. Be sure and bring your brass knuckles, in case things get out of hand again."

He hung up the phone, sat looking vaguely at his class portrait on the wall opposite his desk. He could just make out Claire McManus' blunt, pugnacious features, framed with dark blonde hair and dominated by striking greenish-gold eyes. Somewhere down in his heart-of-hearts, Paul knew he loved her, though it wasn't easy to accept or admit. Why else, he thought, would he have purchased a practice in Tualatin, just south of Portland, unless it was to be near Claire, who worked less than a mile away, for Westside Dental Group, a DMO? His family was still upset he hadn't come back to Central Oregon.

Regardless of his motives, unconscious, subconscious, or otherwise, there was never a doubt where you stood with Claire, and that had proved to be both curse and blessing. She was just so *damned* overwhelming.

She was a lot of other things, too, Paul admitted, thinking of the past weekend, when they'd gone for an early morning run together, then ended up back at his condo and back in bed. He might never get used to Claire's intensity during sex. He never wanted to, either. In rare soul-searching moments, Paul thought about Claire and children -- *their* children -- but that seemed unlikely.

Claire'd probably eat 'em.

14

THREE

When the doorbell produced no results at the Janos residence, Emmett McManus used his key to open the gate to the side yard. Shutting the gate behind him, he walked along a narrow concrete pathway surrounded by rhododendrons which had not quite stopped blooming. Last year's leaves had been completely removed from the bed, and a fresh layer of bark mulch layered over the ground around the individual bushes.

McManus approved of that tidiness and attention to detail. In its way, his job at Westside Dental Group was not unlike being a gardener. His official title was Operations Oversight Coordinator, but what he actually did were those things outside the purview of regular company business, let alone the practice of dentistry. A post-Vietnam Army Special Forces background provided just the sorts of skills needed for his employment. In very common terms, McManus was a leg-breaker, though he thought of himself as an 'options purveyor,' aiding those whose lives had grown in an undesirable direction, and helping them make enlightened decisions concerning their future.

Passing beyond the corner of the big house, McManus followed the path as it curved toward a much larger slab of aggregate concrete bounded by a low metal railing. He stepped to the railing, and looked down upon the over-sized swimming pool below.

The pool never failed to bring a smile to McManus' unremarkable features. Shaped in outline like an enormous upper molar, it was perhaps the one tacky thing owned by Konstantine Janos, the CEO of Westside Dental Group.

The middle, or palatal root, longer than the others, housed a very complete and exotic spa. Resplendent in the center of the frothing waters lay the long, tanned form of McManus' employer, a book in his big hands and a small cooler of beer on the deck beside him.

McManus strode quietly down the wide spiral steps to the pool level, and stood beside the spa, his hands in the pockets of his tan dockers.

"Want a beer, Emmett?" Janos asked, without looking up from his book. McManus seldom succeeded in sneaking up on the tall Greek immigrant. The man possessed uncanny hearing.

McManus shook his head. "A bit early, Kon."

"Migod, man! You're Irish! C'mon."

"We're not all drinkers. As you well know, I personally dislike the loss of control. Besides, I have some news of possible import."

Now he had Janos' attention. Dark brown eyes flashed with curiosity as the big man set the book aside and picked up a large bath towel from beside the cooler. "Tell me," Janos said, levering to his feet, and wiping his sweaty features. The bubbling water continued to swirl around his lower body, which appeared unencumbered by a swimsuit.

McManus hunkered down, and tried to select his words carefully. "Your friend, Doctor Lu, has engaged an east coast consulting firm, Phelan Associates."

Janos' habitual smile faded slightly. His handsome features grew concerned. "What's that mean exactly?"

"He's up to something."

The tall Greek snorted. "That's nothing new, Emmett.
The little sneak's *always* up to something."

"The Phelans are a nasty piece of something, Kon. They're like badgers or ferrets."

"*Lawyers*?" Few dentists or physicians found the practice of the law anything but enemy territory, and mined, at that.

16

McManus chuckled. "No. They winkle out things, things away from the ordinary, hopefully buried by time and effort, hidden from the hand or eye of man. Things thought to be *safe*." His voice turned grim. "They roll over stones to find what's beneath, and they don't much care how they do it."

"Violence?" Janos understood violence. He'd been in a LRRPS unit in Vietnam as a very young grunt.

"On occasion. But mostly, they are resourceful and persistent. Or at least the old man was. This current bunch may be more action-oriented."

"You seem to know a lot about them."

"My Grandmother, back in the Old Country, was a Phelan. When my parents came here, to the West, we kept in touch with our shirttail family in the east, though we'd almost never seen them. Christmas cards, the rare letter or phone call. Now, here they are, three of them."

"Will they talk to you?" Janos draped his towel over his shoulders, reached for his unfinished beer.

"Probably not much," McManus said, shrugging. "They're in their twenties, I'm forty-five. I'm old and out-of-date."

"You're five years younger than me."

McManus' reply was very soft. "We're in different lines of work, Kon. Age doesn't matter so much in yours, though the young bucks and buckettes may *think* you're an old fogey, you control the single largest source of new dental jobs in the Portland area. They *have* to respect you."

"The Company pays well, provides up-to-date workplaces, good equipment, and great benefits," Janos replied, climbing up the single step out of the spa. He wrapped the towel around his waist, stood dripping on the concrete. "It's what I wanted when I got out of Dental School, and that's what the

17

Company's going to provide." He grinned at his leg-breaker. "But you've heard all this before."

McManus nodded. "I'll talk to the young Phelens. Perhaps they'll tell me what Doctor Lu is up to."

The two men began to walk up the spiral steps toward the large, sprawling house. "Lately," the Greek observed, "Benny Lu seems to be fixated on the Mormons. Sozye Dental Associates is growing faster than his company, Considerate Care."

"The Saints can be very aggressive in business."

"Each graduating class at Oregon Health and Sciences Dental School is damned close to half-Mormon. A lot of them go back to Utah or Idaho, but, from his start-up in the Sixties, Nephi Sozye made it a point to hire every local Mormon he could entice on board."

Janos opened the sliding door to his home's bottom level and ushered the shorter man inside. They walked through the long, lower family room with its overhead projection television, pool table, and climate-controlled herpetarium. A large Black Tegu, yellow-striped and over three feet long, stared malevolently at the passing humans through the thick glass of the herpetarium. It pushed up onto its front legs and turned as they walked by, watching with unblinking black eyes filled with hunger.

McManus ignored the big lizard, happy that it couldn't get through the glass. "It seems strange for the large group practices here to be sharply divided along such incredibly ethnic and religious lines," he told his boss. They'd reached the elevator to the upper levels of the home, and Janos punched the button.

"Always has been, but the groups came and went. Painless Parker, Harry Semler, Larry Bernard, the Brodsky kid. The old names, the ones with all the good stories. Mostly the downtown was Jewish. The Asians were Japanese then, east out toward Gresham,

18

or west by Aloha and Hillsboro. Farm kids who'd gone to dental school. Roman Catholics in the northeast and southeast. West side was a mix. When I got out of dental school and started the company, there really wasn't a big group on the west side. We bought out some people, made a few payoffs, built a couple offices."

The elevator door opened. "And the rest is history," McManus said.

The two men stepped inside the cage. Janos smiled and nodded as he pushed for the third floor. "And luck. We've kept the company lean, held the paperwork down -- damn paperwork is the bane of health care -- and I keep my finger on the pulse of docs in the trenches."

"My niece mentioned you took the Tualatin office to lunch on Tuesday."

"Yeah, nice bunch of people out there, work together real well. I try to keep them happy, listen to their thoughts on how the company should evolve. And *only* the docs go to lunch with me. They'll tell me all I need to know."

"Claire seems very pleased."

Janos grunted, white teeth flashing against his tan. "Well, she's real dedicated, just works her butt off." The elevator opened on the third level, and they started down the hallway to Janos' private study. "Say, Emmett, I've been meaning to ask. Why do they call your niece 'The Creep?' I mean, she's a swell kid, maybe a little aggressive, but the staff and patients love her. 'Creep' seems unfair, somehow. Wrong."

McManus gave a rare laugh. "It's a pet name from the family. My brother and his wife provided it. Claire practically came out of womb crawling. By the time she was three months old, she could reach any part of their small home. The first thing my brother Patrick would ask when he arrived home from his workday was, 'Where's the Creeper?' Over the years, it

19

got shortened to 'The Creep,' then followed her into school and beyond."

"Well, that's better." The tall dentist bent down, let the door scan inspect his right eye. A dull whir, followed by a click, and he opened the study door. "I understand she's quite an athlete, too. Played at OSU?"

"Yes. Basketball mainly, but she tries to win at everything she does."

"Give me a jock every time," Janos replied, and took a seat behind his desk. He motioned McManus toward the opposite chair. "Now, tell me what you can about these cousins of yours."

The ex-soldier gathered his thoughts as he sat down, deciding what he *could* tell, and knowing full well what he *couldn't*.

FOUR

By the time Paul Tiernan arrived at the Oregon Medical Association building on southwest Corbett, the line along the no-host bar was two-deep. Trying to spot an accessible crevice somewhere between the packed bodies of his peers, he reflected that the monthly meeting of the Multnomah County Dental Society was ever-thus.

It wasn't that dentists were a bunch of drunks, but for a fair number of practitioners, Friday was a day for golf, fishing, or other recreation, and the Thursday evening dinner meetings were the kick-off of a three-day weekend.

Unbruised and only slightly battered after fighting the mob for a glass of Oregon Pinot, Paul located Marty Pastore at a small table in a far corner and dropped into the opposite chair. "No riots yet?" he asked Marty, then took a long swallow of his wine.

Marty wig-wagged his right hand about six inches above the table top. "Not yet, but Stan Lund was crowing about his 'mercury-free' practice within earshot of a couple of State Board guys, and they were givin' him the fish-eye."

"They'll make a mental note, pull his file tomorrow, stamp it 'Suspicious.' Then when his 'mercury-free' fillings start coming out in a few years, the first patient complaint will bring the Board investigators down on him big-time."

"That's okay," Marty replied. "Lund's a prick."

Paul agreed with that, maybe tacking the word 'arrogant' in front of 'prick.' "Still," he said, "nobody wants to see the Board's blackshirts in their front office, cleaning out charts, quizzing the staff, and chaining the front door shut."

"The Dental Gestapo," Marty said. "But even *I* do the occasional posterior composite, one or two surfaces, real conservative, and I know you do, too. Hell, *everybody* does."

"Sure. As long as you keep an eye on them, the patients understand they're more toxic than amalgam, and they don't hold up like silver amalgam or gold, it's acceptable."

"Here comes 'The Creep,'" said Marty, suddenly more animated and cheerful, looking over Paul's head into the crowd. He began waving.

Paul started to turn, felt a familiar hand squeezing his right shoulder. "Hey, babe," said Claire McManus in her usual throaty tones, bending down to his ear. Paul smiled, watching Marty react to Claire's voice. Even when guys teased him about Claire, or were uneasy around her, they all *loved* that voice.

"Hi, Marty," Claire said, deliberately an octave higher, and sat down at the third chair. She wore tan slacks and a greeny-gold blouse that matched her eyes, with a navy blue blazer hanging over her broad shoulders.

"You got your hair cut," Paul said, looking her over. She looked great. A nice, warm feeling developed in his stomach, one that had nothing to do with the wine.

"Yeah." She fluffed her dark blonde hair. "Whenever I can't see my ears...well, *you* know." Her wide mouth curved into an urchin's grin, personal and private, for Paul alone.

Even watching Claire, Paul felt Marty's antennae go up. She knew their classmates razzed Paul about her, and whenever she could stoke the fires of speculation, she did.

"You want something to drink?" Paul asked.

Claire glanced over at the crush of bodies at the bar. "No, that's okay, dear. I'll share yours." She grabbed Paul's wine and finished it in one gulp.

"Yes!" Marty crowed, thumping the table with a fist. "'The Creep' strikes again."

"You know, Marty," Claire said, her pale gaze shifting from Paul to Marty as she licked wine off her lips. "If you don't make nice, Paul and I won't let you be Godfather to our first-born."

Marty's imagination had apparently never gone past the sex part. He goggled at Claire, speechless for once. "Babies..?" he finally choked out.

"What, you think we don't *want* kids?" She pantomimed rocking an infant in her arms. "Of course, we need to find *you* a wife first, so the baby can have *Godparents*." She looked briefly at Paul. "Did you remember to tell Marty about my sister Kathy? She'd be perfect. They'd make a sweet couple. We could have a double wedding!"

Marty had now turned a stricken shade of bilious white, a color which Paul hadn't thought occurred in nature. He reached across the table and gripped Marty's right forearm. "Relax, Marty. She's kidding!" Marty looked anything but reassured, reaching automatically for his drink while Claire cracked up.

Conversation around the trio slowed as attention turned to Claire. Paul thought the sight of a tall, rather elegant, well-dressed female dentist having a laughing fit must take precedence over talk about crowns, root canals, new dental materials, stock options, vacation homes, and large German automobiles. Fortunately, his back was to the crowd, leaving a now red-faced and spluttering Marty with a dozen or so people looking directly at him and wondering what he'd done that was so damned amusing.

Interest subsided as Marty regained his composure. He sat scowling at Claire and Paul, both of whom grinned back unabashedly. "You never told me anything about you two getting married and having kids," he complained to Paul.

"Today's the first *I* heard about it," Paul replied, wishing Claire had left him some wine.

"Me, too," Claire added, "but I think Paul's got the basic idea down to the point where I could *get* pregnant."

Her remark cheered Marty up immediately, and Paul guessed there were going to be unfair comparisons made between Italian and Irish Catholics, at least the men. He shoved his chair back and got to his feet. "I'll go get us some more drinks while you two discuss things." He pointed at Marty's glass and lifted his eyebrows. "What're you drinking?"

"Seven and Seven."

"And since you're buying, that Pinot was okay," Claire added with what was, for her, a sweet smile.

Paul stuck his tongue out at her and headed for the bar. The earlier crush had largely dissipated, and he quickly got their drinks. Juggling three glasses wasn't the easiest thing, however, and his progress back to the table was slow, erratic, and cautious. Dentists weren't the most nimble people at best, and a horde of them milling about drinking and telling lies to one another struck Paul as a collection of accidents waiting to happen.

He'd just selected a safe route back to the table, when he noticed the slim, dapper figure of Benny Lu speaking with two other Asian dentists, a young couple. They stood about twenty feet from Paul, just out of earshot in the ongoing gabble. What caught Paul's eye more than the smooth, congenial Lu or the couple were the two heavyset dark-suited guys standing silently behind Lu. One paid close attention to the conversation while the other idly watched the crowd. Interesting. Paul had never heard Lu kept a posse around him. The guy seemed too slick, too confident.

"Who are the two bruisers with Benny Lu?" he asked Marty when the drinks were safely on the table.

Marty stood halfway up, looked across the room, then sat back down. "Oh, that's the Ha brothers, Justin

24

and Dustin. Oral surgeons in Lu's Hawthorne office. Wrestlers at Iowa. Martial-arts dudes." Marty grinned. "They're acting out, I think. My goombah relatives could take 'em."

"They need those little Oddjob derbies," Claire observed, taking -- for her -- a very feminine sip of wine.

"Huh," Paul said. "Maybe there'll be a pitched battle with the Mormons later."

"Hyrum Gregorson and his Sozye homies aren't real big on meetings that serve alcohol in copious amounts," Marty replied. "Gregorson's supposedly real straight even for a Mo. But you're right about a confrontation. Lu'd like nothing better than torpedoing his main rival, but he takes a long Asian view, and probably prefers to discredit Gregorson."

"Speaking of the big boys," Paul said, "where's your boss, Claire?"

Claire shook her head. "Won't be here. He wanted to avoid the speaker tonight. Guy's been plaguing hell out of him, trying to sell the Old Man on 'remineralization.' You know, the fluoride varnish thing they do in Scandinavia. Kon just knew he'd be pigeon-holed."

"Who's the speaker?" Paul asked. He hadn't even thought to ask earlier.

"Tom Barnum."

"You know," Marty added. "'P.' Thomas Barnum, the Holistic Guru. New Age Dentistry. Charge the patients for doing essentially nothing. Or damned little."

"Wait a minute," Paul said, holding his hands up to chest level, fingers spread. "This is the thing where you put this fluoride goo on the teeth when there's no radiographic evidence of caries through the enamel into the dentin? It's supposed to re-mineralize the enamel?"

"Yeah," Marty replied, nodding. "And it works, too, if you're dealing with a homogeneous cradle-to-the-grave socialist health-care system where the patients come in regularly and do what they're told. Which is to say Scandinavia. Doesn't do so well here, where the patients would rather buy a new drift boat than go to the dentist, but it is catching on. Prevention is good."

"Barnum's been calling Janos regularly," Claire said, "even coming by Admin, and Janos is too nice to grab him by the scruff of the neck and toss him out. It's Admin's big, new giggle. And Barnum, of course, is oblivious."

"In that case, your boss *is* too nice a guy," Paul said, starting on his wine.

"He's almost *too* public, *too* well-liked," Claire replied, shaking her head. "I've watched him for five years, and the man's totally genuine. Outgoing, up-beat, a real family man, supports education, Portland, and the Greek community. I couldn't tell you the last time he took a vacation."

"His daughter's up at the school?" Paul asked.

"Yeah, she's a senior this year, graduates in a week. She's going into the Air Force, three years in Germany."

"I saw her once," Marty said. "She's a real babe."

Claire shook her head again, glaring at Marty. "The whole family is photogenic as hell. Tall, tanned, with all those white teeth. Just pisses me off."

"And they're some kind of Catholic?" Paul asked.

"Greek Uniate. Same as Orthodox, basically, except they recognize the primacy of Rome. St. Apollonia's is a small parish in Southwest, between Portland and Tigard. It's kind of cool, all the icons and stuff. The priest is married with two kids."

"Jeez, a *married* priest!" Marty exclaimed. "That'd be hard. My mom and my aunts would *hate* that."

"For sure that'd change the dynamics of an Italian parish," Paul said, laughing, thinking of Marty's tales of bribing priests for favors with traditional Italian cooking. 'Pasta for Plenary Indulgences,' as Marty put it. Out of the corner of his eye, Paul saw bodies beginning to head in the direction of the far end of the room. Most Multnomah County meetings were now catered buffet-style, so the caterers must have just trundled out the heavily-laden tables.

"I'm gonna throw one of those hard little biscuits at Barnum," Marty announced, as they left their drinks on the table and joined the throng assaulting the food.

When Claire looked at Marty with something like approval, Paul became concerned. Once every year or two, some major dental meeting in the Portland area broke up in a food fight which escalated into a real brawl. The police had frequently intervened when the battle spilled into the streets. He'd never been involved, and he didn't want to be now. Sharing a paddywagon with a bunch of rioting middle- aged and older lunatics didn't appeal. "No, Claire," he said, using the same tone of voice he'd use to an errant pet.

"Don't worry, dear," she replied, giving Paul a wide grin. "It's just that I've heard Barnum speak before. They don't call him Doctor Morpheus for nothing. I'll have Marty hit *me* with the biscuit to keep me awake."

That made sense.

FIVE

A little over an hour after they got back to his place, Paul and Claire lay alongside one another in the darkness, satisfied and tired, yet not ready for sleep.

Claire lay uncovered on her left side, looking out the window at the night sky. Scattered light from the stars and the crescent of the new moon silvered her long, smooth body.

"It's been ten years, Paul," she said. "Why haven't we gotten married, settled into domestic tranquility?"

"Beats me," he replied, stroking her right hip. *This is something new*, he thought. "I love you."

"I know. And I love you. It's not *you*. It's not even *us*. We're great together. I look at our friends who've gotten married, and none of them gets along as well as we do. It's *me*, Claire the Creep. I just can't quite take that final step."

"Don't be hard on yourself. I've never proposed."

"Exactly. You *knew* I'd waffle." She rolled over and looked directly at him. Her normally pale eyes seemed darker. "Isn't that right?"

Paul shook his head. "I'd never pressure you. I've always figured when the time came, it'd just sort of happen. You're as independent as a cat, and I'm not much better."

That seemed to mollify her. She chuckled ruefully. "Yeah, there is that. Or maybe it's the fact that I'm an only child and you've got siblings." She touched his lips with her left index finger.

"What about your sister Kathy, the firefighter? Marty seemed adequately terrorized." He began to suck on her finger.

"Imaginary sisters don't count in the real world, dear."

"The real world. Good you brought that up." Paul pressed her hand to his chest. "In the real world, we're two individuals who get along extraordinarily well, despite the fact that most people we know can't fathom our relationship. Which is fine with me. In my opinion, that's kind of a hoot. Bottom line: I can't imagine being married to anyone but you. Probably I've known that the whole ten years."

Even in the darkness, he saw her eyes widen in surprise. She regarded him in silence for several seconds. "That's *really* sweet," she said finally.

"Hey, I'm a sweet guy. Ask any of my previous girlfriends."

Surprise turned to skepticism. "Did you *have* previous girlfriends? You never talked about it."

"They've pretty well faded away, Claire, if they ever existed. Ten years is a long time, even when it's just right."

The ringing phone prevented her answer. Paul rolled onto his back, and picked it up on the second ring. "If this is you, Marty, you're in *big* trouble."

A chuckle sounded in Paul's ear. "Sorry to call so late, buddy. It's me, Wismer. I need some clear thoughts -- and your memories of our ranching childhoods."

If Paul hadn't been wide awake a moment earlier, he was now. "Ron? You and Margie okay?"

"Yeah. Everything's fine. I just need your help. You ever know a kid named Byron Duncan at the school?"

"Yeah, I think so. Behind me two or three years. Short guy? I think. 'Dinky' Duncan."

"That be him. Got himself seriously killed this morning while out for a jog on the Wildwood. Looks like it might be a cougar. Real messy."

"Jesus! He was a nice guy. You run dogs in?"

The chuckle came again. "You're swift as ever. I gather you weren't asleep. Say 'Hi' to Claire for me.

But, yeah, we got right on it. They milled around for about half an hour, never got more than a couple hundred feet from the death-scene. Kept coming back to the trail. Handler finally threw up his hands."

"Cougars can jump thirty feet horizontally, more downslope."

"Downslope, upslope. Didn't make any difference. No scent. And another thing: you ever see a cougar didn't stash its prey, if it had time? That's *really* why I called."

Paul considered the question. "No. They run an economical lifestyle. Waste not, want not."

"Might be an exception, though. Young animal, habits not so ingrained? Knows there're plenty of runners."

"Sure. Give it a few days, though, see if it kills again."

Wismer's chuckle turned bitter. "Gee, thanks, Doc."

"Sorry, Ron. But if it didn't hide the kill, it may have left the area. Might even have made it all the way to the Coast Range by now."

"I hope. The Captain was *not* pleased."

"He understands you're dealing with a wild animal, not some predictable felon, doesn't he?"

"Oh, yeah. There's not a lotta heat -- *yet*. But you can bet your ass there will be. It was on the news tonight, and the papers'll be full of it tomorrow morning. The ban on hunting with dogs opponents will be in full cry."

"Sorry I can't be more help."

"Hey, I just needed to talk to somebody outside work. Somebody with a straight head."

"Let me know how it goes. And my best to Margie."

"Sure. Same to Claire. And thanks." The line went dead.

Paul sagged back on his pillow, looked at the ceiling. Wow."

"What?" Claire asked. "That was Ron Wismer, right?"

"Yeah." He told Claire what'd happened. When he'd finished, they lay in each other's arms for a few minutes.

"Makes our problems seem insignificant, doesn't it?" Claire said at last, nuzzling his neck.

"Marry me," he replied.

"Okay."

"That was easy."

She lifted her left leg across to straddle him, grinning, her teeth gleaming in the dim light. "So's the next part."

He laughed. "You *think*. I'm *never* easy."

"Better be, or the wedding's off."

SIX

Emmett McManus sat across the restaurant table from Riona Phelan and could think only of his grandmother. Set in lean, olive-skinned features framed by ragged coal-black hair, haunting dark eyes eerily recalling his ancestor watched him in a kind of grimly amused assessment.

"What do you see, Cousin?" she asked, her voice low, husky. She had the same wariness as his grandmother, too, he decided, that gauging tilt of her head, as though deciding whether to fight or flee.

He tried a disarming smile. "You greatly resemble my grandmother. More than I expected."

An answering smile slowly spread over her young face, barely overcoming her cautious reserve, the smile at its finish little more than a hunter's grimace. Her amusement ratcheted up a notch or two without warming that cool expression. "Blood will tell, I understand," she said. "I see us in you, also."

"Not surprising," McManus replied, nodding. "We are, after all, something like second cousins." He looked past the tacky Mexican decor of Esparza's Tex-Mex, seeking a waitress.

Riona's smile widened a few degrees, showing more of her white, efficient-looking teeth. "Blood is thicker than water, too, cousin."

"In my experience, yes," he said, looking directly into her dark gaze. "Do what you will for Doctor Lu, but confine your attentions to his immediate enemies. Leave my employer untroubled." He kept his voice down. The place was noisy, but crowded enough so that other tables and their occupants were close.

Her smile vanished. She lifted her water glass, took a swallow, her eyes never leaving his. "So soon. I thought we could play at being family a bit longer. I would show you pictures of my brothers, Sitric and Senan. Fine, strong lads, the both of them." One eyebrow lifted in question and challenge.

"We're playing the numbers game, then?"

"Three against one? Hardly necessary. Your employer interests us not at all. We have provided Doctor Lu a mighty weapon against the Mormons, should they be gullible fools, as their recent history occasionally shows. Do you remember the Mark Hoffman affair?"

McManus nodded. "The Magic White Salamander letter, wherein a magical creature -- not the Angel Moroni -- appeared to Joseph Smith in his First Vision. An incredible fraud that many reputable Saint scholars accepted until Hoffman began killing people, and shat in his own messkit." He took a drink of his water, and gave Riona a thin smile. "Documents, is it?" Through the doorway behind his cousin, a waitress finally seemed to be heading in their direction.

"The religious love words," Riona affirmed. "And, who knows? This seems genuine. I'll keep you informed." Another eyebrow arch. "Perhaps Doctor Janos may profit." She picked up her menu as the waitress appeared beside their table.

They ordered, their conversation paused until the waitress had departed.

"You have a niece here locally?" Riona asked, and McManus heard more than casual interest. The Phelans searched for strengths as well as weaknesses.

"Claire. My brother's daughter. A dentist. She works for Janos, also."

"So I have heard. Is she like us?" He could practically smell her concern, her need to *know*.

He shrugged. "Perhaps. I have no first-hand knowledge. Beyond a certain level, our blood's power dilutes and ceases. If you saw Claire, she would seem only a tall, muscular young woman with dark blonde hair." The former Special Ops soldier permitted himself a fond smile. "She is aggressive enough, certainly, but the McManus bloodline is like yours in that."

"Is it?" his cousin replied, a question not requiring an answer, and he sensed in her words a touch of the uncertainty of youth. Something he much preferred over arrogance, which was all too common among modern children. Perhaps, indeed, he had nothing to worry about from his cousins. Or perhaps Riona was still doing the math, and that determination now stood at three-to-two. Possibly with a question mark. One couldn't be certain about Claire, though in a one-on-one against Riona, McManus thought Claire's extra inches and pounds would tell, all else being equal. For, like every Phelan he'd ever encountered -- or himself, for that matter -- Riona stood at something close under six feet, compact and wiry, with a long-muscled distance runner's build. A hundred-fifty low-fat pounds at the very maximum.

"What document did you procure for Doctor Lu, if I may inquire?" he asked.

Her gaze locked with his again as she took another slow drink of water. McManus thought her intensity admirable. "Since you knew about the Salamander letter," she said, "you must be familiar with the basic tenets of Mormon belief, that Joseph Smith translated the golden tablets containing the Book of Mormon. In doing so, he produced hundreds of written pages. He lent the first one hundred sixteen pages to Martin Harris in June of 1828. Harris intended to use them to convince his skeptical wife, Lucy, of the veracity of Smith's new faith. The pages were lost, and Smith was forced to have a timely revelation telling him not to retranslate the lost pages. The Book of Mormon was published without them, but incorporated their basic wording."

"And you have recovered them?"

Her answering smile showed modest pride. "So it would seem."

"Why sell them to Lu to taunt Gregorson, then? Why not simply approach the church directly, or through a trusted intermediary?"

"After Hoffman, the Saints are leery. They would attempt to keep the price low, even with adequate testing." Her white smile flashed for an instant. "Lu paid well, with few questions asked. Gregorson has a distant older cousin on the Quorum of Twelve Apostles. Lu believes Gregorson will attempt to procure the lost pages to either curry favor or simply do the correct thing."

McManus nodded. "According to Doctor Janos, Doctor Gregorson is an honorable and honest man."

Evil pleasure surfaced in Riona's dark eyes. "And easier to deceive because of that. He will pauper himself, Lu expects."

"And thereby weaken his company."

"Indeed."

"And Phelan Associates receives a percentage above a certain amount, am I correct?"

"Very astute, Cousin. Fifty percent of anything over three hundred thousand."

"Phelen Associates already *has* three hundred?"

Her pleasure tripled. "Of course."

Phelan acquisitiveness was something McManus understood, as long as the trait didn't escalate to greed. Riona's grandfather had always run a tight ship, and he still ruled the roost back in Philadelphia. Riona and her brothers might feel the freedom of distance and the lengthened tether, but likely the old man still kept both eyes open and a firm hand on the wheel of the family enterprise. He must be close to eighty, yet he was hale and hearty, and no Phelan ever held the reins of power without usage and constraint. Though Riona might be a bit precipitous and less careful, youth excused that.

"I'm impressed," McManus admitted.

35

Her laughing response was full-blown, reminding him of Claire's explosive guffaw. People at adjacent tables noticed, smiling at the slim, dark young woman. "Grandfather's doing," she assured him. "Not mine."

"Still and all," he replied, "it's scarcely beer money." As Riona smiled modestly, their waitress appeared through the doorway behind her, carrying a platter with what McManus hoped were their meals. This was a rather late lunch for him, and his metabolism was letting him know it.

Riona's, too, evidently. She began eating with no more than a cursory attempt at formality, not saying another word until she was a third of the way through her salmon burrito.

"You were military?" she asked, between mouthfuls.

"Still Reserve," he replied, nodding.

"Gulf War I?"

"Yes."

"What were your duties?"

"Baghdad and to the east, prowling for intelligence."

"I envy you." She sounded sincere, the attraction of danger for the young, he guessed. Arab culture, and the lure of adventure, too, of course. The Brits had given the Irish a healthy measure of fascination with the corners of the old Empire. And Freud may have been right when he stated that the Irish couldn't be psychoanalyzed because they were too fond of fantasy. He smiled to himself. For most of humanity, he and Riona Phelen *were* fantasy.

"It was...*interesting*, shall we say," he answered at last, smiling for her. "In fact, *you* could join up. There are always places in Today's Army for those with special talents."

She shook her head. "The discipline might be difficult."

"Not a problem. The discipline our kind all must have is sufficient. And the Special Operations people ask few questions. Results count for a great deal, more when the Republicans are in power. A word from me in the right ear, and you'd be in after six weeks of boot."

"Very tempting," she replied, with an unaffected grin, and again he was reminded of his grandmother. "Were there others of us with you?"

"No, but there was a man named Knox in Baghdad who was definitely not a standard-issue human. Didn't *smell* right, if you know what I mean. But I never did find out what he was. Brilliant operative, absolutely effective at gathering intelligence and keeping our location secret."

"Did he kill?" she asked, and McManus sensed an *interest*. Did she *like* killing? he wondered.

"One of his primary skills, I believe, as well as languages, a perfect memory, and immense strength."

He chuckled at the memory. "A fine cook, too, although he personally seemed to prefer his food very *fresh*."

"Not so different from us."

"Very true," he agreed, nodding again, leaving unmentioned the fact that Knox had instantly known McManus was no garden-variety Irishman.

They finished their meal quickly, with Riona showing him a small clutch of family photographs, groups of near-identical Phelans. They were a handsome clan, the lot of them, and he told her so.

She frowned. "We stand out a bit too much, Grandfather says. Better if we blended in more." A delicate shrug as her frown vanished, replaced by a knowing smile. "A blade which cuts both ways, however. Sometimes the Phelan reputation helps."

McManus understood that. He paid their bill over her polite protests, and they shortly stood on the sidewalk, making small talk. He promised to have

37

dinner with Riona and her brothers, and asked that she keep him informed of the Lu-Gregorson project.

"To be sure," she said, then pointed across the street, grinning, where a young woman walked two handsome German shepherd dogs. "Do you think, cousin, that there are were*wolves*?"

He laughed. "Anything is possible, I suppose." But his gaze searched the street for something else, and quickly found what he sought. A hundred feet away, on the opposite side of the pavement, a tall, dark woman with striking green eyes sat against a big KTM dualsport motorcycle.

McManus had noticed her earlier, some distance behind his Toyota on his way to meet Riona. Now her long leather-clad legs were crossed at booted ankles, and her muscular hands cradled a full-face Bell helmet whose color matched her eyes. Seeing him watching her, she donned the helmet and an MSR Gore-tex off-road jacket, electric-started the bike, and pulled out into the street.

She winked at McManus as she rode by.

SEVEN

In Doctor Benjamin Lu's estimation, early afternoon on Friday was not when he should be opening *The Oregonian* for the first time that day. On the other hand, his morning meeting with Hyrum Gregorson, held on a park bench in Laurelhurst Park, feeding the ducks, had gone well.

Even distracted by the predator-related death of one of his many employees, the tall, quiet Gregorson had been visibly shaken when he held a few copied pages of the lost Saint manuscript. Lu, who'd been relegated to keeping the ducks from nibbling at the papers while the stunned Gregorson perused them, wondered silently if every Mormon was intimately familiar with the personal hand-writing of whatever individual had set down the words of the Prophet. He imagined Joseph Smith, seated at a table behind a curtain, the sacred golden plates concealed in his upside-down hat while he translated by looking through a pair of seer-stones. It sounded so improbable, it unaccountably made Lu think of the Great and Terrible Oz, another man behind another curtain. Only Smith had had magic spectacles, golden plates, and an upside-down hat.

And the Saints wondered why the rest of the world's faiths looked at them askance.

Of course, the other faiths were secure behind centuries or millennia of that other curtain, the curtain of time, whereas Mormon theologic oddities took place in the era of recent history, practically the here-and-now, in front of the public and whatever gods that public revered.

Lu had been raised Presbyterian in Pendleton, Oregon, a fourth-generation descendent of Chinese miners who had worked the northeastern Oregon gold fields in the Nineteenth Century. He found

Gregorson's faith more than passing strange, even compared with the Presbyterian tenet of predestination. The man's straight-arrow eagerness to acquire the lost pages of the Book of Mormon, Lu found nearly as strange, even if it played right into his hands. *He* would be more cautious. Gregorson apparently wouldn't.

Whatever. The good Doctor Gregorson would either come up with the money, or he wouldn't. The man had gulped when Lu told him the price, but he'd swallowed again afterward, and Lu recognized acceptance when he saw it.

Gregorson would need a bit of time to make up his mind. Lu didn't expect to hear from him until the first of the next week, if that soon. The manuscript was tucked away in a safe deposit box several blocks away from Lu's main office. The Phelans would deal with the transfer and fund acquisition.

The Phelans. Lu considered them as he worked his way through the 'Arts and Entertainment' section. There was something about them that made him nervous, something he couldn't quite put his finger on, and wouldn't dare to, even if he could. The brothers were bad enough, quiet and dangerous-looking, but Riona Phelan resembled a cat that wanted the world for her mouse. At forty, Lu could understand that feeling. At twenty-five, when he'd been Riona Phelen's age, he'd only been damned glad to be out of dental school and ready to get on with the rest of his life.

He continued to work through the paper, aware at some level of post mid-day activity in the rest of his headquarters; faxes chiming, telephone conversations, the subdued chatter of printers, and occasional laughter.

By the time Lu finished the comics section, his stomach had begun to make definite demands. Even his promising meeting with Gregorson couldn't slow his energetic metabolism's need for food. A bag of chips and a diet soda on the way back to the office had only postponed his lunch, not prevented it. Well, he could read the account of Byron Duncan's untidy demise, then maybe sneak out to the Bento deli down the street.

The front page was largely Duncan. Lu had watched a Six a.m. segment on Channel Eight featuring a 'carnivologist' from Oregon State. The man, with the unlikely name of Odward Haggen, favored the ursine side of the carnivore spectrum. A huge, hirsute, scowling fellow whose voice sounded like boulders crashing together underwater, he greeted each question with a frowning pause and a dark kindling within small, deepset eyes, and was clearly unhappy to be wearing a sport coat and tie. He kept tugging at the tie. Yes, he had read the police report leaked to the television station, and yes, if the killer was of fauna native to Oregon, it was a cougar, probably a younger animal displaced from its mother's territory. It was entirely possible that the animal might strike again, but the fact that Duncan's body hadn't been hidden or covered was significant. In cougars, the instinct to cover is strong, so that might well mean the beast was still on the move.

The interviewer, a young woman who gamely persevered in her questioning, had then asked about cougar size.

The largest cougar ever recorded, a male, weighed two hundred seventy-six pounds -- *after* being gutted, Haggen said -- with a rare smile. Most modern male cougars weigh a hundred-fifty, females only a bit over a hundred. Still, the big biologist cautioned, a hundred pound female cougar can easily take down an eight hundred pound elk.

Haggen was also extensively quoted in *The Oregonian* article, along with a few lesser lights among northwest mammalologists. After reading the cougar lore filling several columns of the front section of the paper, Lu made a vow to never go into any non-urban circumstance even remotely considered a forest.

He'd just refolded the paper and laid it on the corner of his desk when April Kwong, who more or less kept track of Considerate Care's daily operation, strolled into the office.

"Afternoon, boss," she said, dropping casually into the leather chair on the front side of the desk after shutting the office door. "My spies tell me there's been no lunch for our fearless leader today."

Lu smiled at her. Hard not to. Though nominally third generation Chinese-American, April had been raised in San Antonio, and her demeanor was *all* Texan. She could 'aw, shucks' and 'bigod' with the best, and she was so outgoing that more recent immigrants found her overwhelming even as she charmed them into accepting a slightly lower rate of pay than the usual and customary.

Today, April wore her long, black hair in a French braid which hung alluringly over her right shoulder. With her hair tied back from her round face, her large brown eyes commanded even more attention than usual, and her smile would just break your heart. Lu, faithfully married, lusted after her.

"I'm starving," he replied, "and you look wonderful today."

She beamed. "China boy like looky-looky at China girl?"

Lu shuddered. "Do you *have* to do that? It's so damned demeaning."

She laughed, batted her long eyelashes, and lifted one sneaker-clad foot up to rest on top of his desk. "Want see golden gully?" The fingers of her right hand toyed with the end of her braid, and she licked her lower lip with the tip of her pink tongue.

"No!" But he smiled as he spoke. It was both the best and worst he could manage with April's carnal teasing. Cunning and manipulative in business, Benny

Lu privately remained a good Presbyterian, dutiful to his wife and family. April might regularly get him a little hot around the edges, but that was just her nature and there would never be any impropriety between them. They both understood that.

"Okay, then," she said, letting her foot drop back to the floor. Her smile made her look like a teenager. "So, we gonna screw Gregorson big-time?"

This was safer ground, if a bit strongly phrased. He nodded. "Yes, I believe so. I watched the hook set itself."

She considered those words for a few moments, her thoughtful expression for once entirely Asian. "Have you considered the possibility of this back-firing? Could he *sell* the document to his Church, thereby reaping rewards of both a spiritual and financial nature?"

"Possibly, but he is very high-profile among the local LDS. His inclination would be to donate the pages to the Church. Most Mormons would, and that would certainly be like Gregorson. He possesses a level of unselfish nobility."

Her voice was a velvet razor. "A window of vulnerability."

"Exactly. And an expenditure of this magnitude should slow down his expansion into southeast Portland by at least two years."

"Long enough for us to open new offices on Division Street and Johnson Creek Road." She shook her head, bemused, then grinned. "It's like a chess game."

"Chess is a game of war," Lu replied. "And make no mistake. This is war -- oral war."

"It sounds better as a plural. *Oral Wars*."

Lu admitted that it did, chuckling. "Have you had lunch?"

"Just a snack. I need to keep my appetite. I have a dinner date tonight. With Miz Phelan."

Stunned, Lu asked, "A *date*?"

"Easy, boss. Not a *date* date. Just dinner. Though she might be interesting."

"Do you think she's..?"

April chortled, a most un-Chinese sound in his experience. "Oh, yeah. Unless I'm real wrong, Riona Phelan walks both sides of Sexual Preference Boulevard."

Lu stroked his chin. "I had not thought of that."

"You wouldn't. You're as straight as Gregorson."

"Please!"

"Sorry." She stood up. "I'll get back to managing things. You go get lunch. And I should mention that I'm wearing my Feng Shui panties tonight."

He watched her leave the room, moving as freely and smoothly as a Han Dynasty courtesan. *What an amazing woman*, he thought. 'Looky-looky,' indeed.

EIGHT

April was surprised at Riona Phelan's choice of restaurants. Capriel's Bistro, in Sellwood, the borderland between Portland and Milwaukie, was one of April's favorite places, but the Phelans had only been in town a little over a week, and there were plenty of better-known spots.

"This would've been one of my first five picks, Riona," April told the tall, graceful woman when they'd been seated.

Riona gave her a bright predator's smile, with quiet invitation around its edges. "I queried Doctor Lu, saying I wished something not strictly Asian, but with strong Asian inflections." Her smile became more personal. "I did not say you and I were the diners."

"That's okay," April told her. "I mentioned it."

"And he was amazed, was he not?"

April laughed. "You've got him figured."

"Perhaps it's a dental thing, his conservatism," Riona replied, examining her menu. "What do you recommend?"

"I generally have the sea scallops, but the venison is excellent. The ravioli is good, too."

Riona closed the menu. "The scallops it is. You select the wine. Even those of us in staid Philadelphia have heard of Oregon wines."

"A good Mersault then, probably," April said. She grinned at Riona, and lifted an inquiring eyebrow. "Sky's the limit, right?"

"Of course. For you."

"Don't think I'm that easy, Yankee girl."

Riona's deep, dark eyes seemed suddenly deeper and darker. "Easy. Never. *Possible*, perhaps."

As those words crossed Riona's intriguing lips, April felt her face flush, and became conscious of a scent washing across the table, an exciting scent that made the hair on the back of her neck raise. Riona. Not perfume. <u>Riona</u>. She inhaled long and slow through her nostrils. "That's *you*, isn't it?"

"Ah," Riona replied, her smile growing even more languid and seductive, "you are one of the sensitive ones. I forgot myself, and let my hopes overwhelm my good, Catholic nature." She extended one slim hand over the table, let it rest on April's right wrist. Her eyes were intense, gauging. "I apologize. Let us see what happens."

April looked down at Riona's hand, felt the heat from it almost literally permeate her skin, and grinned. "We may just have ourselves a fine time." She pronounced 'fine' something like 'fan,' which she could tell tickled Riona. The incongruity of a Texan accent emanating from someone so obviously Asian always made people smile, and April used it shamelessly.

They ordered their scallops, the wine came, and, after a moderate amount of small talk over their first glasses, Riona questioned April about the operation of Considerate Care. Not the dental practice aspect, but the organizational and financial apparatus. That a twenty-five-year-old would know exactly which questions to ask, and that she would also know to stop before asking things which -- if answered -- would amount to compromising company secrecy, April found simply amazing.

"You're damned sharp," April told her, not bothering to mask her admiration.

"For my age, you were thinking."

"Oh, yeah. That, too."

Riona shrugged. "The Phelans have been in business for three generations in this country, and countless more back in Ireland, so my background is deep, even if my years are not. My grandfather refers to us as 'hunter-gatherers,' and that sums our business up well."

"Which are you?" April asked, laughing.

"I prefer hunting, but gathering is good enough. Afterward."

As she spoke, Riona's expression remained technically a smile, but April felt a cold knot in her gut, one that the wine did not eliminate, only diminished. She gulped reflexively, saw Riona's smile thaw slightly in response, and decided to change the subject. "Can you tell me about finding the lost Saint manuscript?"

"Not a problem. There have been rumors, of course, over the years. Our grandfather had been tracking the descendants of the original families who had actually *seen* the lost pages for over fifty years, since the conclusion of World War II. He affects a hearty, rural manner, friendly and outgoing, plainly but well-dressed, and is adept at putting people at their ease. He made his original contacts in the Fifties, would appear occasionally to re-direct his search. Their family members became used to seeing him, and, eventually, a decade or so ago, when some objecting and concerned senior died, word of it came to Grandfather's ear."

Riona took a swallow of water before continuing. "He made further discreet inquiries, discovered the heirloom trunk with the manuscript, offered the owners a one-time fee of a quarter-million. No questions asked, and no fingers pointed. They assumed he was a Saint, he didn't disabuse them of that delusion, and they readily parted with their guilty secret. A valuable item perhaps stolen well over a century ago."

"Wow! So your grandfather just *kept* it, all these years since?"

"He weighed giving it outright to the Church, a publicity bonanza, perhaps even more than he wanted. Then he saw the wisdom of using it someday to influence a future transaction involving a Saint or Saint-owned firm."

"Your grandfather sounds like one interestin' fella."

Riona chuckled, shaking her head. "Well, that's certainly a valid thought. He is kind, knowledgeable, intelligent, trustworthy, and ruthless. The last has much to do with the Phelan success." Her brown eyes flashed with pride, showing only a touch of the cold certainty of earlier, and April felt another wash of that impossibly compelling scent.

"I've never been able to find a substitute for it, that's for sure," April agreed, finishing her second glass of wine to drown the pheromones filling her nose.

"I thought not," Riona said, and April saw invitation and interest surface again. *Well, ain't this just real promisin,'* she thought, then shivered mentally, not from fear exactly, but an emotion akin to it. Plus anticipation.

Their meal arrived shortly, and they occupied themselves with the food and a running conversation consisting of Riona's questions and April's answers about Portland and Oregon.

And when dinner was done, back at Riona's rented place, in leather and silk bonds, April's fine time came breathlessly true. A trickle of unease remained in her brainstem throughout the experience, only heightening her pleasure. April ignored it and let the hunter complete the stalk.

Her turn would come, and when it did, she would be *most* inventive.

NINE

Just after first light on Saturday morning, Al Chambers began his run up Mount Tabor, in east Portland. A wonderfully clear day, a half-hour before sunrise, and here he was, at age sixty-three, hoofing it doggedly up the pavement toward the first trail section on the north slope of the old volcano.

It seemed weird. He'd hardly imagined being old, and sure as heck not old and halfway fit, and never a time when the kids would be grown and gone, when he and Elisabeth would be on their own, free as birds. Next week they'd be driving down to Logan, Utah, to see his brother Don and Elisabeth's folks, who were, by the grace of God, still alive.

They had a good life, he and Elisabeth. Forty years married, thirty-eight since Al graduated from dental school, seven grandchildren, and their youngest son, Heber, out of the nest for two years. And his job with Sozye Dental Associates had worked out well. A stocky, muscular man with a whole bunch of Type A traits, the low-key but busy group practice had been a natural, non-stressful fit for Al.

He felt pretty darned good as he chugged over the crest of the road and jogged onto the first trail section. Then, two hundred feet in, his breath coming back nicely, Al became aware of something on the trail behind him. Footfalls, for sure, but not the two-legged variety. A dog, he figured, mildly irritated at the interruption, more at people who didn't look out for their pets. He slid to a halt and turned to confront the animal, hoping it would be a Golden or some other easy-going breed, not some sort of half-wild wolf thing.

But it was a cat, large, intent, and heading straight for Al at a gentle lope. Not a cougar, he saw, yet easily as big. Marked with stripes over fawn fur, sturdy fangs, with big flat paws. It seemed to be grinning at him.

All the rules for dealing with dangerous cats snapped into Al's mind. You didn't run. You didn't look away. You made noise, *lots* of noise. Not taking his eyes off the animal, he bent down and scooped a skull-sized rock from beside the trail, took a deep breath, and yelled as loud as he could. No effect. The creature gathered itself and sprang.

Al side-stepped, struck at it with the rock while the beast was in mid-air. A glancing blow to its shoulder, no damage. It landed, spun away, then back, lashed at him with one of those big paws, spitting and snarling, its claws raking across his right thigh.

Back-peddling, Al kept away from the thing, holding the small boulder in front of him to keep it at bay, and yelling his head off. He felt warm blood coursing down his leg, but no weakness. Darned animal was *quick*, though, slapping at him first from one side and then the other, connecting more times than not. Both legs bleeding now, no real damage yet, but it stung like heck.

The thing wouldn't stay away, though, just kept working Al backward, along the trail, it squalling and him yelling. Al wished he had a heavy stick instead of the rock, but he wasn't about to let go of his makeshift weapon.

Then he looked into its brown eyes, saw true intelligence and intent, and realized what it was doing. He was being *herded* away from the pavement, to be killed further back into the trees.

An instant later the creature leapt at him again. Al overbalanced, fell onto his back. He swung the rock as he fell, missed, lost his grip, and the rock bounced away. The big cat seized him by the throat and held on, crushing his larynx, its full weight on his body. Al flailed at it helplessly, trying to scream and failing.

50

The beast brought its rear feet up to his chest and disembowled him with a single powerful thrust.

Al Chambers spasmed twice.

Elisabeth--

Ron Wismer had just exited the shower when the call from Mount Tabor came in. He listened carefully, threw on his clothes, combed his hair, kissed Margie, hugged one of the kids, and was out the door, toast in his mouth, on his way to pick up his partner. He did not kick the cat, even though, at the moment, he was no fan of their kind.

Resisting the urge to speed through his edge-of-Beaverton neighborhood, the Lieutenant still hit Highway 26 with moderate velocity, and worked his Camry through the gears as rapidly as possible. Which, during morning rush hour, was not rapidly at all.

Wismer consoled himself with the thought that the victim wouldn't be going anywhere, although the case had -- right into Twilight Zone or X-Files territory. His gut said they were dealing with the same killer, the same beast that had wasted Byron Duncan, unless the initial contact team had given him some extremely bogus information. He doubted that. Munoz and Carlton were too sharp. He was certain they had reviewed the Duncan case. Everybody had, it was so unusual.

He hit 405 South, then slanted east to Boothe's condo near the waterfront. Carlton had assured him she'd called, and Wismer knew Boothe would be watching for his car.

Sure enough, as he pulled into the north-south street paralleling the Willamette, here she came down the stairs fronting the street, all long-legged and loose-jointed easy grace, wearing black slacks and a charcoal blouse. Her CZ 75 showed as a slight bulge beneath the lapels of her black blazer. Your friendly neighborhood Goth cop.

They'd been partnered for eighteen months, and the Lieutenant thought he was only slightly closer to figuring out Boothe Deakins than he'd been initially. Her father had a botany degree from the University of Oregon, and, in order to use his education to provide the highest income possible, had become one of the premier organic pot growers in western Oregon. Settling in Cherry Grove, in the foothills of the Coast Range just west of Gaston, Leroy Deakins quietly became a legend.

Of course, his activities eventually caught the eye of the local law and the DEA, raids ensued, and only multiple sites on federal forest lands kept Deakins Enterprises afloat. Leroy had never done time, primarily because their operation was truly a family one, and the Deakins children were as close-mouthed as their daddy. No one squealed, no one used the product, and all sales were well out of the area. Freckle-faced, big-eyed innocence had proven quite effective. Now Leroy taught at Pacific University in Forest Grove, the younger kids tended the legalized cash crop in remote forest meadows, and the family prospered.

Boothe grew up heavy on woodslore and weaponry, and the prospect of having access to and usage of serious firepower had sent her into a career in law enforcement. She was apolitical and amoral, but with *rules*, rules which kept her partner safe and secure while presenting the scofflaws and miscreants they encountered with the prospect of justice swift, certain, and low on appeals and lawyers.

"Mornin', partner," she said as she slid into the passenger seat, sunglasses in place, grinning.

"Likewise. You're real chipper." She was pretty, too, Wismer thought, in a severe, narrow-eyed, frightening way. He reminded himself that both his wife Margie and Claire McManus *liked* Boothe Deakins, oblique stamps of approval that defied simple analysis. Or common sense, in the Lieutenant's estimation.

"Nice day."

"Except for the cougar thing."

"Maybe not the same cat. *If* it's a cat."

Wismer turned around in the middle of the block, then glanced sharply at his partner as he stomped the gas pedal. "Don't start with the Sasquatch-type stuff, Boothe. Your folksy, legendary critters don't exist in the real world."

"So you say. Me, I'm not so sure." He felt her cool steel gaze bore into him. "Ever see a cougar?"

"Once. At a distance. Beautiful thing."

"We had a female denned near one of Daddy's crop sites. I spent days when I was in Junior High watching her and her kittens. At some point she became aware of me and tolerated my presence, for whatever reason. I *loved* her. Maybe that was it. She *knew*."

"You were half-wild then, Boothe."

A short laugh. "Still am. Some things don't change, Ronald. I just bathe more regularly and dress better now."

He didn't reply, instead turned right toward Highway 26 over the Ross Island Bridge. They'd be going east when traffic was mostly heading into the city, which should speed things up.

Ten minutes later, they turned off 60th and headed up Mount Tabor on Stephens. This time, besides the EMT rig and a black-and-white, a knot of curious neighbors had gathered, along with a few early-rising runners who looked put-out that they couldn't get onto the trail. Wismer and Boothe smiled and nodded at the group, then hot-footed it down the trail.

Munoz, a tall, blond surfer kid, met them about fifty feet from the covered body. Carlton, a slender black woman almost as tall as Munoz, waited with the EMTs by the body. The forensics people hadn't arrived yet.

"Morning, Lieutenants."

He gave Munoz a tired smile. "Morning, Robbie. I don't suppose this is another Mormon dentist?"

Munoz gulped, nodded. "Yessir. He had a fanny pack with water, car keys, and ID."

Deakins made a soft sound that might indicate surprise. Or maybe 'I told you so.'

"Oh, Christ!" Wismer exclaimed. Bad enough that the Willamette River and something on the order of twenty miles of city separated Forest Park from here, worse to think that somebody -- or something -- was targeting a very definite segment of the population. "For sure an animal again?" They began walking toward Carlton and the others.

"Oh, yeah."

"Bad?"

"Oh, yeah."

"Make any sense to you?"

"Nossir."

"You pass it on to the Captain?"

"At his earlier request. He'll be out with that Haggen guy, the predator expert."

"Saw him on TV. Just what we need, a big, hairy, grumpy civilian." They were almost to the waiting group, who seemed uneasy, except for Carlton. Wismer knew he looked sour. Hell, he *felt* sour. And just plain pissed. He didn't care. Duncan had been a novelty homicide, sort of an act of God, a one-of-a-kind. This wasn't. *This* was fucking weird.

"You don't be too hard on Professor Haggen, Loot," Carlton said, with a big, white grin. Her dark brown cornrows shone in the morning sun, and, in spite of his bleak mood, Wismer felt his spirits lift a little. "He talked to us at the Academy down in Monmouth. A nice man. That grump thing, it's just an act."

"Well," the Lieutenant replied, "that's just dandy, Janiece, but I'm thinkin' this is the biggest potential tub of shit I've ever seen. You know what I mean?"

"You mean there's a brain behind this? It's not really a cat, at all?"

Wismer shook his head, afraid to look at his silent partner. "I dunno, and I don't want to think about it. We deal with the evidence, we treat it as a separate incident, we let the big boys and girls figure it out. More important, we let *them* talk to the Media." He looked at each of the group in turn, including the EMTs. "Fair enough?"

They all seemed accepting. One or more of the EMTs might fold on the deal, but he had to at least try to keep the big Wacko genie in the bottle. "Okay, let's have a look." Munoz lifted the sheet.

This dead dentist was older, pretty darned fit. Even gutted and with a crushed throat, he looked like the kind of person you'd like to have as a neighbor. Wife, kids, grandkids probably. Lots of people to mourn a senseless, even cruel, death.

"It took the cat a while to get him," Carlton said. "There's blood here and there on the hiking trail." She pulled the sheet further down, exposing the victim's legs. They were clawed to shit, ribbons of sliced flesh.

"Who found him?"

"We did. Neighbor heard yelling, phoned the police."

Wismer studied the corpse. He pointed at the forearms. "A few swats on the arms. My guess is he was fending it off with something, a rock or a stick maybe."

"Gutsy old guy," Munoz said, shaking his head.

"Looks like he did everything he could, too," Wismer added.

Carlton turned to Boothe. Wismer smiled to himself. Funny how they always went to her with the strange shit. "Can a cat be *trained* to do this?"

56

"Don't know," Boothe slowly answered. "Maybe if Siegfried and Roy were involved, I guess." She squatted and examined the victim's hands, then smiled, closed-lipped. "Definitely got some fur here, though. Lab rats'll be able to tell us what kind of cat did the deed."

Wismer sensed from her tone of voice that -- at some level -- his partner was telling Carlton and Munoz what they wanted to hear. The Deakins feral-child brain might already have arrived at a quite different alternative.   His earlier 'X-Files' thought returned, stronger now. *Christ on a crutch!*

That line of thought aborted upon the arrival of their boss, accompanied by the large, blocky Odward Haggen. The pair resembled an ad for one of those 'Big 'n Tall' stores, one on each side of the titular description. Wismer had expected the forensics people first, but this might work out better, since Haggen appeared shrewd and knowledgeable, and, better yet, not some kind of a showboat who played to the media. There would be no teasers for the eleven o'clock news from Odward Haggen.

"Good morning, Janiece," Haggen rumbled as he and the Captain drew nearer, his deep, growly voice not quite so overpowering in the out-of-doors. He nodded to Deakins, his smile widening, becoming almost fatherly. "Good morning, Boothie."

"Morning, Professor," she replied, straight-faced.

Out of the corner of his eye, Wismer saw Elch's eyebrows lift nearly into his hairline.   His own eyebrows gave an inadvertent bounce. He'd *never* heard anyone address his partner with any degree of familiarity. He'd have to quiz her on this one later.

While Haggen and Boothe visually went over the victim's body prior to the arrival of the forensics team, Wismer gave the Captain a capsule run-down laced with as little conjecture as possible.

"Tell me one thing good about this one, Ron," Elch said when Wismer finished. "Just *one* thing."

"We have fur, Karl," Haggen put in, looking up from his examination. "We'll know what species we're dealing with. There was no fur at the Duncan site."

Elch didn't reply right away, and Wismer knew better than to jump in with anything. The Captain's eyes narrowed as he gazed at the corpse without seeming to really see it.

"Why is that, I wonder?" he asked. "Duncan finished up on his back, too."

"Duncan was attacked from behind," Haggen said, as though he were giving a classroom lecture. "He ran. He was dead and on his back *before* he had a chance to defend himself. This gentleman's neck was crushed from the front, also a fairly normal cougar method against larger mammals, but he made noise and fought back. The fur is the consequence."

The Captain merely grunted acceptance, and Wismer knew the sound of shit impacting the fan filled the tall man's head like sugarplums at Christmas. Thoughts of what the media would do with this second death, with implications so obvious the most brain-dead reader could make the connections, even without written conclusions. *Christ*! The conspiracy-theory nutcases and supernaturalists of every stripe were going to have a field day!

He looked at Deakins then, and she regarded him without speaking, merely shook her head once, as if cautioning him. Wismer thought he'd never seen her expression so guarded and thoughtful around her fellow professionals.

At least she didn't look as all-at-sea as he must. *Christ*!

ELEVEN

Later that morning, still doing paperwork in the roomy four-desk office Wismer shared with Deakins and two other detectives, he realized Boothe had been absent more than usual. Her typical pattern involved a half-hour or so of furious activity, a short break, phone calls, maybe a longer break to go somewhere else in the Police Bureau building to check on something, then back.

Now, however, she'd been gone close to an hour. In the past, when this happened, it usually meant she was up to no good. So, when she reappeared, slipping behind her desk without saying anything, very close to their alleged lunch hour, Wismer cleared his throat and spoke.

"Been out for a walk, *Boothie*?"

No guilt or embarrassment showed in her level gaze, only mild amusement. He hadn't caught her doing anything she thought wrong, then. Of course, there wasn't much Boothe Deakins considered wrong, especially if the cause was right.

"Right, took a stroll up to talk to Vinnie Messick at 1500 SW First. Even on Saturday, he was in the office."

Messick was the local FBI's ace forensics man. If Vinnie liked you -- and he both liked and respected Deakins -- sometimes a covert request for his expertise would be honored. The feebies here were generally inclined to help law enforcement who wouldn't climb up their butts, which the local cops wouldn't. For their fellow feds, on the other hand, it was pretty much 'eat shit and die.'

Wismer looked over at the door to make sure it was shut. "So, you cobbed some of the fur at the scene, took it to Vinnie? Excuse me. I mean 'Senior Technician Messick.'"

"Yeah. Signed for the running gear from the Duncan homicide and gave him that, too."

"Oh, *that's* cute. What's all this supposed to accomplish, exactly?"

"Just wanted to know what kind of cat we have." Not one ounce of remorse in her voice.

"We have a fur sample going down to the labs at OSU already, with Haggen. Besides, how is Vinnie Messick gonna tell us this? Don't the feds generally identify *people*?"

She started to smile. "Vinnie has a local hotshot geneticist who works with Customs on illegal trafficking of animal parts. Feathers, hides, horns, stuff like that. Occasionally does things for the feebs. I called in a favor he owed me from the pistol competition last year."

Wismer had to laugh. The FBI, burned in two consecutive competitions by his lanky, blonde, sociopath partner, had brought one of their best national-level shooters into the Portland office on TDY the previous year. Coincidentally just in time for the All-Law pistol shoot. The guy was damned good, but in the end, Boothe Deakins had prevailed. The feebies had gone home with their tails between their legs, and Chief Albright and Karl Elch had chuckled for a week -- in private, being too kind to beat a dead federal horse. Later Wismer found out that -- prior to the match -- Boothe had discovered Vinnie Messick's attempt to stack the deck for the feds. She'd said nothing, merely made a sizeable side-bet with him. Cleaned Messick out. Now she probably had five years' worth of favors on the docket.

"How soon are we gonna get results?" Wismer asked.

"The genetics lady won't be back until tomorrow night. She's speaking this weekend at some World Wildlife confab in Vancouver, B.C. Vinnie got her on her cell-phone and made the arrangements. You and I will meet with them Monday afternoon."

Wismer sighed. "By that time, we'll be lucky to get out of this place without the media circus descending on us big-time. The Sunday papers'll have opinions and conjecture from everybody from the Captain and Chief Albright down to that gal at the Church of Elvis."

His partner regarded him with frank disdain. "We'll catch *nothing* compared to Albright and the Mayor. And you can be glad that Rose Festival is pretty much over, so we don't have five thousand sailors in town, like last weekend."

"True enough. But why'd you go to Vinnie? We basically *know* it has to be a cougar. If it's native. And nobody's reported losing a large exotic cat in the area."

"I'm not sure why I went to Messick," Deakins replied, shrugging. "If it's not a cougar, say maybe a leopard or jaguar, then the investigation changes focus. I guess I just want independent confirmation." She grinned. "Plus I don't want Vinnie to forget he owes me."

"Pistol competition's coming up in August," Wismer said, reminding her, then had a another thought. "Why couldn't it be a lion or tiger?"

"They roar. Lions, anyway. None of the neighbors heard any roaring, even though they heard the victim's yells. Besides, I don't think your average human could fend off a really big cat for as long as Al Chambers apparently did."

"You probably got that right," he admitted, looking at his watch. "'Bout time for lunch. You up for some Bento?"

Stupid question. His partner only smiled. Provided she was hungry, Boothe Deakins would eat anything, anywhere, any time. Then burned it off in the weight room or in martial arts classes.

61

They put on their jackets and went out into typically uncertain Rose Festival weather. A few drops fell out of the overcast sky, but at wide intervals, with the temp in the low sixties. The old rule about northern Oregon weather was if you couldn't see Mount Hood, it was raining, and if you could, it was about to rain. This was generally true from October to late June.

The vaguely triangular area just south of West Burnside, between Police Bureau offices and west to Southwest Broadway contained numerous eclectic businesses, some of which were eateries, both trendy and non-trendy, and the lieutenants strolled to one of those, Big Daddy Bento, operated by a family of mixed-Asian origins, mainly Chinese. The restaurant's otherwise non-denominational decor was dominated by views of various Japanese landmarks, however, chief among those Mount Fuji.

Boothe was well-known to the owners. Some of the younger family members were into martial arts and greeted her with broad smiles and deep bows. She bowed back, only not quite so low, and Wismer knew there were some serious protocols going on. As they headed for a rear table, no one said anything about the murders, and that was probably another example of Asian propriety. The media had arrived at the homicide scene at about the time Doctor Chambers' body was being loaded into the EMT rig, so the whole town knew.

The Captain had insisted on speaking with the widow, accompanying Wismer and Deakins to the Chambers' home. Elisabeth Chambers, seeing Elch's readily-recognizable saturnine features when she opened the door, turned white as a sheet. Boothe supported the older woman as they went into the well-appointed living room, and offered to get her a glass of water when she was settled into a chair. Elisabeth Chambers had waved Boothe away, and the Captain did the honors while Wismer examined pictures of various generations of Chambers hanging on the wall by the fireplace. All clean-cut, all happy, all likely nice folks. It was just a frigging shame, he thought once more, as he took a seat opposite Boothe in the little restaurant.

They always ate the same thing, Chicken bento with veggies on the side, and green tea, so the kid who escorted them to their table headed back to the kitchen after another bow, leaving the two officers alone for the moment.

"Tell me about the 'Boothie' thing," Wismer asked, folding his hands together on the table top.

"Not much to tell," his partner replied. "Professor Haggen worked for my dad during the summers while he was playing ball at Oregon State. I was like in first grade."

"So your folks called you 'Boothie?'"

"Still do. Natural enough that Odward did, too. He's a great guy. Like Carlton said, he uses that gruff shit to keep the public at a distance."

"What'd Haggen do for your dad?"

"Drove the product to market down in Peoria, southeast of Corvallis. That was the distribution center. Odward was clean-shaven in those days, had a crewcut, played tackle, and always, *always*, wore an Oregon State T-shirt, with OSU decals and stickers all over the delivery truck."

Wismer nodded. "Smart move. Pretty much Beaver country all the way from Forest Grove down through McMinnville to Corvallis." The beaver was the Oregon State mascot, just as Donald Duck was at the University of Oregon in Eugene. Both critters well-suited to the local climate.

Deakins chuckled, glanced toward the kitchen. "Whatever, it sure worked for Odward." She unfolded her paper napkin and placed it in her lap. "And two upstanding members of the law enforcement community should *not* be having this conversation."

"Right," Wismer agreed, then favored her with his best imitation of her implacable, flat stare. "If we can't trust each other, Boothe, we can't trust anybody."

"Thanks for sayin' that, Ronald. Though you didn't have to. I know how you play the game." She looked in the direction of the kitchen again. "Here comes our grub."

When the food was safely arranged on their table, their tea poured, and the young waiter bowed away, Deakins spoke again. "What kind of shit do you think we're in? As the ranking investigative officers in these homicides." She picked up a small slab of chicken breast with her chopsticks.

"Deep and tenacious. These deaths aren't coincidental, particularly if forensics shows the killer was the same animal."

Deakins nodded. "And if two killers were involved?"

"That simplifies things. One notch. Still, why were Mormon dentists targeted? That implies direction, intelligence. The Saint community should be justifiably concerned."

"So, no matter what, it's shit up, down, and sideways?"

Wismer chewed thoughtfully for a few moments. "Yeah, I think so," he replied finally. "So what do *you* think?"

"I think somebody's killing Mormon dentists. Not Mormons, not dentists. Mormon dentists. That's the whole deal. Somehow it's convenient and confusing to use big cats to do the whacks. I'm not ruling out two different animals. And even if it's not cougars, we *will* say it is, until we find out otherwise. Maybe even after that. That's my take on the thing. Elch and the Chief may handle it differently."

His next forkful of rice stopped halfway to Wismer's mouth. "We aren't heading into mythological creature territory?"

She shook her head, laughing around her food. "Not yet."

"But we might be, at some point?"

"Maybe." She reached across the table, touched his left wrist with the long fingers of her right hand. "Tell you what, though. If it gets weird, and we solve it anyway, I'll wear one of those little belly shirts the chick cops wear in the movies -- into the Day Room."

Wismer snorted. "Thanks for not saying that while I was drinking my tea. Woulda blown it out my nose for sure."

"Hey! Ray says I have nice abs!"

"I'm a believer. But he's been going out with you for three months, and either knows which side of his bread the butter is on, or he's an uncomprehending moron." He flashed her a nano-second's smile. "I should also point out that Raymond Gubrud is in the Public Defender's office, and his judgment is skewed. To my mind, his sole positive feature is that you see something in him." Another smile. "Or somewhere about his person."

A slight flush crept over Deakins' angular features, and her eyes narrowed. "Shithead," she said softly.

Wismer shook his head as he took a sip of tea. "I just hope to hell you're serious about that belly shirt thing."

TWELVE

Paul and Claire sat opposite one another on the balcony of his condo, enjoying their wine. A small teak table stood between them, their bare ankles intertwined under it. Darkness gathered in the eastern sky as Saturday drew to an end. Overhead, the orange contrail of a jet momentarily seemed to form the demarcation between blue day and black night.

"An August wedding sound about right?" Paul asked.

Claire's answering smile was lazy, sated. "Sure. I told Mom yesterday. Dad called me this morning, all concerned."

"Concerned?"

"Concerned and happy. Mostly the latter. They *like* you. Plus, you have 'good prospects.'"

"They didn't say that!"

"*Dad* did. You have to understand, this is important to the born-Irish. The desired maiden needs a cozy weather-tight bungalow, a bit of land and stock, lace curtains, and good china." She dug her toenails into his ankles. "You tell *your* folks?"

Paul nodded, his voice a bit defensive. "Yeah. Talked to Mom after you went to softball practice this morning. Dad, Henry, and Eric were out moving irrigation pipe and throwing feed to the cattle. Mom liked the idea fine, no big surprise there, since I'm the last to marry. Henry and Eric tied the knot with their respective spouses after their first couple of seasons in the NFL, so this is kind of a load off my folks' backs."

Claire laughed. "F.X. probably thought you were gay."

Paul shook his head. "I don't think so. Francis Xavier Tiernan thinks gay men only come from urban environments. But there was definitely an advantage to

66

being the youngest and the smallest. Expectations were not unbearably high."

"'Small Paul.' *Cute* nickname."

"I'm taller than *you*."

"In your dreams," Claire retorted, "but you're a damn fine passer."

"Thread the needle." He nodded emphatically, thinking he'd had more than enough wine when he began bragging even a little. "Most assists at OSU since Jim Jarvis."

"Good hands."

"You, more than anyone, can attest to that."

She reached over and stroked his left cheek. "I can."

The phone in his kitchen rang.

Claire glared as Paul rose to answer it. "If that's Wismer, tell him you'll call back."

"Too early for Ron," Paul replied, as he vanished into the condo. "He never calls until the kids are in bed. Besides, they had another cougar death this morning, so he's busy. It's probably Dad."

Ten minutes later, he rejoined Claire, the remainder of their bottle of wine in his hand. He filled both glasses after sitting down.

"Not your Dad?" Claire asked. "You were awful quiet."

"No. Answering service. An irate patient. Harold Fenstermacher, slightly-psychotic Vietnam veteran."

Claire regarded him quizzically, her eyebrows together. "You didn't have much to say. You just sat there."

Paul shook his head. "Mister Fenstermacher generally does all the talking. He's really a pretty nice guy until he breaks a tooth or loses a filling. Then he goes ballistic. He knows exactly who put in every restoration in his mouth, and when something goes wrong, to his way of thinking, at least, he unloads."

67

He took a long drink of wine. "Post-traumatic Stress Disorder, with manifestations linked to his oral condition."

"Nothing you did?" Paul could tell she was holding back laughter.

"No. This particular offending situation was an MO on tooth number three, done in 1982 in Eugene by one Ralph Pinardi, General Dentist."

Now Claire laughed outright. "So, what'd he say?"

"Four-letter words beginning with 'F.' A few other things. When he calls, he's always had a few drinks, always has a Sergeant Barry Saddler CD on, singing 'Ballad of the Green Berets.' And he just goes frigging berzerk." He gulped the rest of his wine, regarded her bleakly.

"God, that's weird!"

"He always cries at the end. When he quits sobbing, I tell him to come in the next morning -- in this case, Monday -- and we'll fix him up."

"He *cries*?"

"Every time. He'll come in, I'll take care of the problem, he'll thank the entire staff -- a perfect gentleman -- and I'll tell him to be sure and wear his nightguard."

"And everything's cool until the next time?"

"Yeah. He was in a LRRP unit in 'Nam, just like your boss. I think he saw some heavy action. "It took its toll." He shrugged. "I don't mind. Really."

Claire studied him in silence for a few moments, then emptied her own glass. "You're a nice guy, Paul," she said quietly.

He mustered up what he hoped was an acceptable smile. "You want nice, you should meet my fiancée'."

Picking up their glasses and the now-empty bottle, Claire got to her feet, pulled him up. "C'mon.

I'll give you a back-rub, and I'll tell you about the middle-of-the- night call *I* had recently."

"We need to talk about dead Mormon dentists, too. This morning's victim was another Sozye doc. They didn't say that on the news, just his name, but I recognized it. Remember Al Chambers? Older guy, taught one day a week in the Operatives Department, like I do now."

Claire thought for a few seconds. "He had the A-L half of the class, not ours. They all liked him."

"Well, he won't be back for Fall Term, and you can bet Ron Wismer and Boothe Deakins are in the hot seat."

"Let's go have your back-rub, Doctor Fatalism," Claire said, tugging him into the great room. She indicated the carpet. "T-shirt off. Face down, please."

Paul removed his shirt, dropped to the floor, pillowed his head on his arms, and closed his eyes. "So, tell me about your call. While you rub, of course."

Squatting on the backs of his thighs, settling her thumbs into his trapezii, Claire began to knead slowly. "Well, I got this call over the weekend from the ER at Providence. A nurse, actually, apologetic as hell. One of our patients I'd sent to the Oral Surgeon, her daughter had taken all her Vicodin, and they were in getting the kid's stomach pumped."

"How old?"

"Sixteen, and as soon as the mother's voice came on the line, I knew it was some kind of bogus."

Paul laughed. "She had the 'voice?'"

"Yeah, the *drug* voice. Every drug seeker has it. I don't think they know they all sound the same. It's like a flag. But, anyway, the mother was calling because, of course, since her daughter had taken all her Vikes, she needed *more*." She bore down harder on his shoulders. "Did you know you're getting hair on your back?"

69

"Did you phone in a script?"

"Sure. You have to buy the story. There's no way around it." She paused, and he could almost feel her frown. "You didn't used to have hair there."

He shifted slightly under her. "I thought we were swapping funny patient stories."

"That was before I found out I'd accepted a proposal of marriage from Kongo the Gorilla."

"It's all that testosterone."

"You're looking for an upside to your ongoing hirsuitism. Aren't you, Doctor?"

"I'm only thinking of your happiness."

Claire leaned down and kissed the back of his neck. "That's *so* sweet, Paul. Too bad I'm not buyin'."

With an effort, he rolled over, still beneath her, and lay looking up at her face. "With all that hair," he said, "maybe the kids won't need heavy winter jackets."

Her expression changed, became momentarily unreadable, as though he'd said something serious. Then she grinned. "Yeah, okay," she replied at last, bending down to him.

What was that all about? Paul thought, as they kissed.

THIRTEEN

When Ron Wismer and Boothe Deakins arrived at the entrance to the FBI's Portland offices after lunch on Monday, Vinnie Messick waited just inside the glass doors fronting Southwest First. Vinnie's thick hands were stuffed deeply into the pockets of his white lab coat, and he looked entirely too pleased with himself.

The two detectives exchanged looks, and Boothe lifted a cautionary eyebrow at her partner. "What's up?" she asked the blocky forensics specialist.

"Well, things ain't exactly what I expected," Messick replied, grinning as he shook their hands. "Thought I better clue you in before we get talkin' with Miz Milton, who, I want to point out, is generally one unflappable lady. However, she is currently somewhat flapped, since we got ourselves what the Bureau calls an 'MS' situation."

"'MS'?" Wismer asked.

"Yeah. 'Mulder-Scully,' like on the TV program. Something inexplicably mysterious." The grin on Messick's broad features turned sly as he led them to the elevators. "Damned glad it's yours and not ours."

"Thanks loads," Wismer replied when they were inside the elevator, going up.

Messick shrugged. "Hey, I never saw your evidence and I don't know nothing. If I didn't owe Annie Oakley, here, I wouldn't of got involved. As it is, my bosses find out, they're gonna shit." His deepset brown eyes danced. "It *is* damned funny, though."

"Thanks loads," Wismer said again. Deakins said nothing, merely watched the lights on the panel march upward, a thoughtful expression on her angular features.

Rose Milton turned out to be a medium-sized, round-faced woman with calluses that matched

Boothe's. She regarded the two detectives with the same level of joy most people reserved for potentially poisonous snakes. Still, Wismer saw genuine curiosity and a healthy level of calm determination in her brownish-green gaze. They had apparently thrown her a curve, but she thought she'd at least hit a solid dribbler into the infield.

"Is everything Vinnie told me the truth?" she asked, as she stepped up onto a small platform and took her place behind the podium. As she spoke, she absently polished her wire-rimmed glasses on a sleeve of her beige cotton blouse.

"So far as we know," Deakins replied.

The geneticist leaned on the podium after replacing her glasses, her hands folded. "Then you are well and truly screwed, officers. You have given me something I *can* explain -- up to a point -- but nobody in this room is going to be one damned bit happy about it." She nodded to Messick. "Except Vinnie, who finds your situation amusing. Of course, he's a twisted individual. At best."

Messick smiled happily in acknowledgement.

Rose Milton turned more serious. "There are no slides, folks, and this conversation is so far off the record it's not even within the boundries of the continental United States." She sighed. "How much do you two know about genetics?"

"Some," the detectives admitted. "Not a lot."

"That's okay. You've probably heard that most mammals -- as well as a lot of lesser lights in the animal kingdom -- share genetic commonality with humans. Horses, for example. Their Number Nine gene-pair is *exactly* the same as Human Number Eight. Domestic cats are even more so. Sixteen of their nineteen gene-pairs are comparable to human. Cats and primates are closely related. We are not as special a creation as our theologic advisors have long preached."

72

Her smile flashed on and off. "Still, I would not have suspected that your killers would be something *truly* unique in my experience." Her smile returned, rueful this time.

"'Killers?'" Wismer asked.

Milton nodded. "Oh, yes. What we have here -- whatever they are, and they *aren't* cougars -- is a boy one and a girl one. The fur came from a male. The running gear DNA belonged to a female."

Wismer felt his stomach drop. He couldn't bring himself to look at his partner, whose instincts had proven so spectacularly right. "Any guesses?"

"Oh, sure. Did you know that cougars -- the logical but wrong culprit in these murders -- are closely related to cheetahs? More than any other form of large cat, at any rate."

"Uh, no," Wismer admitted. Deakins was quiet.

"Well, they are. However, unlike all other cats, cheetahs don't have fully-retractable claws."

"But the killers did."

"Indeed. So they weren't cheetahs. *Modern* cheetahs, at any rate. But, as I said, they weren't cougars, either."

Boothe leaned forward, her elbows on her knees. "So what were they?"

Milton frowned. "I don't know, and Vinnie will tell you he has never heard me say that before where any animal is concerned. There were, however, *other* species of cheetah -- or cheetah-like cats -- in the fairly recent past. The North American versions -- *Miracinonyx inexpectatus* and *trumani*, had more fully retractable claws. And some scientists believe the European *Acinonyx pardinenis* may share that trait. Though it is closely related to modern cheetahs and has been included in the same genus, it was a *much* larger animal. As were the two North American varieties. So what we have here are creatures who are *almost* modern cheetahs."

"An *extinct* animal killed our victims?" Wismer asked, thinking he sounded whiny.

Beside him, Vinnie Messick grunted with delight. "The enviros'll *love* that, huh? That's even *better* than endangered. The accidental re-appearance of a critter thought to be gone forever. Wow."

When it returned, Milton's smile was grim. "Except that the killers were also both human, each with a complete complement of human chromosomes. Or, if one looks from the other end, a complete complement of mystery cat. The sharing of those sixteen chromosomes I mentioned earlier accounts for that..." She paused for a moment, took a deep breath. "...*design efficiency*. Along with much less 'junk DNA' between the important stuff."

Wismer's world turned on its side for an instant, flipping into nightmare. He swallowed, took a deep breath, licked his lips. "What do they look like?"

"He means cat or human," his partner added.

"Well, they've obviously got claws, and are at least partially furred," the geneticist answered. "Beyond that, I couldn't begin to guess."

"Shit," Deakins said disgustedly. "Lycanthropes."

Wismer looked at her, trying to remember where he'd heard that term. "What the hell is that?"

For the first time Milton laughed. "Like werewolves, detective. Part-time in both worlds."

"Told 'ya," Vinnie chortled. "It's seriously weird shit. *Your* weird shit."

Leaning forward, Deakins looked across her partner's front at Messick. Wismer knew that flat stare. He and Deakins never played 'good-cop/bad-cop' with their suspects. Boothe would sit alone with the perp in the interrogation room, wearing that look, talking, just talking, in a low voice. Until the perp couldn't take it, until his gums -- or maybe his fingernail beds -- started to bleed, and he buckled.

74

Captain Elch called it 'The Dueling Sociopath Challenge.'

Vinnie, however, understood the look easily enough. "Don't you give me that crap, young lady!" he exclaimed, shaking a finger at her. "I'll put you over my knee!"

Deakins grinned at him. "Seems unlikely." Her gaze shifted to Milton. "So. Two for the price of one, huh?"

Milton nodded. "Looks that way. Too much good DNA in there for just one species."

"Shit!" Boothe replied. She drew her CZ, held it in her lap, regarding it thoughtfully. "Guess it doesn't matter, though. Put a big enough hole in 'em, and it won't make any difference. They'll still go down."

"There's my girl," Vinnie said. He sounded relieved.

"Up yours," Deakins replied cheerfully. "Not that I don't appreciate your help." She smiled at the geneticist. "And yours, Miz Milton."

"Excuse me, here," Wismer added, raising his right hand. "But we seem to have developed some additional problems in our investigation. Like just what the living hell are we looking for here? Two people or two animals?"

"Both," the other three replied together.

"C'mon," Wismer said reasonably. "We still have *no* witnesses amongst the living. Do the killers have to look *either* human or cat-like?"

"So, Ronald," Deakins said, grinning at him. "You want something like out of the 'Howling' movies?"

"I want this conversation not to be happening. And I *really* don't want to be hunting something that switches back-and-forth at will."

"'Full-moon fever,'" Vinnie said.

Deakins shook her head. "No, they do it when they want. We're not talking Lon Chaney here. Either

75

they switch, or they're always a cat. And the running gear sort of argues against the single form."

"So you're sayin' they switch, and they do it whenever they're in the mood?" her partner asked.

"Yeah, but the process could take a while."

"Shit." He turned to Milton. "You know Odward Haggen?"

"Sure. There aren't that many people on the west coast who do our kind of work. It's not Odward's whole income, like it is mine, but he's damned competent."

"He's got a fur sample. He gonna figure this out?"

She nodded. "Yes, almost certainly. And he'll do the tests and examination himself, so the total number of people who know about this will be five." Milton stood up straight, gripping the edges of the podium. "The hard question is what to tell your Captain and Chief Albright."

"Tell 'im the whole story," Messick put in gruffly. "He'll still say the right things to the media. Two different animals is a *good* thing."

"Both cougars," Deakins said.

"I probably shouldn't tell you guys this," the FBI man said, leaning forward to rest his elbows on his knees, "but we really *do* have an investigation division back on the east coast -- something like a half-dozen people -- that looks into this sort of weird stuff. If you get stuck and need help, I *might* be able to pull some strings. Just a little favor, what with the pistol competition comin' up soon and all."

Rose Milton stepped down from behind the podium. "I'll be glad to take a look at any additional samples, too. Off the record again, of course."

"Thanks," Deakins said. "Professor Haggen will definitely have some useful suggestions. He's about a common-sense as they come."

"How about maybe I just go and throw myself in front of a MAX train," Wismer mused, looking up at the ceiling.

"Margie and the kids'd be pissed," his partner replied, grabbing his left wrist, "not to mention me."

"You? Pissed? Oh, that'd be *real* bad," Messick said.

The funny part, Wismer thought, was that Vinnie seemed absolutely sincere.

FOURTEEN

By the time they'd arrived back at the Central Precinct, Wismer's mood had lifted somewhat. Boothe had kept mostly silent, letting him come back to level on his own, and he appreciated that. Unspoken communication was one of her strong points. She knew when to leave people alone.

On the other hand, Boothe doubtless had her own thoughts on their situation. Hers, of course, were unencumbered by standard-issue moral constraints, and she was a total linear thinker. Procedural steps were taken in numerical order, though somewhere around steps five or six, the CZ usually made an appearance, and all that would be left was paperwork.

"You think Haggen's phoned the Cap?" he asked as they approached the precinct entrance.

"Yeah. The Professor's not much of a procrastinator. There'll be sticky notes or voice-mails, if the Cap's around."

There were both, and five minutes after they were in the building, they'd replaced the evidence and were seated in Karl Elch's office. They'd passed the Mayor on their way up, and the little gap-toothed guy seemed cheerful enough, so Wismer thought maybe this wouldn't be too bad.

Elch proved him wrong. "Sit!" he said first, then, when both detectives were seated, added, "Where the *hell* have you two been?"

"Talking to Vinnie Messick," Deakins answered, before her partner could.

Their boss was anything but slow. "You gave some of the fur to Messick." Anger underlaid his flat words.

"There were *two* killers," Wismer said, hoping to deflect Elch's displeasure before he really got his wind up.

"What!"

"Duncan's was female," Boothe said quickly.

Speechless for the moment, the Captain stared at them. Finally, he said, "*Two* different animals?"

"Two different *people*," Wismer amended.

Elch looked briefly at the ceiling, a 'why me, God' expression on his craggy features. Then he looked back at his officers. "Yeah, Haggen mentioned that." He eyed Deakins. "The running gear, huh?"

"Yessir."

"Crap." He picked up his phone, punched in some numbers, waited for what was obviously some kind of voicemail, then left a message about there being two killers involved. "The Mayor. He and the Chief've got a press conference tomorrow morning. This'll make both their jobs easier."

"All due respect, Sir," Wismer said, "but this just buys us some time."

"I know that," Elch replied, grimacing. "Plus there are a couple more things. Car prowls and home break-ins were down dramatically over the weekend. Also, there were twenty-seven cougar sightings in the Portland Metropolitan area."

"Would that be a *good* thing, then, Sir?" Deakins asked.

Elch allowed himself a small grin. "Depending upon one's point of view, I guess." He leaned back in his chair, lifted his long legs, and rested his crossed ankles on one corner of his desk. "So what next? How're you two gonna haul my sacred butt outa the fire?"

"Yeah, Ronald," Deakins said, turning to Wismer, one eyebrow elevated. "How we gonna do that?"

Wismer glared at her. "Okay, we know there are two different killers, that they're apparently some kind of two-for-the-price-of-one were-cat things. Which I hate to admit. Politically or otherwise. I can't believe

I believe this, but facts are facts and evidence is evidence. If they have a human form, and the running gear argues for that, then we have to figure out how to identify them when they look like us."

"They'll probably look a lot alike," his partner added.

"Why?" asked the Captain.

"Oh, yeah," Wismer said. "Vinnie's expert said they're closely related, at least cousins, maybe even brother and sister."

Elch considered that for a few seconds. "Do tell. Too bad we can't work up physical appearance from DNA yet. A couple years from now, I hear, but not yet."

"There is one thing," Deakins said. "We know they've got big fangs. Where do those go when they're in human form?"

Both men looked at her in puzzlement. "What?" the Captain asked.

"They'd dissolve back into the body," Wismer replied. He glanced at Elch, as if for support. "Wouldn't they?"

His partner shrugged. "I dunno. Tooth enamel is crystalline, with *no* blood supply. The rest of the tooth doesn't have much. I wouldn't think they could just build a new set of teeth at the drop of a hat."

"I'll ask Paul," Wismer said.

The Captain raised his right hand in caution. "Let's keep the circle small, Lieutenants. Who's Paul?"

"Paul Tiernan. Guy I grew up with. He's a dentist. He'll set me straight on how teeth form, and I won't tell him more than he needs to know."

Elch shook his head. "More dentists. We keep coming back to that segment of the populace." He chuckled. "And not one of my favorite segments, either." Then he paused. "'Tiernan?' Weren't there Tiernans at OSU a few years back?"

"Yeah. Paul was the youngest, the basketball player. The two older brothers played football. Henry and Eric."

"Henry was the quarterback? Had a real arm?"

"Right. Played pro seven-eight years. Eric about the same, only on the line."

"'Ox?'"

Wismer laughed. "Yeah. Big, quick, smart, aggressive."

"I *hate* football," his partner said quietly.

Elch regarded her with amazement. "But it's *violent*! You *like* violence."

"She'd like football, if they let you use guns," Wismer added, grinning at Deakins.

The straight line of Boothe's lips slowly curved up. "Oh, *yeah*," she said.

"If you two didn't do a decent job," the Captain said, giving Deakins a pointed look, "statements like that would worry me." He pulled his legs down, slid back into his chair, and sat up straight. "So, as it stands, the Mayor and Chief Albright and I will treat these as separate incidents, the Mormon dentist thing as coincidence, and let the chips fall where they may."

"The number of jogging Mormon dentists has dropped off, I bet," Wismer said, watching Boothe out of the corner of his eye.

"*I'm* bettin' the killing keeps up," she said in very flat tones, "except it won't be cats doing the whacks. That game'll only work twice. And, if it does continue, we need to talk to Hyrum Gregorson. Somebody may be trying to cripple his operation."

"That's the longest speech I've ever heard you make," Elch said, his expression impressed. "And you're right about needing to question Gregorson if it keeps up. Which I sincerely hope it doesn't." He scratched his sizeable nose. "Never occurred to me that this might be pointed at his company, frankly."

"You don't have my partner's devious mind," Wismer said.

Elch eyed Deakins. "Is that what it is?" He chuckled. "Well, Lieutenants, you might as well get back to your real jobs in the real world now. Just keep me posted."

When they were back out in the hall, Wismer began softly laughing.

"What?" Boothe asked.

"You were just Little Mary Frigging Sunshine in there, kiddo."

She gave him an arch look. "You think we're done with this, Ronald? I don't." She held out her right hand. "Betcha!"

Wismer sighed, felt frustration well up through his entire being. He shook his head. "No, I agree with you. And I wouldn't place any bets on all this for anything."

FIFTEEN

Paul Tiernan was taken completely aback when Ron Wismer and Boothe Deakins walked into his office fifteen minutes before quitting time on a Monday. "Oh-oh," he said from behind the reception counter. He looked from one serious face to the other, trying to smile. "Is this an official visit, guys?"

Wismer grinned, but not widely or for more than a moment. "Sort of. We need to know about tooth formation."

"O-kay. We're done here for the day, except one hygiene exam. You want to wait in my office while I do that? Take me five-ten minutes."

"Sure," Deakins replied, and Wismer nodded.

Paul led them to the back of the office, got them seated. "This real important?" he asked, standing briefly in his doorway before leaving to do the exam.

"Maybe," Wismer said.

"Mind if I look at these?" Boothe asked, gesturing at a quartet of tooth models on Paul's desk.

"No, not at all. Back in a bit." He shut the door behind him, wondering what in hell this was about.

When Paul had done the exam and returned, Wismer asked, "Teeth are all more or less the same in higher mammals?"

Deakins still studied a pair of models, both cut away to show internal tooth structure.

"Yeah, more or less," he answered, taking a seat behind his desk. "Enamel on the outside, dentin beneath that, surrounding a hollow core. Incisors in the front, then canines, then premolars and molars as you go toward the back of the mouth. Function determines shape to some extent. Cattle, sheep, and horses all have large, flat molars with broad grinding surfaces. Heavy-duty carnivores have big canines that both guide the teeth together and hold their prey.

Humans and most other higher primates are fructivores -- fruit eaters -- so our teeth aren't horribly specialized beyond the basic differences." He looked at them. "Why is this important? What's the deal?"

Wismer shook his head. "Can't tell you, bud. Has to do with an ongoing investigation."

Paul grinned at him. "Just a tip, Wis. Cougars have really big canines."

"Tell me about impactions," Deakins said, before her partner could reply beyond a sour look.

"They can be either full or partial. Partial is when a portion of the tooth is visible in the mouth. Full is when the tooth is completely covered by tissue or bone, or both. The key is that further eruption and exposure within the oral cavity are unlikely."

The blonde detective nodded. "What if a nearby tooth was removed. Would the impacted tooth erupt then?"

"Sometimes. Particularly if stimulated, like putting a denture over the tooth. Impacted Wisdom teeth almost always erupt when a denture is placed over them. Within a few months at most, they're in the mouth."

"A few months," Deakins said. She looked at Wismer before turning back to Paul. "What's the quickest you've seen a stimulated tooth come in?"

Paul considered her question. "I had an impacted upper lateral incisor come in less than two months after I placed a partial over it."

"So eruptive forces are slow at best?"

"Yeah."

"How about enamel? Does the body ever dissolve it away?"

"The body makes it, it can take it away. I've never seen enamel resorbed, though. Dentin, yeah. Happens all the time. It has some blood supply. It's metabolically available. Internal, external resorption. Body goes a little wacky, turns on itself, starts eating tooth structure. And remember, the permanent teeth cause the baby teeth to resorb as they erupt under them."

Boothe leaned forward, her eyes narrowing. "But just the dentin, not the enamel?"

"Right. When the baby tooth is shed, the enamel is intact."

Wismer folded his arms over his chest and sighed. "Too damned slow."

"If this has something to do with the deaths of Byron Duncan and Al Chambers," Paul said, "You have completely lost me."

"Sorry," Wismer replied, a touch of bitterness in his voice, along with obvious frustration.

Paul knew his answers hadn't been the right ones, for all that they were absolutely correct. He glanced at Boothe, but she looked inscrutable, her gaze flat and introspective. There were times when he wished he knew her better, could see a little of what went on in her head, but he also knew Ron would say not to go there. Probably good advice. Claire was tough enough to fathom.

* * * * *

"And Ron wouldn't tell you *why* they were asking about tooth formation?" Claire asked. She leaned against the counter in Paul's kitchen, drinking a Diet Coke, watching Paul scrape stir-fry around inside a skillet on his stove top.

"No. But they just kept coming back to eruption rate and resorption rate. And the weird part was that it had something to do with Duncan and Chambers."

"That doesn't make sense. They were killed by some kind of cat."

Paul lifted the skillet from the flame, and clicked off the gas. He began spooning the stir-fry onto two plates. "Well," he said, as he ladled. "If I had to guess,

85

I'd say they've got some DNA samples that've confused them in some way." He shrugged, handed her a plate and fork, and gave her a quick grin.

Claire took the plate, her blunt features puzzled. "I don't get it. A cougar's a cougar, right?"

They sat down at Paul's little kitchen table. "Except when it's not, apparently."

"Maybe it's an adolescent. Still got deciduous teeth."

Paul shook his head. "It's something more than that. I can't read Boothe at all, but I know Ron pretty well. Whatever it is, it's got him worried."

"Huh," Claire grunted, taking a forkful of food, and chewing thoughtfully.

They ate not exactly in silence, but only with intermittent small talk about their days' patients. When they'd finished eating, Claire rinsed her plate and fork and stuck them in the dishwasher. "I need to give my Uncle Emmett a call. I meant to call him from the office, and got side-tracked. Just take a minute, okay?"

"Sure," Paul replied. "I'll go through my day's interesting mail while you chat."

Claire moved out onto the balcony with her cell phone, sliding the door shut behind her. Paul watched her through the glass as he sorted his mail, wondering why calling her uncle was important just now. He knew the two spoke only occasionally. Perhaps it had something to do with the projected wedding in August. Her gestures during the conversation seemed awfully animated for that, though. She even paced. Oh, well, he thought, picking up a copy of the Oregon Cattleman's Association quarterly magazine and admiring the cover subject, a comely Hereford.

Nice-looking animal.

SIXTEEN

Claire was not habitually an early riser, but her uncle's concern on the phone the previous evening brought her to his secluded rowhouse home a little over an hour before her workday began, ostensibly for breakfast.

They were halfway through their waffles and eggs before
Emmett McManus broached the subject he'd alluded to ten hours earlier. "I hate to be abrupt, Claire, but *can* you? Your father has never said." He coughed between the two short sentences.

Claire put down her fork and swallowed her current mouthful of egg. "Yes, but I haven't for over ten years."

"Did you *enjoy* it? The sensations, I mean."

"Sure." She grinned. "There's *power* there. Speed. Strength. Heightened senses. A mind-set only remotely human. Damned *right*, I enjoyed it."

"I see. Then why the ten-year hiatus?"

She shrugged. "Really haven't thought about it a lot lately, but I think I worried about the possibility of addiction." Even talking about it made her uneasy.

Her uncle nodded. "Ahh. There is that. Did your father never speak with you about it, then?"

"When I hit puberty, he and Mom sat me down for a serious talk, showed me how to do the Shift, took me out a few times, then said it would be my decision as to when and how frequently. The whole rigamarole seemed like another version of the 'sex lecture,' except there wasn't a pill to protect me."

An expression of vexation momentarily crossed McManus's narrow features. "So perfectly proper. Very like my brother. He can be rather trusting." He smiled fondly at her. "But he can be excused in this instance. You have always seemed so *capable*. I might have done the same thing."

Her face warmed. "I think it scared me some. To suddenly find myself in the body of something designed to hunt and kill. And *feed*."

"And you an adolescent, with a human adolescent's uncertainty. It must have seemed a kind of *possession*."

Claire chuckled. "I think I outgrew that part pretty quick. But you know how kids are. It was something my *folks* did, of course, so I didn't want to so much. If I'd had other Shifters around, ones my own age, it would have been a different story. We could have run together, hunted together, like you and Dad did, back in the Old Country."

Her uncle leaned back in his chair, rubbing the back of his neck with one hand. He smiled. "Ah, yes, I remember those days. I remember those *nights*. Splendid times." His features sobered. "What about Paul?"

Claire shook her head. "He doesn't know. No reason for him to. On the other hand, he wants *kids*."

"Cause for concern?"

Total incredulity flowed over her features, as though she couldn't believe his words. "Damn right. The gene's dominant. I'm a Double, got it from both sides. *All* our kids will be what you and I are."

"It may not be the problem you fear. Paul is a fine young man. And we have to be *taught*. There are likely many of our kind who have never been informed and instructed."

"Do you really *believe* that?" Claire scoffed. "My mother and father are *proud* of it. I'm not sure I want to tell Paul to give the baby a ball of string and he or she'll be happy for hours."

In spite of the gravity of their conversation, McManus laughed at the thought. "Wait until puberty, then, as did your parents."

"*Yours* didn't!"

"No, and this conversation has strayed from the point I intended. I am going to suggest you practice privately. A showdown of sorts may be coming. The people I told you about, the Phelans -- our cousins -- may be behind the deaths Paul's friend is investigating. If so, they will be intelligent enough to realize that you or I could implicate them. Riona Phelan *asked* about you, wanting to know. I think her frankness illuminated her concern."

Claire considered his words. "Yeah, and Paul thinks the cops have some DNA evidence that's got them going."

"A cat which isn't. Or a human which isn't."

"Makes sense."

"Altogether too much, I'm afraid. But the Phelans cannot know of your connection to the police."

"What if they find out?"

"If they are somehow responsible for these deaths, then they may well decide to eliminate a potential problem."

"*Us.*"

"Indeed."

SEVENTEEN

That evening Emmett McManus drove carefully around the sleek KTM motorcycle parked in his driveway, studying its functional knobby-tired efficiency. *A week on one of those is just what I need right now*, he thought. A total escape from his current reality. He continued looking nostalgically at the big machine until his garage door dropped down to block his view.

In the kitchen, his shoes off by the entry, McManus smiled to himself as he saw the Gore-tex riding jacket draped over a dining room chair, the tall boots neatly sitting at the edge of the carpet. A sticky note on the rim of a wine glass simply stated: 'deck.' A good bottle had gone missing from the rack beside the refrigerator.

His smile grew broader as he picked up the glass and strolled out into the darkness, then broader still when he saw the long-legged figure slouched on a teak lounger.

"A grand motor-bicycle you have," he said, taking a seat in a matching chair as she wordlessly filled his glass from the missing bottle. "And fine leather pants, too," he added, letting his gaze wander over her.

"You'll turn my head, Emmett, with your flattery." Her voice was deep, warm, compelling.

He took a sip of wine, chuckled. "More than your head, my dear."

"Ah, the cunning tongue. How long has it been for us, then?" She drank some of her own wine.

"You know how long. Thirty years. I was a boy. And you, you look the same as those long years ago."

She sighed. "When you dashed the crystal of my virgin purity on the hard stones of your burgeoning

90

sexual needs." Her pale jade eyes flashed amusement in the gleam of a distant street light, causing his heart to skip a beat.

Now he laughed. "I believe you have it wrong-way-to. I remember a different set of events. *I* was the innocent."

"Men are ever thus," she replied, laughing with him. "The fault lies always elsewhere." Her tone sobered, she touched his arm. "You look careworn, Emmett. Is something amiss?"

He held his glass in both hands, nodded slowly. "I spoke with my niece today, warning her. Some of my own kind may have gone rogue, I fear. Have killed locally."

"The dentists, is it then?"

His curiosity spiked. "How did you guess?"

"I work part-time for the Board of Dentistry."

"No!" he gasped, practically choking on his second swallow of wine. "What name did you give them?"

"Mai Killian. One I've used before."

"But, *dentists*. Why on earth?"

"I needed work to occupy my time when I wasn't in class at Portland State. The task seemed simple." She smiled, shook her head. "A mostly male conservative group free of complications, proper gentlemen. I didn't count on the profession harboring so many active and interesting people. This year's State Dental Convention was little more than a free-standing riot. Water balloon battles. Nitrous oxide fests. Toga parties. The dean at the school was behind that last."

"And now someone is killing the Mormon ones."

"You believe your folk are responsible?"

"The facts fit, and the Police know they have something strange, according to my niece. And some of my Philadelphia cousins *are* in town."

"Would you be needing help?"

91

"Perhaps. I'll investigate a bit. Will you keep in touch?"

She stood, pulled him to his feet, then undid her belt and let her leathers slip down her body. "One of the reasons I'm here, Emmett." Her smile went beyond invitation to promise. "To keep in touch."

EIGHTEEN

Family Home Evenings were Heather Spitzley's favorite times. Usually on a Monday, during the summer months Tuesday worked better for the Spitzleys because of the boys' Little League. While she tossed the fresh vegetable salad, Heather smiled out the kitchen window at her husband Jim as he adjusted the gas on their new Coleman range. From the front of the house she could hear basketballs bouncing, the boys getting in a last game of H-O-R-S-E before dinner.

Heather chose that moment to reach for a bottle of Extra Virgin Olive oil, so she didn't see the range explode. She felt only an instant's pain as the cloud of glass shards from the window enveloped her face and upper body, then the collapsing window frame smashed her across the kitchen. The back of her skull indented the front of the refrigerator.

The frightened boys ran in from their game, found their dying mother, and called 911. The police examined the scene and began to collect what was left of their father.

Then they notified Deakins and Wismer.

NINETEEN

Enough yellow 'Crime Scene' tape festooned the Spitzley back yard to wrap a couple good-sized mummies. That was the first thing Wismer noticed when they arrived at the residence. The second thing was the stench of Marzipan. "Oh, fuck!" he said under his breath, as the two detectives surveyed the ruin of a particularly tidy example of American middle class domesticity.

"Semtex," Boothe said, before he could. "Our guys were right."

"Not just a faulty meter on a propane tank."

"Another Soyze staffer, too. Been with 'em over ten years."

"You were right. They've moved past the cats."

"Whoever 'they' are."

"We are so screwed."

Deakins shot him a sardonic smile. "Maybe not. We're gonna have something besides fur this time."

"Some kind of identifiable timer, maybe."

"Sure. The wife was collateral, probably. The kids were out front shootin' hoops." She looked around them, into the distance. "Argues for a line-of-sight. Finger on the button." She pointed to the west. "Mini-mall there, about a quarter-mile away, on higher ground. Easy enough to watch through binoculars, wait for the right moment."

"Tar roof, looks like," Wismer said, shading his eyes against the late evening sun with his right hand. "At least some of it."

"I say we go take a quick look right now."

"*Now*?"

"Sure, just a quickie, before it gets dark. The forensics guys are gonna be busy for a while. Doctor Spitzley contracted a bad case of the come-aparts. C'mon."

Ten minutes later, the two stood beneath a swing-down fire escape ladder at the back of the little mall. Deakins smiled as she looked up at the recently-painted device. "We put somebody here tonight to keep the local hoods off it, then run the forensics people over the fire escape and the whole roof tomorrow morning. Sound good, Ronald?"

Wismer didn't reply immediately, instead looked up at the edge of the roof. "A cougar can jump twenty feet vertically. But I don't suppose one could work the buttons on the remote."

"That's a good thirty feet, and 'no' on the remote," Boothe said, chuckling, an amused expression on her features. "It's a game of Cat-and-Mouse, isn't it?"

"Only *you* would say that."

"Like you wouldn't at least *think* it."

"I think we need to talk to Doctor Gregorson when we're done here tomorrow."

"Yeah. Ask him who might bear him a grudge."

"And if he likes cats."

"You say *that*, and you have the gall to diss your partner!"

Wismer grinned at her, not showing any teeth, trying to be smug. "Guess your attitude's finally startin' to wear off on me."

Boothe snorted. "Like *that* would ever happen."

"*None* of this should be happening."

"Oh, yeah," she replied, "but it's gonna be a good ride, huh?"

He repressed a shudder. "So it's a challenge?"

"Sure." The flint-hard sociopathic mind behind her level gaze showed for a brief moment, glinting in the evening sunlight. "Find the kitties." She grinned. "Now let's go."

TWENTY

Doctor Benjamin Lu lay on his back on the *Tatami* mat, disoriented and drenched in sweat, trying to catch his breath. It wasn't that he had slowed in his years of martial arts training, he told himself, but rather that the younger dentists were quicker. He shook his head to clear it, took a deep breath and accepted the offered hand up from his opponent, Waldo Matsuda.

"Are you all right, Doctor Lu?" Matsuda asked, inclining his head slightly as he spoke. A hint of nervousness pervaded his words. Decking your boss, even in friendly practice, might be a foolish act.

"I'm fine," Lu assured the younger man as they walked to a bench near the wall of the Dojo. "I didn't get inside your moves quickly enough."

Matsuda, compact, muscular, and somewhat taller than his employer, merely nodded before handing Lu a towel. "I am frequently lucky, also," he replied finally, with a minimally modest smile.

"You were also Byron Duncan's classmate. Did you attend his funeral?" The two men sat down.

"Yes. It was a fitting tribute." His expression seemed troubled. "A terrible death. A tragedy. The more so because their strange Christianity prevents the unmarried from attaining the highest levels of their Heaven."

Lu had not heard that, even though a fair number of his long-ago classmates had been Saints. "To me, a Presbyterian by birth and experience, that seems quite odd. To you, a practicing Buddhist, it must seem more so."

Wiping his face with his own towel, Matsuda nodded. "Truly. Byron was a fine person, though obsessed with finding a spouse." He glanced at Lu. "I understand that death is the end of a life, and do not expect life to be fair, but I do think the rules of one's faith should be. Brian's potential lack of stature in his faith's eternity has nothing to do with his thoughtful, kind nature or laudable work ethic."

"Theirs is an American faith in all ways. Christ came to this hemisphere after His Resurrection. The Garden of Eden was located near Independence, Missouri."

Matsuda gave a short, barking laugh. "Then my friend's *American* faith betrayed him."

"Your own beliefs should preclude bitterness," Lu chided. "*My* faith, after all, includes the Calvinist doctrine of Predestination."

"'You can and you can't. You will and you won't. You're damned if you do, and damned if you don't.'"

Lu regarded Matsuda in surprise, then smiled. "You, a Buddhist, knows *that* bit of doggerel? Written by a minister, I should add."

The younger man grinned, looking his age for the moment.
"I had a life before teeth, though sometimes I tend to forget that." He looked around the spacious room, at other pairs of dueling Asian dentists. "But that's why we are here this Tuesday evening. To gain knowledge and discipline."

"Indeed," Lu agreed, flexing his sore shoulders, thinking that he had gained the knowledge that he would need six hundred milligrams of Ibuprofen shortly after arising tomorrow.

TWENTY-ONE

The school seemed quieter than usual when Paul arrived for Wednesday morning clinic. The omnipresent susurrus of student activity preparing for nine o'clock patients barely murmured through the cavernous reception area and up the stairwell as he trotted down the stairs to the Clinic floor.

His first step onto the main level always gave him pause. How many feet had trod this path from humble student beginnings to dental greatness? How many mediocre graduates ran million-dollar-plus practices in the Willamette Valley, and how many truly-gifted practitioners labored in small towns in Eastern Oregon? Like any other aspect of the health care professions, dental skill levels, greed levels, and care levels didn't always match.

For Paul, obscurity in a small Tualatin practice was preferable, with weekly half-days at the school. Associating with some of the top names in dental education served as both a skills tune-up and an ethical boost. Of course, some of the top names in dental education were also some of wackiest people he'd ever known. And it got worse when you'd graduated and been accepted as a peer. Then they *really* let their hair down. Only his decade-long relationship with Claire buffered him against the constant zaniness of the dental school. The students themselves, to his surprise, had proven to be a relief to deal with compared to the faculty.

This was his first day back since Al Chambers' death, and Paul half-held his breath as he entered the circular hallway fronting the offices of the various clinical specialties departmental heads. His immediate boss, Joe Coogan, DMD, the chief of Operatives, had been Chambers' classmate in 1965.

Coogan was parked behind his morning *Oregonian*, which was typical, with his feet resting on his desk, also typical. He folded one edge of the paper back and looked at Paul, his round Irish features composed. "Funeral's tomorrow," he said simply.

"I'll be there," Paul replied. "How're you doing?"

"Not worth a crap," Coogan said, snapping his paper for emphasis. "A man in his sixties should be able to go for a morning run in an urban setting without getting butchered by a wild animal, don't you think?"

Paul pulled a chair over and sat down in front of Coogan's desk. "Sure, and I don't blame you for being pissed. Al was a great person, a good instructor, and your friend."

"He was *everybody's* friend," Coogan corrected. "His one clinic day was the most relaxed, pleasant day of the week for both staff and students. Al understood the relationship between teacher and student. He was helpful, kind, non-judgmental, and realized that the dentist-in-training has to be *aided* in the learning process, not pushed or hand-carried." Coogan shook his head. "Al epitomized what makes this institution one of the finest in the country."

"If not *the* finest."

"Exactly."

"But the school was a *lot* tougher in the old days. Requirements were higher, courses more demanding. Department heads had to either be of foreign birth or have a speech impediment to prevent students from understanding their every word. Students had to walk to school through the harsh winter snows to get to class, and it was uphill both ways. An old ex-fighter-jock like yourself probably thinks today's curriculum is watered-down, and the students are sadly mollycoddled."

The look Coogan gave him reminded Paul of his father, a sort of sheepish anger laced with Irish fatalism. "Am I *that* obvious?"

"Yes and no," Paul replied, "but you should look on the first page of the 'Metro' section of the paper."

Regarding Paul suspiciously, the head of Operatives shuffled through *The Oregonian* for the Metro section, then held it up, perusing the front page briefly. "Holy jumpin' shit! Jim Spitzley! His *barbeque* blew up."

"Another Soyze staffer, you'll notice."

Coogan didn't reply immediately, reading the article before speaking. The he folded the paper, set it down, and looked at Paul, his gaze thoughtful. "You're right." He shook his head. "Heather and Jim. Both dead. Nice people. Those *poor* kids. Hyrum Gregorson must be incredibly distraught."

Paul hadn't thought about that issue. "What kind of a guy is Gregorson? He was enough ahead of me in school so we never met."

"Honest, decent, hard-working, fair skills. You know how the Mormon kids are. Not break-out talents as a rule, but so doggedly persistent that they do a good job of dentistry. Well, except for Kenny Cantwell. He was the best operator I ever saw. An amazing talent." Cantwell had been head of the department until the mid-eighties, a dental god.

"Gregorson's lost three people in eight days," Paul said, pulling up a chair and sitting down in front of his boss's desk. "Even if he's thick as a brick, he's got to be wondering who his enemies are."

Coogan looked down at the newspaper, tapping on his central incisors with one index finger. "You've got a point there. I sure as hell would be lookin' over *my* shoulder."

"I grew up with Ron Wismer, one of the detectives in charge of the investigation. He and his partner came into the office to see me yesterday

100

afternoon, asking about dental anatomy, eruption rates, and resorption."

The head of Operatives' eyebrows elevated. "What's your take on that?"

"Something at odds to what the public has seen and been told. Just a guess: funky cougars. They must have gotten some fur or tissue samples that don't add up."

"And you think the teeth are part of it?"

Paul chuckled. "Yeah, but that might be my dental mentality." He stood. "I've got to get ready for Clinic."

His boss swiveled his chair and surveyed the row of pictures on the opposite wall, above the bookcase. He steepled his fingers. "Wonder what *Edgar* would do."

Unable to keep from smiling, Paul surveyed the middle and largest portrait of the group. The dental school's most distinguished alum, W. Edgar Buchanan -- 'Uncle Joe' on 'Petticoat Junction' to most Americans in Paul's age group -- who'd left a thriving practice in Eugene to find another life in Hollywood. Buchanan's photograph, taken when he appeared on 'The Rifleman' as the town physician, showed a stubbled, narrow-eyed cynic who'd seen enough of life to harbor few illusions.

"Hard to say," Paul replied. "What about the man in the picture on his right? Not hard to guess his solution."

"John Henry Holliday?" Coogan laughed outright. "The country's most famous dentist. Judging from the O.K. Corral, not much doubt but what there'd be weaponry involved."

"Might be the best answer," Paul said from the doorway.

"Might be the *only* answer," Coogan replied, grinning, momentarily looking much younger than his sixty-some years.

TWENTY-TWO

Deakins and Wismer stood on the low peripheral wall surrounding the tarred portion of the mini-mall roof, and tried again to reconstruct the actions of whoever had detonated the device which killed Jim and Heather Spitzley. Below and behind them, a forensic collection crew systematically went over the fire escape. The two detectives had borrowed one of the Parks Bureau's cherrypickers to access the roof, thus avoiding contaminating any evidence on the fire escape.

"We can just walk around on this edge, Ronald," Boothe assured her partner, doing a double-pirouette on the wall's metal cap. They had line-of-sight on the Spitzley backyard from this point. No doubt the view would be even better from the opposite side of the building.

"*You* can, maybe," Wismer replied, regarding her with open distrust, and not about to look down. "I'm not so big on heights."

"Yeah, I know," his partner said, laughing as she skipped away along the roof's lip, obviously enjoying his discomfort.

Wismer resisted the urge to grind his teeth. Instead, he turned away from Deakins and walked slowly along the metal cap, exceedingly careful where he placed his feet. When he was on the far side of the roof, a few feet away from where they judged the person with the detonator had watched, he released his held breath and looked at Boothe, who stood a few yards away, her arms akimbo, her gaze locked on the Spitzley yard.

"Here we are," she said at last, pivoting smoothly around to view the tar surface of the roof.

"Fairly fresh tar," Wismer observed. The roof must have been re-surfaced within the past year.

"Double line of tracks. Running shoes. Probably our perp."

"Nice that the access hatch and the heat pump are at the north end of the roof. They've had all the foot traffic."

Deakins shook her head. "Still might not mean crap. Everybody buys running shoes these days, and most times they aren't so dramatically different from one another. 'Oh, this person wears Nikes' doesn't mean a hell of a lot, unless there's some change in the sole that makes this set of footprints unique."

"Best lead we've got, maybe."

"Unless the forensics people find something on the fire escape. Which might happen."

"Fingerprints, maybe."

"You're givin' me a lot of 'maybes,' Ronald."

"Us hotshot detectives thrive on 'maybes.'"

The tall woman laughed. "Yeah, ain't that the friggin' truth. But we *are* gettin' closer. Whatever these things are, something human punched the detonator on this little episode. And *humans* we can find, given enough time and enough evidence."

"Unless we run out of Mormon dentists first."

Deakins snorted. "When we're done here, we call Gregorson, set up an interview, see if he can think of any enemies." Her flat gaze turned from the distant backyard and toward her partner. "'Cause that's what it is, you know. Somebody who's got their sights trained on Soyze, somebody who wants to cripple the company. If it was just Gregorson, he'd already be dead."

"Maybe they want to screw with his head."

"Oh, yeah. That, too."

TWENTY-THREE

Wearing only panties and a rather abbreviated black bra which emphasized her breasts, the tall, slim young woman eeled up the slick, chrome pole, its gleaming metal surface pressed firmly into her crotch. From beneath strawberry-blonde bangs, she smiled over at Levi Klaghorn as she rose completely onto her tiptoes. Her fingertips caressed the pole suggestively even as her smile took on a wanton lasciviousness.

"*Nice*, Carly," Klaghorn said, nodding in approval. He sat at a table near the small stage, his chair turned so he could watch Carly's rehearsal and still see the front door. The *Beaver Dream* didn't open until two in the afternoon, giving its owner an hour or two each morning to critique the strippers' routines. Carly Meadows, late of Green River, Utah, showed real promise, Klaghorn thought. He'd expected the young Mormon women sent to him by Headquarters to be prudish and self-conscious. He'd been pleasantly surprised that many of them, in addition to impressive martial arts and weapons skills, could shake, rattle, and roll with the best.

Klaghorn, the leader of the Church's Danite presence in Oregon, had spent the last five years developing his cover as a titty bar operator in Portland. The result was everything the Danite High Command in Salt Lake City could have asked for. Who, after all, could imagine a representative of the Church's 'Avenging Angels' in the sinister, slightly sleazy ex-Navy Seal?

Formed in 1838 by Sampson Avard, the Danites were a highly secret Mormon society bound by very rigid penalty oaths. Originally intended for action against dissenters within the Faith, the group later shifted its mission to activities against all those opposing -- or deemed dangerous to -- the Church.

Almost no one outside the Faith -- and very few inside -- knew of the Danites' continued existence. They were presumed to be a defunct historical footnote far in the Church's past. A disturbing footnote, in the eyes of many, better gone and forgotten.

Klaghorn cracked his prominent knuckles as Carly slid smoothly back down the lightly-oiled pole. The girl definitely had what it took to drive the crowds wild with whatever people who came to titty bars wanted to be wild with. Lust, presumably, along with a need for fellowship and camaraderie. And, Klaghorn reminded himself, a desire to part with their money. That was most of it. For an official cover, the *Beaver Dream* had proven to be a fountain of wealth. Wholesome young women being apparently *very* unwholesome was the real deal for most of the *Beaver's* clientele. The bucks poured in, and only the top ten percent found its way back to Salt Lake.

Forty feet to Klaghorn's left, the front door opened and what appeared to be an over-aged farm boy walked hesitantly in, blinking as his eyes adjusted from the brightness outside to the more subdued lighting within the building. No doubt this was Hyrum Gregorson, dentist in difficulty.

Klaghorn hauled himself to his feet with a grunting sigh. He didn't like dealing one-on-one with the Faithful. It compromised his anonymity. "Take a break, Carly," he said to the young woman, whose gyrations had ceased. She still leaned casually against the chromed pole, but watched Gregorson, instinctively understanding that this gangly, uncomfortable-looking man was a co-religionist.

Gregorson wouldn't look at her, and, even from across the room, Klaghorn saw the man's face redden. *One of the good ones*, he thought sourly, and sighed again, glad he hadn't worn a T-shirt featuring the club's mascot, Nookie the Beaver. He turned toward the dancer. "Give me a half-hour, Carly. When you come back, we'll try it with the new music."

He smiled at her, not a hard thing to do with any of his little flock. They were all attractive, clean, healthy young animals. As a life-long Mormon, Klaghorn frequently mused about the children these women would bear when they found marital happiness after their time at the *Beaver*. In the meantime, however, he was like a bizarre sort of sorority housemother, responsible for safeguarding the virtue of twelve young women, all of above-average looks. At thirty-seven, even with his Danite training, Klaghorn felt *he* posed the biggest single danger to potential complications of a sexual nature. Oh, well, it hadn't happened yet, and it wouldn't. Danites -- even these young women -- were properly chaste, the closest thing to true monastics in the Faith.

"Doctor Gregorson, I presume?" the Danite captain asked, smiling and extending his right hand to his uneasy guest.

After casting a nervous glance in the direction of the retreating Carly's metronomic backside, Gregorson clutched Klaghorn's hand like a drowning sailor being rescued from the icy depths of the Atlantic, and shook it vigorously.

"They told me you'd be able to help," Gregorson said, as the two men sat down at the table Klaghorn had occupied earlier.

Klaghorn eyed the dentist briefly, wondering how much the man knew about the continued existence of the Danites. Wondering, too, whether being tall and speaking in a deep and slow voice meant the man lagged on the uptake. He looked into Gregorson's serious brown gaze and decided not. Intelligence and concern showed clearly, mostly the latter.

"How much were you told?" he asked.

"That you were a Church representative, that this...place...is not what it seems, and that I should trust your judgment."

"Fair enough," the Danite replied, with a thin smile. "Tell me your problem."

Had Gregorson been able to speak faster, the conversation would have taken less time. On the other hand, his economical speech patterns shortened things somewhat. Klaghorn had been briefed at length by Salt Lake, so his questions at the end mostly involved Gregorson's *impressions* of Doctor Benjamin Lu and how what had happened to the Soyze employees impacted the company.

"Do you believe the documents Lu showed you to be genuine?" Klaghorn kept his voice low, and spoke as slowly as Gregorson, if only to keep his voice from shaking. Salt Lake had not known about the alleged discovery of the missing pages of the Book of Mormon. Though personally not terribly devout, Klaghorn understood the potential importance to the Faith. Quite simply, this would be the most earth-shaking event in the past century-and-a-half of Church history.

Gregorson nodded. "After comparing what I was given to faxed copies of the original dictated pages, I believe so. Yes. The cadence of the text, the actual penmanship, all seemed authentic."

"Some of us have been deceived before," the Danite replied softly.

"I understand. I am no expert, yet everything about the documents bears great similarity to the companion pages which the Church still possesses. An expert could, of course, accomplish such a forgery."

"Would Lu be party to such a deception?" Klaghorn asked, thinking that this represented the most likely possibility. There was no doubt in his mind that Doctor Lu intended crippling harm to Soyze Dental Associates, if only financial.

The tall dentist didn't reply immediately, instead sat thinking for a few moments, apparently considering the concept. "I believe *he* believes them to be genuine. Whether or not they *are* remains to be seen."

"Yet you are willing to gamble several hundred thousand dollars on their authenticity?"

Gregorson thought some more. "Yes," he said finally, his gaze sharp and certain. "I see no other course of action."

"And you believe the financial damage to Soyze, the slowing of expansion, would alone be enough for Lu? He would be satisfied?"

"Yes."

Klaghorn found that level of faith and certainty both naive and compelling, yet he couldn't rule out Gregorson's being right. "So why do you have three dead employees?"

Pain washed over the dentist's plain features. "I don't know." His words were barely audible.

"Lu, again?"

Gregorson shook his head, perhaps too strongly. "I cannot believe that of the man. I am not sure I could believe it of *anyone*, though I know evil exists. Benjamin Lu is cunning, competitive, and greedy, but I do not believe he would *kill* simply to damage Soyze and myself. The money for the documents would be enough for him."

Though he didn't say the words aloud, the muscular Danite agreed, if only in principle. "Then who?"

"I have no idea."

"Have you considered the firm who provided the missing pages to Doctor Lu? The Phelans."

"I met two of them. They were young, well-spoken, reserved. Professional. *Animals* did some of this, Mister Klaghorn."

The Danite shrugged. "*Animals* can be trained, Doctor. Explosives can be purchased. This cannot be

108

coincidental. Someone is clearly seeking to bring you and Soyze down."

Anguish showed in Gregorson's eyes.   "But *why*?"

Now Klaghorn was on more familiar ground. "Perhaps simply because they *can*. Sometimes that's all it takes."

With a choking sob, Hyrum Gregorson buried his face in his hands.

* * * * *

When Gregorson had departed, Klaghorn sat in silence watching the now-closed door.   Something terribly wrong was going on with Soyze Dental Associates, and the Danite suspected that his initial reaction might be all too accurate. A casual, off-hand, cat-with-a-mouse game could be the *whole* story. *Because they can*, his mind repeated.

Lost in his thoughts, he barely heard Carly's approach. He smiled up at her as she paused behind him, resting one hand on his right shoulder. "Did you hear?" he asked.

She nodded.   "We may soon be putting our training to good use." The anticipatory note he heard in her voice sounded a great deal like he and his classmates had sounded at the end of their Seal training. Confident and eager to use their new skills. "Don't be running off half-cocked," Klaghorn cautioned.

Carly chuckled. "Females can't do that."

"You *know* what I mean."

Two more young women, identical dark-skinned brunettes wearing light bathrobes, walked out from behind the stage. "What's up?" they asked.

The Coolidge twins were taller than Carly Meadows, rangy and long-muscled, farm girls from down in Manti.   Supple and loose-jointed, their

109

synchronized routine -- with just a hint of lesbian familiarity -- never failed to bring the patrons to their feet, whistling and throwing money. Klaghorn considered them his best draw. They were also good at breaking things: bricks, noses, arms, you name it. Plus they could fight in unison better than any two people he'd ever seen. Individually he could probably take either twin, but he had no illusions about his chances against both of them, and he hoped it would never become an issue. In fact, the biggest problem he had with the Coolidges was telling Lorna from Barbara, and that was problem enough, thank you very much.

When their nominal leader had explained the apparent situation to the three young women, one of the Coolidges -- he thought Barbara -- looked at the other and grinned. "Looks like we maybe get to kill something, Sis."

"Ut-ut," Klaghorn said, raising a cautionary hand before the other twin could reply. "Don't jump to any conclusions, ladies. Maybe you'll only get to hurt a few people *really* bad."

Carly snorted. "That'll sure beat shaking our rumps and what-all."

"Oh, but you do that *so* well, Carly!" the twins replied, leering.

"You know the rules," the Danite captain said sternly.

"*No catfights*," answered all three women, laughing.

* * * * *

Half-a-block from the *Beaver Dream*, Wismer and Deakins sat watching the front of the place. Hyrum Gregorson had driven away in his Volvo less than ten minutes earlier, and the two detectives remained more than a little perplexed.

110

"He *knows* someone in there," Deakins repeated, for the third time. "They don't start dancing until later in the day. Besides, he was still blushing just *leaving*. This wasn't someplace he *wanted* to come."

"Granted," Wismer replied, massaging the back of his neck with his right hand. "Be nice if we could tap his phone lines, listen in."

"Too late now."

"Check his phone records, then. There might be a sequence that'd tie into this joint."

"Speaking of joints," his partner said, inclining her head toward two women approaching the front of the *Beaver*, "yours might be interested in those two."

Wismer let the remark pass for the moment, instead watching the two attractive young blonde women sauntering down the sidewalk. "I see what you mean," he said finally, after a few moments. "They look like the real dancer McCoy, all right." Actually, he thought they looked better than what he expected, more trim and athletic. "They look kind of jockish."

"More than that," Deakins replied. "Look how they walk in relation to one another. See how they're opening the door, how one is the lookout, how their feet move. The pivots. We are lookin' at somebody with personal defense training. Probably martial arts, too. Oh, yeah."

"Exotic dancers *do* that stuff?"

"Not so far as I know. But *these* two do, and I'll just bet that has something to do with our good Doctor Gregorson."

"Well, it can't be a Mormon thing. A titty bar would be the absolute antithesis to the Mormon lifestyle. Gregorson was humiliated and mortified. You only had to look at the guy to know that."

Deakins remained thoughtful. "I dunno. Most of the Mo's I've known have been pretty damned pragmatic. How about Ray and I go there tonight, watch the dancers?"

111

"The food's probably shitty."
"Ray can pay."

TWENTY-FOUR

Soyze Dental Associates' headquarters were on the northern edge of Portland's Hollywood District, a simple three-storey facility with a specialty clinic on the bottom level, and the company offices above that. The property was beautifully-landscaped, with mature Bigleaf maple trees fronting the street, lower-growing native shrubs closer to the building itself. Wismer thought that whatever had occupied the property prior to Soyze must have been much larger. For this part of town, the considerable distance from the sidewalks was unusual.

"Tasteful," Boothe said from beside him, as the two walked toward the front entrance.

"Better than a strip joint, for sure," her partner replied.

Deakins chuckled. "Probably shouldn't mention that."

"Only as a last resort, in case the good Doctor Gregorson isn't forthcoming."

"Good thinking." She opened the front door and they stepped inside to the air-conditioned foyer.

"No elevator," Wismer said, glancing around.

"There's a service elevator at the rear of the building. I checked the plans."

"Probably a Mormon deal."

"The fitness thing? Taking care of the body the Lord has given you?"

"Right."

"Can't argue with that." She raised a clenched fist. "Climb them stairs!"

"You are an irreverent person."

"You noticed?"

"Some time back."

"You love it."

They reached the first landing. "You remind me of Margie."

"Really?"

"Yeah, at some levels. The motherhood thing, the kids, the hormonal differences, make her a little more mellow, but there's commonality. She can be a real hard-ass, just not to *your* refined level."

"Your mean I need to breed, bring forth live issue? So I can reach some sort of emotional steady-state?"

"I didn't say that. It'd affect your job performance."

"I *like* sex."

Startled, he looked at her, frowning. "One would hope. You have some serious biological needs, I suspect."

She smiled, an introspective and private expression that required no further conversation. They reached the top of the stairs.

The receptionist was middle-aged, greying, friendly. The other employees in view appeared similar, and Wismer wondered if Gregorson preferentially hired Mormon widows and singles. He knew the Faith looked out for its own, and approved.

Another flight of stairs, then Gregorson's office, its door open, with the man himself quick to greet them, much more at ease than he'd appeared exiting even an upscale titty bar.

"Who wants to hurt you and Soyze?" Wismer asked, when they were seated and offers of water or tea had been declined.

An instant's flash of concern and pain showed in Gregorson's mild brown gaze. He shook his head, his hands gripping the edge of his desk hard enough to turn knuckles white. "I don't know," he said quietly.

"Anyone try anything in the past?" Boothe asked.

A pause. "No."

114

"You're in pretty intense competition with Considerate Care for dental contracts on the East Side," she continued. "Any reason to think Doctor Benjamin Lu might be behind some of this?"

"I cannot believe that," the tall Mormon said, his features and voice hard. "Benny Lu is relentless, implacable, and cunning, but he is generally a fair antagonist. I do not believe him to be a killer. Or to approve of killing to further his own ends. We were, after all, at the Dental School in the same era."

Wismer wasn't sure he agreed with that level of wholesale denial, or what in hell being in school at roughly the same time had to do with it. "Who else has anything to gain from this ongoing situation?"

Now Gregorson's gaze snapped to Wismer. "Are you suggesting there will be *more*...deaths?"

He hasn't thought of that, the Lieutenant realized.

At his side, Deakins leaned forward. "Why would they stop? You haven't received any demands, have you, Doctor? No payoffs?"

Alarm spread over the Saint's ordinary features, with a touch of panic. He shook his head, stroked his chin nervously. "No...no. Not at all."

Wismer stood, Boothe a second behind him. "Well, we won't take any more of your time, Doctor." He brought out his card, laid it on Gregorson's gleaming desk top.

"Let us know if anything occurs to you," Deakins added, along with her own card. "Call us 24/7." She gave him a professional smile. "And remember, we're on your side."

"Yes, of course," Gregorson replied, shaking their hands and coming down the stairs with them, even going out into the mid-afternoon sunlight.

When they were back in the car and down the block onto Broadway, Wismer said, "You rattled his cage pretty good, little lady."

115

"He's an innocent. He needs to get thinking, get a plan. This is like a terrorist attack."

"Good analogy."

"Thanks. There's a little commonality here, too. My Great-grandmother was a Mo. From some place called Manti."

Wismer hurried to make the light at Thirty-ninth, swung around a delivery box van. "You lookin' forward to the strippers tonight?"

She regarded him seriously for a few moments, then grinned widely. "Yeah. Wanta see what they have to do with this."

"Think they do?"

"Sure. I don't believe in coincidence. That wasn't someplace Gregorson'd ever been before."

"I agree. And Ray'll probably have fun."

"Jesus, Wis! He's a goddamn *lawyer*!"

"Take a legal pad and a pencil, then. I can hear his lawyer jargon now: 'Look at the torts on that plaintiff!'"

Boothe didn't reply, only gave him a dirty look.

TWENTY-FIVE

"There's a *woman* out there!" Jeannie Simmons said when she came off the stage after her first dance of the evening. "In the *second* row!" She toweled sweat from her face and hair.

"What's the deal?" Carly Meadows asked, shrugging. "We get women in here all the time." She unbelted her robe, hung it from a hook behind the curtain.

Jeannie shook her head violently, grabbed her own robe. "No. You don't get it. She's not some housewife out to see what the hubby gets from this place. Or a dyke. They always sit in the back. She looks like *us*."

Carly nodded slowly, looking down at the shorter woman with her brows arched. "You mean blonde, brunette, or redhead? With boobs and a flexible spine. Or a god-fearing Saint?"

"No, I mean she looks *fit*. Capable. Tough."

"She alone?"

"No, she's with a guy. He's normal-looking, seemed to like the show all right, like most of 'em. She seemed more interested in the choreography."

"Ah. Maybe she's a dance instructor. Or even a stripper herself."

"Remember the course we took on Recognition of Authority?"

"'Cop-spotting?' Yeah, and I remember you were better at it than me. But even if she *is* a cop, she could still be here just for the show. If you believe what you see in the movies, a lot of cop business goes down in places like this. What's she look like? *Really* like us?"

"Yeah. Light blonde hair, freckles, tall, sits *absolutely* still."

Carly shook her head and pursed her lips. "Don't like *that*." She looked down at herself, pushed her boobs briefly up, took a deep breath, then reached for the curtains. "I'll check her out, Jeannie. See you when I'm done."

Deliberately not looking toward the second row, Carly spun through the curtains, and smiled and bowed to the audience, displaying her cleavage. She took two long steps to the vertical chrome pole, gripped it with both hands above the lubricated portion and swung up and around it, presenting the crowd with a circumferential view of her crotch and ass from below. After a second's stunned hush, the ensuing roar threatened to blow the ceiling tiles off.

As Carly touched down on the stage floor again, she chanced a quick glance at the second row, and almost lost her composure. Jeannie had described the woman perfectly. She sat completely still, hands folded in her lap. Steady grey eyes studied Carly with professional detachment.

Carly repressed a shudder, let her gaze flick away as she leapt up to catch the horizontal overhead bar and swung up to provide another tantalizing glimpse of her posterior and nether regions. The roaring built again, to Carly's satisfaction. She might not be an exotic tease, like the Coolidge twins, but her routine was more athletic.

Ten minutes later, glistening with sweat, Carly had removed her bra, to the accompaniment of more hooting and hollaring, and she'd pretty well learned as much as she could about the silent figure in the second row. If the woman wasn't a cop, she was some kind of fed, and if she wasn't either of those, the remote possibility -- and the one Carly didn't want to think about -- was that she was a Danite Elder Carly'd never seen.

Oh, well, Carly thought, she'd have Levi run a search through the ID segment of the geneology

118

archives in Salt Lake. There couldn't be that many freckled platinum blondes working in Portland officialdom. As she reached that conclusion, Carly jutted her flexible pelvis toward the woman and did a little bump-and-grind while grinning wickedly at her. A *looky here*, as Levi called it.

Surprisingly, the blonde smiled back. Big-time.

TWENTY-SIX

"Well," Boothe told her boyfriend as they climbed back into Ray's car, "*that* was an ambiguous result."

"Yeah," Ray agreed, slipping on his seatbelt and starting the Suburu. "The food wasn't that good. But those twins were *really* something!"

Boothe glared at him as she fastened her own belt. "No, bonehead, I mean the strippers *made* me."

Ray didn't look at her as he guided his car from the *Beaver's* lot. He was paying attention to the task at hand. In Raymond Gubrud's world, if you didn't pay total attention, you were likely to be killed at any second. Just because. "What do you mean?" he asked at last, his brow furrowing.

"The first one, the smaller blonde, saw me and told the sorta red-headed one -- the second dancer -- and she scoped me out pretty good."

"The redhead was amazing," Ray said, smiling as they sped toward the I-84 freeway entrance. "Almost as good as the twins."

"What I'm *saying*, Raymond, is that they *knew* I was some kind of authority, that I was there to check them out."

"C'mon," he scoffed. "They're *strippers*! No other job skills, no education. Drug-use history, perhaps. Possibly single mothers." He grinned over at her. "Maybe they thought you were a lesbian."

"You ever see strippers like these?"

Ray thought for nearly a half-minute, as he swung the Suburu to the on-ramp and dropped down it onto the freeway. Boothe could tell from his expression that he was starting to use his larger brain, going on lawyer-mode. "No. Not that I've seen too many strippers, but these were clean, healthy, and *very* fit." He turned to her for a moment, puzzled. "That's unusual, isn't it?"

She chuckled, couldn't help it. "They're not *real* strippers, Ray."

"Gosh, they all seemed *gifted* to me. Particularly the twins." He rolled his eyes.

Boothe gave a huge sigh. "I didn't say they weren't good at their cover, but that's what it is -- a cover."

"I think the crowd was deceived. And I believe their cover to be a financially sound one."

"Wonder what they're up to?"

"You and Ron followed a *Mormon dentist* there?"

"Yeah."

"Interesting. Typically, when possible, Mormons only seek aid and succor from other Mormons."

"A Mormon titty bar staffed with martial arts-trained cuties. Now there's a concept!"

"Most baffling," Ray agreed. They were approaching the Willamette River, no more than five minutes from Deakins' condo.

"You wanta come up for a nightcap?" she asked, resting her left hand on his right forearm.

"Do you have an outfit like that redhead's?"

"Maybe."

"In your 'evidence room?'"

"Maybe."

"Can you dance like that?"

Boothe just smiled.

TWENTY-SEVEN

Karl Elch regarded his two Lieutenants with open amazement at their meeting the next morning. "Just about the time I think you two have dredged up all the weird shit possible, you come back at me with even more."

"It's not a homicide, Sir," Deakins said. "It's not even criminal activity."

Elch grimaced. "Yet. I presume you've looked at the permits and licenses?"

"All in perfect order," Wismer replied. "Better than perfect, in fact. Total compliance. The place is textbook on following food preparation guidelines. They recycle everything. The women who work there are all over twenty-one. No lap-dancing, no prostitution, no neighborhood complaints. The guy who runs the place" -- he glanced down at his notebook -- "one Levi Klaghorn, does not suffer bad actors well. Has been known to escort them to the parking lot in a forceful manner. Ex-Navy Seal."

"Who frequents this paragon of porn?"

"Middle class single males, according to Boothe. Scuttlebutt is that these are the best-looking strippers in the Pacific Northwest."

"The women all live in a small apartment building about two blocks away," Boothe added, "owned by the same outfit that owns the strip joint."

"Not remotely connected to anything like Deseret Industries, I'm assuming," the Captain said. His craggy features had taken on an intrigued look, and Wismer guessed his boss found this lesser mystery more comfortable than the weird cat thing. Though at some level, there might well be a connection, if only in opposition.

"We traced ownership to a private corporation in southern Idaho," Deakins replied. "Not quite down the chain on it, but I expect we'll end up with some obscure link in Salt Lake."

"The heart of the Mormon Empire," Elch said, stroking his upper lip with a knobby forefinger. His right eyebrow raised. "Where are the dancers from?"

"Utah," Wismer said, and both detectives grinned at their boss.

Elch glared at them. "Damn, I hate it when you do that. Makes me feel inadequate." He turned to Deakins. "You're sure they've had self-defense training?"

"Oh, yeah," she replied. "The way they move..."

"...even when they're dancing?"

"Definitely. There's a lot of commonality between dancing and some of the martial arts. My style, *Berisilat*, was created by a woman of the Minangkabau, from Sumatra. The combat form is *Sila_buah*, but there's a sporting form which is virtually dance."

Elch continued to look thoughtful. "Maybe they're training locally. Can you check around, see?"

Deakins grinned. "Already on it. Might be a dead end, though. There's enough of them -- a dozen or so, including the kitchen help and servers -- to have their own *dojo*, train only within their group. In which case, we'll have no way of finding out."

"Wouldn't that be kind of incestuous and predictable?"

"Yeah," Deakins agreed. "Isolation. It's slightly frowned-upon. I'll ask my guru, see if there's a *dojo* on the east side where they might go."

"We already have one that caters to Asian dentists of both sexes," Wismer added. "Almost all of Benny Lu's staff belong."

"Really?" their boss asked, beginning to look slightly distressed again. "Anything else you want to share before I have my morning chat with the Chief and the Mayor?"

The two lieutenants stood. "We'll keep you posted," said Deakins, still grinning.

TWENTY-EIGHT

"Here she is," Carly Meadows told the *Beaver Dream* staffers, clustered behind her in their communications room, looking over her shoulders at the nineteen-inch monitor screen. "Homicide Detective Lieutenant Boothe Deakins -- no middle initial. Been on the force for seven years, with several commendations and a rep for cutting right to the lowest common denominator."

"She's not bad looking," said Summer Archer, one of the servers.

Levi Klaghorn pointed a thick finger at the screen. "Yeah, but look at those eyes. My Grandmother used to say looking into eyes like that made you hear the gravedigger's spade."

"She looks...*interesting*," Carly said, wondering what went on in the brain behind that enigmatic expression and penetrating gaze. Wondering if she was going to find out. Last evening's visit had not been chance, she was certain.

"Carly's got a girlfriend!" one of the Coolidges teased. The other giggled.

Carly shot the twins an exasperated look. "Carly's got a *Mission*, clone-girls. Same as you."

"We *saw* you send her a twat-o-gram last night," Jeannie Simmons said, "right in front of the Lord and everybody."

"Ladies," Klaghorn reminded them gently, "we need to focus on *why* this hot-shot cop showed up on our doorstep with a Multnomah County Deputy District Attorney named Raymond J. Gubrud in tow." He glared at Jeannie. "*Not* something, for the Lord's sake, called a '*twat-o-gram*.'"

"Just bein' cute," Jeannie replied, pouting.

"Nice that Gubrud used his Visa so we have his name," Carly said, her gaze back on the monitor screen, trying to ferret something from the stoic image of Boothe Deakins.

"How about I phone Hyrum Gregorson?" their leader asked. "See if *he's* talked to this lady."

"Dollars to donuts says he has," Carly replied, "which would be part of their investigation, but that by itself wouldn't give her us." She thought for a moment. "Unless she followed Gregorson here yesterday."

"Don't like to think about that," Klaghorn said.

"Don't like to think he might have told her about us, either."

The muscular Danite shook his head. "You were right about him being an innocent, but he's a bright guy. I don't think he'd tell even his *family* about us, let alone someone outside the Faith."

"So," Carly said, "he was followed here by the cops, on a freakin' *hunch*." She regarded the on-screen Deakins again. "And this tough babe was responsible. And she *knew* we weren't just a bunch of pitiful have-nots floppin' their boobs."

"Whose fault is that?" Klaghorn asked, laughing. "You ladies do too good a job."

"Tain't funny, McGee," Carly replied, thinking that this smart law enforcement broad had been entirely too sharp. Which only made Carly more curious. "But she can't have figured out we're going to move to protect Soyze Dental Associates, even if our cover's kind of blown."

"Technically, we're on the same side," the Danite chief reminded her, "except that we're clandestine."

"'The enemy of my enemy is my friend,'" Carly quoted, wondering how she could meet Boothe Deakins on neutral ground and find out what she knew.

No easy route to that goal, and less chance of it happening.

TWENTY-NINE

Benny Lu decided Thursday morning that April
Kwong had never been as quiet as she had this week.
He'd noticed it as early as Tuesday, and was now
convinced. She was cheerful, upbeat even, doing her
job with her usual efficiency, but very quiet for her,
with none of her usual flirting and immodest behavior.
At the first opportunity, when the two were alone in his
office, he asked tentatively, "You seem not your usual
self this week. Is there something amiss?"

She considered his words for a moment or two,
also unlike her. Typically, her responses were crafted
well in advance and delivered carefully and succinctly,
a completely Asian trait despite her Southwestern
upbringing. "There *is* something," she finally replied,
a tiny hint of her usual sauciness surfacing in her eyes.

"I see. I hesitate to ask, but is it Miz Phelan,
perhaps?"

Another pause, her eyes cast down. A faint
blush traveled over her features before her gaze
returned to his and she answered in a low voice. "Yes.
Quite a surprise, actually."

His breath sucked in. "A woman." Astounding,
simply astounding! "I *am* surprised. I did not
consider..."

"That I might swing both ways?" Her normal
grin surfaced as she shook her head. "Not anything I
expected either, frankly. Women have never interested
me much, except for a few near-misses in college.
Riona Phelan is...*different*." Her gaze retreated inward.
She licked her lower lip, her eyes momentarily
unfocused. "*Very* different."

Lu's practical nature overrode his curiosity.
"Will you be leaving the company?"

April came back to the conversation in a nano-
second. Her gusting Texan guffaw filled the small

office. "Not on your tintype! I'm not *that* smitten. Besides, Riona's grandfather is thinking of opening a branch office out here. Assumin' things continue between us, that'd work jus' fine."

"I see," Lu replied, taken aback by his own relief.

"This's too good a job to leave."

He nodded, regarding her with new knowledge. "Ah."

She waggled a forefinger at him. "Doesn't mean I won't want a raise at my annual review, though, Boss. Don't even think about it!"

Lu smiled at her. "We shall see, of course, but I am most relieved."

She smiled back. "You durn well better be."

THIRTY

The Danite leadership's idea of what constituted an adequate mountain bike would not appeal to any young Mormon who had even rudimentary knowledge of bicycles. The Coolidge twins had replaced most of the clunkier running gear on their mounts with lighter-weight components, switched the stock knobs for dual-use tires more suitable for the street, and the results were now acceptable, barely more. Both were saving to buy lighter chrome-moly frames, thereby arriving at machines they hoped would be more useful for following Mormon dentists who bicycled to work.

Just now, the twins cruised a half-block behind Marvin Lockwood, who had stopped for a red light on East Halsey Street. Right after the morning rush hour, traffic had thinned nicely, but their biggest problem remained their overweight steeds. Lockwood seemed to be in excellent condition, nearly equal to theirs, and his bike weighed considerably less. Even the rigorous Danite breeding program which had produced the *Beaver Dream* staffers was challenged.

"Don't get too close, Lor," Barbara cautioned her sister, who sucked on a water bottle while steering her bike with her other hand, blinking sweat from her eyes.

"No prob, Sis, except for keeping a featherweight three thousand dollar unobtainium-framed machine in sight. Plus we have to dance tonight."

"Don't remind me," Barbara replied, grimacing as she swept sweat from her face.

The light changed, and Lockwood sped off, his muscular calves flexing evenly as his narrow, soft tires bit smoothly into the asphalt. The Coolidges sprinted after him, closing the gap slightly, drawing nearer to 102nd Avenue, just before Halsey passed over I-205.

The light at 102nd turned yellow. Rising up off his seat, the young dentist kicked through the intersection. A hundred-and-fifty feet behind, the twins were forced to stop.

"Crap!" Barbara said, her head down, panting. They watched Lockwood pick up speed on the downhill ahead of the short climb to the crest of the overpass.

"We'll catch him," Lorna assured her, breathing just as hard as she reached for her water bottle. "He'll turn right on 92nd, heading for Sandy Boulevard. We'll catch him in that stretch."

As Lockwood rode up the overpass, an older Volkswagen van turned right from 102nd onto Halsey. The twins saw movement inside the blocky vehicle as it accelerated in the dentist's wake, pulling out to pass him on his left as he crossed the freeway, two hundred yards from where the girls waited for the light to change.

To their surprise, the van swerved right alongside Lockwood, matching his speed. Something dark and bulky flew out the open side door and hammered Lockwood in his left side, throwing him across the sidewalk and over the concrete railing. As the twins watched in horror, the bicycle caught on the edge of the railing, hung briefly, then disappeared down onto the freeway below with its rider.

The light changed, and the Danite agents pumped hard for the overpass. They reached the spot where Lockwood had been ambushed, jumped off their bikes and looked over the side in time to see several cars slew sideways to avoid the motionless body crumpled on the concrete below.

The tractor-trailer rig behind the cars had fewer options. It passed directly over both Lockwood and his bicycle as it skidded to a halt, blocking two lanes.

"Oh, crap," Lorna said, turning away, swallowing bile.

"I'll call 911," said Barbara, bringing out her cell phone, "then Levi."

"That cop'll be here eventually. Another dead Saint dentist. She'll recognize us."

"What do you wanta do? We're *witnesses*. Probably the best they'll have."

Lorna rested her hands on the railing, leaned forward and closed her eyes. Her shoulders sagged. "Yeah. You're right. It's our duty. Dammit."

"Find something to cable the bikes to while I finish my call, and we'll get down there and see what we can do. That trucker'll have flares, but he mayn't be in any mental condition to use 'em."

"Right." While her sister called 911, Lorna pulled the two bicycles together, looped her Kryptonite cable-lock around the machines and the heavy concrete railing and snicked it closed. Then the two young Danite agents climbed over the freeway boundry fence and slid down the embankment into the chaos and carnage below.

THIRTY-ONE

When the aftermath of Marvin Lockwood's homicide had been cleaned up and traffic was on the move again, Ron Wismer watched the Coolidge twins hike back up the freeway embankment and shook his head.

"How long were they here?" he asked his partner. Both stood on the grass beside the pavement, well away from the slow-moving flow of traffic. The tractor-trailer rig was still partially in the right-hand lane, until the trucking company sent out a relief driver. The baggers and scrapers had left minutes earlier.

"Half-hour before we were, until now," Deakins answered. "They called 911, then came down here. One of 'em got the trucker out of his rig, the other ran up the freeway with flares, and they had things half under control by the time the uniforms arrived. So, three-and-a-half hours total."

"And they just *happened* to be behind Doctor Lockwood when he got knocked off the overpass?"

Deakins gave a soft snort. "They were *following* him, Wis. Low-level surveillance. Probably tryin' to prevent something like this. They dance at that strip club."

"Jesus! Undercover strippers. Nice concept." He looked as his partner, saw that intent, gauging expression in her eyes that meant her mental cogs were on maximum whirl. "So, what d'ya think?"

"They knew who I was when I got here. Saw it in their eyes."

The Coolidges vaulted the fence, retrieved their bicycles, and vanished to the east. Wismer watched the tall, rangy women leave, then said, "Huh. So the

132

Saints must have some data base for identifying officialdom. Good knowledge for us to have."

"And Ray paid with his card, so they had him right off. More good knowledge: They could have just rode away when the guy they were following got spread over the freeway."

Wismer frowned. "They be good citizens, I guess."

"More than that. They *knew* I'd recognize them. They stayed anyway, and really helped."

"In the wake of tragedy."

"In the wake of *murder*."

"Yeah. That, too. You taped their statements, got a phone number. What's next?"

"*Home* phone, not the titty bar. Part of the pretense. We pretended not to know each other's identity." She looked at Wismer. "I need to get inside their group. Mutual benefit. Particularly I need to co-opt the strawberry-blonde one. I got the impression she's the platoon leader -- of whatever they are."

"What about Klaghorn, the ex-Seal? He the man?"

"Good question. Maybe just the front-man, the muscle, or somethin'. Multnomah County says they all have concealed weapons permits, so somewhere in the strip joint is bound to be a war room of some sort."

"Mormonette Commandoes."

Deakins grinned. "Law-abiding citizens, too, with all their legal T's crossed and I's dotted. You should've seen Ray watching those twins dance. Practically had to tie a drool-screen around his chin."

"I shouldn't wonder. They looked earthy. Maybe Margie and I should get a baby-sitter and go out there and take a look?"

His partner laughed aloud. "Sure. Not a bad idea, really. Then you'd recognize the rest of them under other circumstances."

"Are they all as nice-looking as these two?"

133

"Yup. And the quasi-redhead is nasty along with it. She stuck her snatch out at me with malicious intent."

"A *revealed* weapon?"

"I guess you could say she's got a permit for that, too," Deakins replied, laughing again.

"I'll take Margie out for a good dinner in Northwest Portland first. Or maybe down in the Pearl. Cafe Azul."

"With a bottle of excellent wine. These are high-humidity ladies. Fog up your mind real good."

"Along with the rest of you. Assorted pumps and spongiform tissues."

"You got that right, Ronald."

"Seriously, you think Lockwood is connected? Or just coincidence?"

"Well, hard to say. The Coolidges gave us a good description of the vehicle, a '73 or later orange VW Van with a white roof. The older body style, before the really lumpy square one. The perps apparently opened the sliding side door and knocked Lockwood over the railing with some kind of mechanical device. My gut, despite the unlikely vehicle, is that there's a connection."

"Might be somebody with a personal grudge. We'll have to check Lockwood out." They began walking back to their car, leaving the scene for the uniformed officers, Deakins with her hands in her pockets.

"Sure," she said, after a long pause. "But I bet we come up dry."

Wismer chuckled as they got in their car. "Not like with the strippers."

Deakins started the car. "Definitely not."

"I suppose I'll see."

"Oh, yeah, you bet. You *and* Margie."

THIRTY-TWO

For some time now, Paul Tiernan's Fridays had followed a routine. He finished his work day, went home, showered, and waited for Claire. A decision would be made on where to eat, whether to go to a movie or not, and they would end up at her condo or his, honing their procreative skills or falling asleep spooned together. Or both.

A comfortable ritual, one due to change in August, when each and every waking morning would find them with one another. Or, as Claire put it, "non-alone."

It was going to be weird.

Not as weird as the deaths of four Mormon dentists, however, Paul reminded himself as he poured two glasses of wine, one for himself and one for Claire, who'd be here shortly. He'd had a phone message on his machine from Ron Wismer, a "heads-up," Wis called it.

Marvin Lockwood had graduated with Paul and Claire, and while the guy had been self-contained and kept to himself, he'd made no enemies during their four years of school. No close friends, either. Even the other Mormons had not been tight with the guy, though none of them had ever expressed any frustration to Paul over that. Not that they would, being your basic non-complainers.

Paul looked down at the pair of wine glasses for a moment or two, contemplating the possibility that someone -- or, more likely, some*ones* -- had it in for Soyze Dental Associates. Ron's tone of voice had indicated that likelihood, even though he hadn't said so. The cougar deaths were one thing, the exploding Spitzley barbecue and Lockwood's bicycle crash were quite another. Yet the police apparently felt there *was* a connection. Ron hadn't really explained, and everything in the media so far implied only bizarre coincidence, although that might change with this latest death.

None of it made much sense, except that one segment of the dental community seemed to have been targeted for destruction.

As he continued to ponder, the front door opened and closed, and he heard Claire's voice in the hall. "Honey, I'm home!" A brief silence. "I don' smell no dinner?"

Paul laughed. "We're drinkin' dinner tonight, babe." He picked up his wine and handed her the other glass as she entered the common room, still in scrubs.

"You don't look too happy to see me," she observed, studying him over the rim of her glass as she took a slow sip.

"Marv Lockwood crashed his bicycle on East Halsey. Fell onto the freeway."

Claire searched his face, her eyes wide. "I gather he didn't make it."

"No."

"That doesn't sound like the guy I remember. I don't think I ever saw him make a mistake."

"My guess, from the sort of unspoken part of Ron's message, is that Marv may have had help."

Claire considered that for a few seconds. "Ron and Boothe must be going nuts." She cocked her head at Paul. "Was Marv married? I didn't really know him that well."

"I never heard, but I don't think so, at least not in school. He was in the A-L half of the class, so I never was around him much after sophomore year. Still, an unmarried Mormon..."

"Quiet guy."

"Very."

"Almost withdrawn sometimes."

"A *young* fogey."

She grinned at him, tickled. "Oh, that's good. Aren't you the clever one?"

"If you think I'm sharp, you should meet my intended."

"Your *intended*, Bucko, wants to go out for dinner."

"Reservations have been made. Seven-thirty at Caprial's Bistro. And a shower would be good. You smell like burned chicken feathers."

"An entirely wholesome dental odor. Many find it seductive."

Paul laughed again, louder. "Nobody outside the profession, believe me."

"C'mon, then. Shower with me."

"Already took one."

Now she scowled at him, irritated. "I said *I'd* be *in* there with you, dootbrain!"

It was his turn to look puzzled. "Should that make a difference?"

Claire pulled her scrub top off, then her sports bra, and stood looking at him, nude from the waist up. "Yeah," she said firmly, cupping her breasts. "And these better be compelling reasons."

"I think I like your mouth better," Paul replied, pulling her to him and kissing her.

Pressing up against him, her fingers twining through his hair, Claire sighed when their kiss broke. "Yours ain't so bad, either, bud." Her already deep voice had dropped an octave.

"I love you."

"Maybe we should...you know..."

"Reservation's for seven-thirty, my dear."

"You're no fun."

He stepped around her, began to take off his T-shirt. "You don't believe that."

"No," Claire admitted. "I don't." She grabbed his butt, pushed him toward the bathroom.

They managed to find enough time anyway.

* * * * *

Caprial's was Friday-busy, packed to capacity, a hub-bub of yuppies, yuppified gentry, and high-budget crunchies. The wine display was nearly obscured by perusing bodies clad in natural fiber, and Paul could hear bottles clinking from the racks on the other side of the display shelving. "Made the reservations last Tuesday," he said to Claire's unasked question, as they were led to their table on the north side of the room, opposite the bar area.

"Ya know," Claire murmured in his ear, "this marriage thing might work out."

Paul smiled as he sat down and picked up his napkin. "It will if I remain in charge," he said, draping the napkin on his lap.

"Boy, are you a dreamer," Claire replied, chuckling as she spread her own napkin.

"How about alternate weeks?"

"How about you're in charge when I'm not around?"

His smile turned rueful. "That'll be the best I can do, isn't it?"

"Yes. This discussion is over, and I'm going to have the halibut."

Their waiter appeared shortly after that, effectively preventing any response, not that Paul had an adequate comeback to a statement so perfectly delineating Claire's personal philosophy.

They made small talk over wine and appetizers until their dinners arrived, their conversation continuing as they ate. At some point near the end of his fish, Paul noticed that Claire had grown quiet and was glancing across the room frequently. "What?" he asked, his gaze following hers, trying to see who or what she was watching. It wasn't like her to be distracted while eating.

She gestured with her fork toward a table in the corner next to the front windows. "Isn't that Benny Lu's company manager over there, April whats-her-name?"

Paul looked across the room, studying the couple. "Yeah. April Kwong. The woman she's with doesn't look Asian, so she must not be a Considerate Care employee." April's dark-haired, impeccably-dressed companion had her back to them, but her height and hands, gesturing as the pair talked, hardly seemed Asian. "I don't recognize her at all."

Claire's eyes narrowed gradually as she examined the tall woman. One corner of her mouth jerked up. "Yeah, well, she looks familiar to me, though we've never met. And even if this might not be a business meeting, she works for a company that's doing business with Lu."

"How do you know that? You *know* who this woman is?"

"Let's just say I know *of* her, and leave it at that. I'll tell you when I can."

"Over dessert?"

Claire shook her head. She seemed momentarily to bristle at the woman seated with April Kwong. "No, lover, but I *will* tell you. Just not now. Okay?"

"Sure. You bet. I'll have the Creme brule'."

Frustration spread over Claire's blunt features. She reached over the table to him. "I don't mean to be a shit about this, but I haven't decided what I know, or how to tell you about it."

"The chocolate fudge tort looks good, too."

"Turd!" she grated, but she grinned as she said it.

Paul pretended to go down the dessert list, pursing his lips and frowning. "That item is not on the menu, Madam. Just the tort."

THIRTY-THREE

With the Coolidge twins and Jeannie Simmons behind her, Carly Meadows entered the East Stark Street Combative Arts *dojo*. The entry door closed, all four young women paused and took deep breaths, releasing them before climbing the stairs to the *dojo* proper. Carly felt calm descend over her mind and body. Seven generations of very selective marriage and resultant progeny seemed to well up through her, suffusing her being with power and certainty. The flow of time paused for a few moments before regaining its normal pace. Without speaking, the women headed up the stairs. Mormon missionary traders had brought martial arts techniques back from the eastern rim of the Pacific in the days just after the Civil War. Inclusion into the rigorous Danite curriculum had been quickly approved by the elders of the then-young faith.

Misha Voortees, their sometime teacher, stood quietly near the entry into the hardwood-floored *dojo*. A compact, muscular woman of Dutch-Sumatran ancestry, Misha's tanned features split into a welcoming smile at the sight of the Saint women. "Ah," she said in her soft voice, "This will indeed be a most auspicious evening." Chuckling, she took Carly's elbow and steered her around the nearest of two *Tatami*-surfaced squares currently occupied by practicing students. "I have someone I wish you to meet."

"Who?" Carly asked, puzzled, glancing back at the Coolidges and Jeannie, who shrugged in reply. Then she saw the back of a familiar blonde head atop a tall black-clad form seated in a *sempok* posture by the second practice square.

"Boothe," Misha said, touching the seated woman's left shoulder. "Here are the young women I mentioned on the phone."

"Whoops," whispered one of the twins, as a grinning Detective Lieutenant Boothe Deakins uncoiled smoothly to her bare feet and faced the Danites.

There was no missing the satisfaction in the policewoman's grey eyes as she shook Carly's hand after Misha's introductions. No missing the black headband, short-sleeved shirt, and sweat pants. The only thing missing was the *bengkong* belt. Another *berisilat* practitioner, Carly would bet. Her pulse quickened more as she took Deakin's hard hand in hers, sensing the loose-jointed strength in the relaxed body beyond that hand.

"Quite a coincidence," Deakins said, grinning even wider as she greeted the Coolidges after releasing Carly.

"Simply amazing," the twins agreed dryly, never easily-flustered, the snots.

The Lieutenant introduced herself to Jeannie, then returned to Carly. "You keep good company," she said. "These ladies really helped us out last Friday."

Though not as tall as the twins, Deakins was a touch taller than Carly, so Carly had to look slightly up at her, which was a bit disconcerting. "So I heard," Carly replied, thinking no matter how she tried to avoid it, this smart cop was going to find out more about the Danite presence in Oregon. The curiosity lighting up the speculative grey gaze meeting her own would not be easily denied or deflected. She must already know quite a lot. Somehow she'd found this place, and the Danites weren't here that often.

"Perhaps you two would like to contest one another?" Misha asked, with her trademark gentle

141

smile. "I believe your skill levels to be quite comparable."

"I'd like that," Deakins said, raising an inquiring hopeful eyebrow at Carly, a low-level dare.

Still, the policewoman was being polite. In Carly's book, that counted, and she was not about to be intimidated. "Sure," Carly answered. "Just let me do a few warm-ups."

"Of course," Deakins said. "All right if I join you?"

The five of them walked over to the other side of the mat and ran through their standard warm-up *Djurus*. Deakins fell right in with their pattern, her body and limbs moving freely, relaxed and totally at ease.

"You've been doing this a while," Carly said when they'd finished, mopping light sweat off their faces. As she spoke, the other three Danites watched Deakins silently, the twins alternately smirking at Carly.

"Ten years," Deakins affirmed, rubbing a knuckle on the end of her nose. "Since I was in college."

"Shall we, then?" Carly asked, gesturing toward the now-unoccupied *Tatami*. The detective nodded, then folded her towel carefully and laid it on the floor. The two women stepped onto the mat, and Carly noticed that the usual sounds of activity in the dojo began to dwindle down. Not unusual, but she guessed that Deakins might be well-known to local martial artists, and watched her opponent as they gave the traditional *Silat* salutation, the striking surface of right fist into the vertical left palm. The lieutenant's pale freckled features had picked up some color during their warm-up, and Carly remembered what Jeannie had said the other night: 'She looks like *us*.'

And, had Levi Klaghorn been here, he'd have said, "Watch your ass, kid."

142

Carly intended to do just that. Hands up in front of her chest, she took a step toward Deakins.

As did most non-flashy martial arts, *Silat* required its practitioner to relax. Body tension was the antithesis to good practice. Base, angle, and leverage were the secrets, operating on the centerline of the opponent's body. Deakins took a short strike with her right hand. Carly moved a few degrees to the outside, leaned in, and deflected the move with her own right. She caught the detective behind the trapezius with her left wrist, levering the taller woman away. Deakins continued the move, pivoting on her left foot, spinning rapidly back at Carly, moving Carly to her left with a forearm.

They sped up, probing for weaknesses, testing knowledge and experience. Elbows, hands, wrists blurred. When Carly and the other Danites had appeared at the *dojo*, months earlier, one of the more traditional Chinese martial artists had sneered, saying *Silat* looked like two gay males having a hissy-fight. Carly had changed his mind forcefully over a brief five-minute exercise on the mats.

No one would suggest anything of the sort now. Deakins was *good*. Quick and sure. She and Carly moved faster and faster, but remained evenly matched. When Carly managed to throw the taller woman, Deakins flipped clear, back at her in an instant. Leg sweeps failed. Deakins was too balanced, too precise, bouncing closer, trying to get inside Carly's moves. And nearly succeeding. *Guru* Voortees had been right; their skill levels were virtually identical. For Carly, it was like fighting herself in a mirror.

After ten minutes, both women were sweating heavily, their absorbent clothing approaching sodden. Deakins, grinning, stepped back at the same moment Carly did. "Nice," the lieutenant said, palms together in salute, her breathing only slightly elevated. "Most fun I've had in a spell."

143

"Yeah," Carly agreed after pressing her own palms against one another, bowing as she returned her opponent's bright grin.

"You see?" *Guru* Voortees said, her tone delighted, as the two younger women left the mat.

"You shouldn't be so pleased with yourself," Deakins admonished. "You would *scold* me for that."

"Hah!" their teacher replied. "That was a match of souls. Nothing I have seen recently compares."

"Thank you, Misha," Carly said, bending down to her towel and water bottle. "You are too kind." She settled on her butt against the wall, Deakins alongside her, companionably close, the warmth of her body bathing Carly's bare neck. The Coolidges and Jeannie took the mats. Carly let her eyes close as she sucked on her water. "That *was* fun."

"Almost as much fun as watching you the other night."

Carly chuckled, briefly embarrassed, glad for the workout-flush coloring her pale skin. "You could have gone all evening without saying that...Boothe."

"I try not to let the significant stuff go unsaid, particularly not the naughty bits. You are quite a piece of work, Miz Meadows."

Regarding her recent adversary through half-lidded eyes, Carly grinned evilly. "And *you* aren't, Lieutenant?"

Deakins shook her head, meeting Carly's gaze. "I'm not as spectacular as you. No way." She sucked on her bottle.

"But just as naughty?"

"Well, yeah, there is that. And you've got serious wickedness."

"You've seen me nude, too."

"Like I said: spectacular."

"I'll bet you're pretty nice."

"Maybe when all this is finished, you'll be able to find out."

144

"*'This?'*"

"When we figure out who's killing your brethren."

Carly felt her breath suck in. *Deakins knew.* Oh, well, no big surprise there. "How close are you?"

The policewoman shook her head again. "Not that close. We're getting some ideas on methods, but not motive. Who benefits if Soyze Dental Associates goes down? The obvious candidates don't quite add up."

"Considerate Care."

"Probably not. Like I said, doesn't add up. Ought to, but doesn't, or so my gut says. We're missing a piece of the puzzle." She rested her right hand on Carly's left wrist, and Carly felt her breath catch a second time. "Just don't forget we're on the same side," Deakins continued. "We both want this to stop."

Carly sighed. "We do." She paused, looked more directly at the other woman, inhaled before she spoke. "Did you mean that part about my finding out about you?"

"Sure. I'm not a tease, like you and those twins."

"You're not just trying to get my help?"

"Dedicated cops don't do that. I'm all business. I'd *never* trade my bod that cheaply."

"Oh. Then what's your price? Boothe."

"Make me an offer. Carly."

"Promise to be gentle?"

"No."

Carly laughed, took another swig of water. "Then we may be able to work something out."

THIRTY-FOUR

The Danites walked everywhere they didn't ride their bicycles, though they occasionally used public transportation to get to Portland's west side. Now they strolled the two miles or so back to their quarters through the warm late spring twilight, trying to fathom the circumstances which had connected them up with Boothe Deakins.

"C'mon, Carly," Jeannie implored. "Give!"

Carly shrugged. "What's to give? She and her partner followed Gregorson, more or less because they were curious about him, had some spare time, and not a whole lot was adding up for them. Just happened to be when he came to talk to Levi. Pure coincidence. They saw you and Marianne come into the building. Boothe realized you weren't the average strippers...and there it is."

"Well, 'Boothe' didn't seem to upset *you* too much," put in Barbara, leaning over Carly's shoulder.

"Hey, I can put up with you, I can put up with her." Carly put her arm around Barbara's shoulders, giving her a shit-eating grin. "Besides, her great-grandmother was from Manti. And she thought the last name just *might* be Coolidge."

The twins, as usual, were unimpressed. "Must be the white side," Lorna scoffed.

"*White* side?" asked Carly.

"Yeah, Great-great Grandfather was in a plural marriage. One wife was white -- the *white* side -- the other was, to judge from the family pictures, a freed slave, either mulatto or quadroon."

"The *black* side," Barbara added. "*We're* from the black side."

"Both wives were really *pretty*," Lorna said.

The four women walked in silence for a half-block. "So if that's true, what would that make you

146

guys and Boothe, then?" Carly asked. "Fourth cousins?"

"Yeah, maybe."

"That would explain some of her physical abilities," Jeannie Simmons said. "Still, that's only third generation in the Program. At most. Must have been about 1880, a little later. How much shared genetic material would there be?"

Barbara thought for a few moments, while they waited for a light. "One-sixteenth, I think. We'll check the records when we get home. The website should have information that far back, even if the last three generations of the Program were never included, for security reasons."

The quartet trotted across the intersection. When they'd slowed to a walk on the other side, Barbara began to snicker. "Welcome to the family, Meadows."

Carly scowled. "If I hit you with my gym bag, clone-girl, it's gonna hurt."

"We'll tell Cousin Boothe!" the twins said in mock distress, clutching one another fearfully.

In spite of herself, Carly had to laugh. It was so bizarre. "First we catch the killers. Which means we share with the police."

"And the police will share with us?" Jeannie asked.

Carly nodded. "So Boothe says. Unofficially."

"Ooooh!" the other three Danites replied, grinning at their companion. "*Boothe!*"

"I am so going to club and skin the three of you when this's over!"

"Oooooh!"

* * * * *

Stretched out in her over-sized bathtub, steam rising around her, totally relaxed and pleased with

147

herself, Boothe Deakins dialed her partner on her cell. "Found 'em, joined their posse."

"What?" Wismer asked. He sounded a little bleary, like he'd fallen asleep in front of the TV.

"At the East Stark *dojo*. They're *damned* good. That strawberry blonde is every bit as good as me. And those twins have almost developed their own art."

"Okay." He yawned audibly. "Sounds swell. 'Joined their posse?'"

"The redhead and I agreed to trade information. And why are you yawning? You just had two days off."

"Margie and I went out to see the strippers Saturday night after dinner downtown. Place was a madhouse. We didn't get home until after midnight." He managed a grim chuckle. "Margie'd never seen anything like it. Me, neither. Those gals made the strippers in movies look like cows." Another chuckle. "Kind of thought we'd have a real adventure when we got home. But Brandon was sick, she spent half the night up with him. I got the duty last night."

"How's he doing?"

"Better. Just a shitty kid flu. He's asleep now. So's Margie. I should be, but I had a feeling you'd call."

"Well, they're the real Mormon McCoy, and it's some kind of official group, probably secret. I didn't press the issue, but Carly Meadows -- that's the red-blonde -- has some deep heavy-duty search capabilities. She'll tell us what she wants to tell us, but that'll be quite a bit. She's forthcoming, and all of them understand that we're on the same side."

Wismer grunted. "Our own secret strikeforce. We don't tell the Captain, right?"

"Maybe some of it, but if we tell him everything, he'll pop a valve. There'd be 'liability issues.'"

"You think they're real asskickers?"

148

"Oh, yeah. *Hungry* real asskickers. This's gotten personal. They wanta grind some hind. Those twins are *mean*, and Carly's no shrinking violet."

"I'm considerin' a vivid personal experience here with those twins. I agree with Ray. How many are there of 'em?"

"I got the impression there were six first-line, four there last night. But my impression also was, and you can probably confirm this, even the servers and preparers are fit and capable."

He didn't answer for a few seconds, apparently mulling his words over. "Everybody I saw, and I went to the john twice, peeked into the kitchen, even had a few kind words with your Mister Klaghorn. I think he figured me out some, but Margie and I stayed in the back, so the Coolidge girls couldn't spot me."

Deakins laughed, wiggling her long toes under the water, watching little wavelets break over her knees. "Won't make any difference now, Wis. I think I blew the gig big time."

"So, what's all this mean? Me bein' too tired to actually work it out for myself." He yawned again.

"We have an asset that won't be known to the other side, whoever they are. The bad folks hafta know we're searching, and they may even find it amusing, thinking we're chasing our tails and not theirs."

"Makes sense. Can I go to bed now?"

"Sure. See you in the morning." They hung up, and she settled deeper in the tub, closing her eyes as she smiled to herself in satisfaction. A now-familiar face sprang into her mind, a symmetrical blue-eyed face framed by short, feathery strawberry-blonde hair. Deakins' smile widened. Her left hand crept between her thighs. She sighed with pleasure.

Carly, Carly, Carly.

THIRTY-FIVE

When Paul arrived for Clinic the next Wednesday, the eminent Doctor Coogan was bent over a small group of fishing flies, poking at them with a thick forefinger.

"Going out?" Paul asked as he hung up his jacket.

"Been out already this morning. Hit the Tualatin at daybreak, practiced with my new rod for an hour, just to get the feel."

"And the feel was good?"

Coogan grinned up at him. "Just like doing restorative dentistry. It's all in the wrist." An eyebrow raised. "Did you go to the latest funeral?"

Paul sat down opposite his boss after putting on his white clinic jacket. "Yeah. Marv had married since we graduated. Two small kids, both girls." He shook his head. "A pretty miserable affair. Just so damned sad and unnecessary."

"Gregorson there?"

"He and his wife. She managed to hold it together. He didn't."

Coogan nodded. "Typical. He's a good man. You think he's gettin' pissed yet?"

"Not so's I could tell. Claire was, though."

"No surprise there. So's the Dean."

"Really?"

"Sure," Coogan replied. "You have to remember he's fourth generation in the profession. Great-grandfather Dorfman started the practice in Harrisburg in the late Nineteenth Century. The Dean's dad is in his eighties, still practices two days a week with the Dean's older brother, Fred, and Fred's daughter."

"A legacy."

"Yup. Anyway, the Dean is sort of generically upset, wants to come out swingin,' and doesn't know who to swing at."

"Understandably. Any other faculty news of note?"

"Doctor Barkley's in renewed love." Giles Barkley was the Head of Removeable Prostodontics -- dentures -- a flamboyant, theatrical, silver-haired man who resembled Vincent Price, the late actor.

"*Renewed* love?"

"You know Lena Laluka, the detail gal for Finnish Denture Teeth?"

"Demonstrates most of Newton's laws of motion just walking across a room?" Like many of his peers, Paul found the Finnish Denture Teeth system generally left the happy recipient looking a great deal like the TV horse, Mister Ed. "She's a babe."

"Agreed. So Giles is caught between his dislike for the teeth and his lust for their sales rep. Every time she comes in, he buys just enough -- out of his own pocket, not with school funds -- to wangle a dinner date, then makes every effort to do what the Russians failed at -- capture Finland."

"No luck so far?"

Coogan shook his head. "Not that I've heard. Giles fancies himself as much of a gentleman as he does a ladies' man, though, so he might be mum on the subject."

"My chief memory of him is that he hated being called the 'Removable Head.'"

"What's your chief memory of me?"

Paul leaned back in his chair and surveyed the ceiling, his fingers steepled over his chest. "Gee, what to pick. There's so *many*. Kind, understanding, patient, compassionate, filled with knowledge and a love of learning. Sweet-natured. The list just goes on and on."

"With that list and a few bucks, you could get a good cup of latte'," Coogan grunted, glaring at Paul. "Your fiancee' has influenced your bullshit level unduly."

"Dear Claire."

"'Dear Claire' is as tough as boiled owl shit." The older man leaned forward, his elbows on his desk top.   "The part of me that doesn't envy your relationship with her wants to run like hell."

Paul ran the fingers of his right hand through his hair, thinking he must look perplexed. "I know that feeling, even after ten years."

"Not to sound too fatherly or anything, but you'll be quite happy together."

"I think so. Most of the time. It's just that, when Claire's around, she seems to use most of the oxygen available. Sometimes I can't seem to get my breath. And we're going to be around each other *all* the time, outside of work."

"The heady, hormonal days of youth devolve into anoxic middle age? I think I remember something like that, as much as I can remember middle age, let alone bein' a kid. But, you know, I don't think you have anything to worry about. Strong women stand the test of time."

"It's *me* I'm worried about being tested, not Claire and not time."

"'That which does not kill us makes us stronger,'" Coogan said, grinning still wider.

Paul shot the Operatives Chairman a dirty look. "All due respect, Doctor, but I'm the one on the hot seat here, not you."

"True, and that reminds me that the Radiology Department sent over some faculty records yesterday, films taken of you and Claire when you were students." Coogan reached into a desk drawer and brought out two manila envelopes. "They're culling the seven-year-old stuff. Rather than throw away

Claire's, knowing you were here, they included hers with your records." He handed the envelopes over his desk.

"Thanks," Paul replied, taking the records.

"Have you ever seen those supernumary impactions your intended has?"

"What?"

Coogan looked momentarily guilty. "I snooped. Claire's panograph and that sample Orthodontic tomograph from your sophomore year show what appear to be supernumary canines in both the maxilla and mandible."

Frowning, Paul undid the clasp and slid the long films out of the envelope. He held the big panograph up so that the light from the outside window shone through the film. Four additional large canines -- two in each jaw -- showed clearly above and below the much smaller normal canines. He felt his own lower jaw drop open as he stared at the unnatural images.

"Holy shit! How *long* are those things?"

"I measured 'em," Coogan replied, his expression still somewhat sheepish. "Forty-five millimeters. The longest conventional canine *I've* ever seen came in at thirty-two millimeters, and that was on a really big guy."

Continuing to stare at the incredible film, Paul forced his mouth to close. "Okay, they're big, but have you ever seen supernumary *canines*?"

"Maybe," Coogan replied slowly. "One or two in different mouths. Usually supernumaries are incisors, premolars, or the occasional fourth molar behind the thirds. Not that it makes any difference in this case. These are large, symmetrical, bilateral, and completely formed." He leaned forward over his desk, lowering his voice and waggling his eyebrows. "Wanta take 'em up to Doctor Zieper in Pathology, have them look, maybe run a computer search?"

An uneasy feeling crept up Paul's spine, almost akin to fear. "Uh, no, I don't think so. Claire'd be pissed, if she found out."

"She'll never know."

Paul laughed. "Get thee behind me, Satan."

Joining Paul's laughter, Coogan sat back in his chair and clasped his hands behind his head. "Yeah, I guess. But ask her. It's some hereditary thing, probably rare." He let his smile grow wider, more conspiratorial. "You could *publish*!"

"I *will* ask her, but I'll have to pick the time. Something like this, Claire will see it as an invasion of her privacy. Even coming from me."

Now it was Paul's boss's turn to be puzzled. "That doesn't sound like her. As a student, she was always so matter-of-fact, so confident. The younger instructors were half-scared of her. She'd stand and listen, then do it right the first time. I remember once down at the *Furca*, I overheard three of them trying to figure her out."   The *Purple Furca* was a local dental hangout. When he'd gotten to the school, Paul had been surprised to discover that, just as cops had their own bars, so did the dental profession, except the drinks cost more and the wannabees and hangers-on were maybe a little classier. No buckle bunnies.

"She seems forthcoming and straight-forward," Paul replied, "but she's more reserved and private than most people think. There's a line. You don't step over it."

To Paul's surprise, Coogan seemed to understand. He nodded. "'Enter at your peril.' My wife Kathy's that way, a little. I think it's an Irish thing."

Grinning, Paul got up and tucked the X-ray envelopes in his briefcase. "Wouldn't surprise me at all. And now I have to go out and earn the pittance the school pays me to educate the dental stars of tomorrow. While you play with your fly."

"That's *flies*," Coogan corrected tersely, as Paul left.

* * * * *

There was no wine out when Claire boiled through Paul's front door at six-fifteen at a half-run. Wednesday evenings were a short jog down to the nearest outside basketball court followed by an hour or so of hoops, then back to the condo to shower and relax.

Of course, Claire spotted the X-ray envelopes immediately after she kissed Paul and shucked her scrubs. "Whazzat?" she asked around their second or third kiss, pointing at the counter.

Paul decided this was as good a time as any. "Our old panos, your funky canines. Radiology dumped them in Coogan's office. He passed 'em on to me."

She stiffened in his embrace, an instant's rigidity. "You *looked* at them?"

Trying not to gulp, Paul said, "I looked at mine, too. *You* can look at mine. If you want."

"You *saw* my impactions." Her tone was flat, bordering on anger, but he could tell it wasn't entirely directed toward him. It went deeper than that.

"Big suckers."

She looked directly at him, took a breath, calmer now, hints of a smile appearing around the corners of her mouth. "When they took the panos on us, you remember old Doctor Fixott had to vet every one?"

"Yeah."

"His vision was getting a little worse then, and he spent a lot of time tryin' to find winning Lotto numbers. I took it to him, asked him if he thought I'd need Ortho if those impactions ever decided to erupt. He agreed, but none of it really registered. He was

155

distracted. Signed off on it, instead of showing them to Pathology or Oral Surgery."

"And you skated."

"Yeah." She led Paul to the counter, her arm still around him. "Let's take a look at these."

To Paul, the films looked the same as earlier, so instead of examining them, he studied Claire's features as she raised the panograph to the overhead light. "You look like you did the other night when you saw that woman in the restaurant."

Her forming smile gradually turned sardonic. "I bet I do." Her pale gaze flicked to him and away.

"I don't suppose there's a connection." That seemed a safe statement. Paul knew there couldn't be.

She lowered the film and wet her lips, her hazel eyes abnormally serious. "Yeah, there is," she said very quietly.

"What!"

"Remember what I told you at Caprials?"

"That you'd tell me when you're ready?"

"I'm kind of ready," she said, holding up her left hand with her thumb and index finger about a half-inch apart. "That woman in the restaurant. She's my second cousin, once removed. I think. Her name's Riona Phelan, and her family's doing some work for Benny Lu. My uncle is concerned about them."

"Concerned how?"

"Can't tell you that. Yet."

"This Riona, does she have funky canines?"

"Oh, yeah."

"Will our kids have funky canines?"

Her gaze seemed to darken. When she spoke, Paul could barely hear her. "Yeah." She put the palm of her right hand against his left cheek, and kissed him. "And that's all I can tell you now, lover."

"Okay. I'll go get the ball."

Claire laughed, half-chipper again. "You are *so* easy."

156

Paul paused on his way to the bedroom, and shook his head, grinning at her. "You'll find out on the court, you odontogenic mutant."

Claire was still laughing when he came back out with the ball, but, typical Claire, she killed him at the park, never missing a shot.

THIRTY-SIX

Claire's office day began at seven o'clock, and Paul didn't see patients until eight, so after she left in the morning, Paul sat outside on the kitchen deck, quietly reading *The Oregonian* and sipping his cooling coffee.

He did not consider himself a particularly good linear thinker. Working logically through something wasn't Paul's strong suit, though it could be accomplished. He'd discovered early in life if he dumped all the facts into some sort of mental hopper and then went on to other tasks, the solution, or some greater part of it, eventually dropped into his consciousness.

In the wee hours of last night, the Mormon deaths, the connection between Considerate Care and Claire's cousins, even Claire's weird radiographs, swirled though his mind for a half-hour after Claire fell asleep. Finally he'd clamped the lid over what he knew, spooned against Claire and joined her in slumber.

Now, his mind clear and the coffee doing its trick, Paul put the sports and comics aside and returned to the two big X-Rays. The Orthodontic film showed a different lateral view of Claire's jaws than the panograph, depicting her slight prognathism and its probable cause -- the position of those huge canines -- all four set just to the rear of the roots of her normal canines, as if waiting to slide into place. The sutures between the premaxilla, the maxilla proper, and the base of the skull looked a bit wide too, as though they hadn't closed fully as Claire matured. That was interesting, and Paul was momentarily glad that Claire had hoodwinked Doctor Fixott. A pathologist or genetic odontologist would do flips the moment they saw these films. The Radiology chief had not realized he was seeing some odd genetic anomaly, thank God.

Paul didn't know what he was seeing, either, or the total implications involved, but he did know that the trait ran in Claire's family. She'd admitted that. He stood slowly, took the empty coffee cup and the films back indoors. He had reached a conclusion.

Placing the cup in the dishwasher and the films back in their envelopes, Paul took a white paper towel and a small baggie from the kitchen, then went down the hall to the main floor bathroom where Claire kept the spare set of toiletries she used when she was here. Her hairbrush lay on the counter next to the sink. He picked the brush up and examined it, smiling thinly with satisfaction at the amount of hair lodged between the bristles.

He carried the brush into his small library-office, held it under the desk light and carefully removed fifty percent of the individual hairs from the bristles, depositing them on the paper towel. When he was satisfied he had enough, he funneled the hair into the baggie and slid the seal closed.

Once the baggie rested safely inside a locked desk drawer, the towel deposited in the waste basket, and the brush back in its place, Paul stood quietly in the doorway to the deck, his hands in his pockets, and wondered why he'd done what he'd just done. Not sure. But he trusted his inner sense. There might come a time when the genetic information residing inside what he'd taken from Claire's hair brush would make a difference in their lives.

How that could happen seemed a bit vague. Maybe the information would show up during the next info-dump inside his head. Or maybe not. One thing for sure, he wasn't going to scamper to Wismer and Deakins with the hair samples. A connecting thread ran though the events that had killed four Mormon dentists, and

Considerate Care and Claire's cousins were somehow involved, if only peripherally.

Perhaps more than peripherally, Paul decided. No matter, Claire must be protected.

He smiled at the concept of protection for Claire. Not too likely.

THIRTY-SEVEN

Technically Westside Dental Group's headquarters on Cascade Avenue lay in Tigard, but most of the staffers thought of it as being in Beaverton, whose city limits were several hundred yards to the north. No matter. The Dental Specialties Office, a general dental services clinic, and administrative office sprawled around the periphery of a spacious parking lot dotted with mature Lodgepole pine and other more low-growing evergreens, even a few Greek cypress.

Konstantine Janos had purchased the property in the late seventies to be the seat of his dental empire. It allowed him to practice dentistry for as many hours a day as he wished, yet he was close enough if his administrative staff required his presence.

The only difficulty the location presented, to Emmett McManus' way of thinking, was the lack of route variations to get there. One arrived on Cascade, either from the north or the south. Any person parked within sight of the Westside entrance easily knew exactly which employees were present at the complex and their time of arrival and departure.

The careful and cautious McManus approved of their nearest neighbors, however. Two upscale motorcycle dealerships and an office supplies outlet meant that traffic was heavy and few people parked on the street. Only one of the motorcycle shops possessed a line-of-sight to Westside's entrance, and McManus had long ago memorized the vehicles belonging to the business's employees. Janos chided his security chief for being paranoid, but McManus knew the older man secretly approved.

One could not be too careful in this time of dental deaths, even though the attacks had been limited to Soyze staffers. The unique nature of the first two

161

deaths had been an alarm bell to McManus, signaling the almost certain involvement of Riona Phelan and her two brothers. He did not feel that his warning to Claire had been the slightest out of practical. The young Phelans might not hew to their grandfather's rulebook, might feel the chafing of archaic and out-dated regulations. They might then come for the only persons who they thought could betray them -- their relatives. Forgetting, as do the young, that their relatives would also then be betrayed.

Still, he was far from certain of that Thursday mid-morning as he pulled out from the Westside entrance and headed south on Cascade. There were no vehicles behind him and a sturdy biker type on a slow-moving Harley the only thing in the opposite lane.

As the heavy motorcycle passed his Toyota, the front of his car gave a small lurch, followed a split-second later by an explosion which kicked the front end of the car two feet into the air.

The steering column slammed into his right leg. The car lurched sideways to a stop. McManus felt almost a sense of relief. The time of guesses had ended. The battlelines had been drawn. Through a red haze of pain, he switched off the ignition and sagged back into the seat, ignoring the smoke pouring out of the engine compartment around the buckled hood. The armor-reinforced firewall he'd installed had held. The hiss of automatic foam fire-retardant billowing around the engine sounded clearly.

Question: How physically close to him were they? Pushing the pain away, McManus drew his 1911A .45 automatic from its place under his seat just as the man on the passing Harley ran up to his side of the ruined Toyota.

By the time the EMT team arrived eight minutes later, McManus was still trying to decide who'd been more surprised, himself or the Harley rider, Frank Wheeler, MD. He never doubted that Doctor Wheeler might have saved his life, though, preventing the bomber from checking on his or her handiwork.

Preparation was only part of the defensive task, after all. In the end, luck still played a role. Wheeler's trip to the motorcycle shop to buy new boots on his day off proved that axiom.

And McManus would never forget the look on the good doctor's face as he stared down the muzzle of the .45.

THIRTY-EIGHT

Hospitals were not familiar places to Claire. She'd gone to ERs with friends or teammates in high school and college, but never above that ground-floor level. The nature of her people precluded any great medical problems, and their lives generally ended surrounded by family in the privacy of their homes.
Uncle Emmett had been lucky in one regard, delivered quickly to St. Vincent's and under police protection because of the bomb. Konstantine Janos had called Claire about the attack, assured her that her uncle was going to be fine, then told her to leave the office two hours early so she could visit him. Just like her boss to do that. Every employee was part of his extended family. Janos himself might take her patients for that missed two hours.

She'd parked in the several-storey parking garage across from the hospital and taken the elevator up to Uncle Emmett's floor. His room was easy to spot, the one with the police presence standing by the door, a hefty young cop frowning a bit as Claire approached, trying to figure her green scrubs. Most versions of officialdom connected green scrubs with ER staffers, something with which they were familiar, and Claire was willing to use that easy level of acceptance to access her uncle.

The cop nodded at her smile, his brief frown vanishing, and she walked into the room. Uncle Emmett lay propped up in bed, a *People* magazine open and upside-down on the white sheets over his stomach. A tall, dark woman wearing shorts and a T-shirt sat between Claire's uncle and the window, and Claire realized she'd interrupted their conversation.

"Hi, Unc," Claire said. "Thought I oughta come up and see how you were doing." Other than a little more bulk to his right leg -- probably a cast -- he didn't look too bad, his color good and thick brown hair neatly combed.

"I'll be fine, dear," her uncle replied, a hint of embarrassment in his answering smile, "just as soon as I escape this place." There were a couple of bruises on his face, she saw, but no obvious swelling.

The dark woman stood, Claire's size and looking dangerously fit. "I'm Mai Killian," she said, "an old friend of your uncle's."

Claire studied the woman as they shook hands, thinking most people would kill for those beautiful green eyes, so striking against Mai's mahogany skin.

"Where's he been hiding *you*?" Claire asked, lifting her right eyebrow at her uncle.

"I only come around when I'm needed," Mai answered, with a flash of white teeth in what was clearly *not* a smile.

"Okay," Claire said, wondering just what in hell was going on here.

"She *knows*, Claire," Emmett McManus said softly.

Now Claire's gaze returned to Mai. "But *you're* not..?"

Mai shook her head. "No."

Inhaling deeply through her nose, attempting to filter out the pervasive hospital stench, Claire replied, "But you're something funny."

The dark woman smiled, a genuine smile this time, with real warmth. "Yes, I'm something *quite* funny."

"Maybe you should stop badgering my friend, Claire,"
her uncle interjected, but without any sting to his words.

"No matter, Emmett," Mai said. "Your niece is entitled to be concerned about you." She glanced at her watch. "And I need to make a stop at my office before I go home. I'll be back this evening, after I eat

165

and do some paperwork. Nice to meet you, Claire." She bent down and kissed Emmett. Then, with a mischievous grin for Claire, left.

Claire brought the chair around to her side of the bed and sat down. "So, who is she, Unc? More important, *what* is she?"

Her uncle's smile was weary. "You'll have to ask her, my dear. I am not really at liberty to say, beyond the 'old friend' bit."

"She looks nasty."

"Sometimes she *acts* nasty. Mai, I'm afraid, makes a good friend, but a *very* bad enemy."

Claire grinned at him. "I didn't mean *that* kind of nasty. I meant the other kind, but we can skip that for now. How are you feeling? I mean, besides a broken leg, which is pretty obvious. Plus being generally banged-up."

Her uncle shrugged, rapped a knuckle on his cast, creating a hollow sound. "I'm quite sore, in addition, but once I'm out of this room, the final mend will take but a few minutes. Removing the cast will be the time-consuming part."

Claire nodded in quick understanding. "Dad told me once about that little trick. Never had to use it, though." She leaned toward him, lowered her voice, and let her expression turn serious. "So, was it...?" She left the next words unspoken, thinking of the officer standing just outside the door.

"One would surmise," her uncle confirmed, nodding.

"One would surmise what, cousin?" said a husky feminine voice behind Claire.

Spinning up out of her chair, Claire confronted a slender business-suited woman a couple inches shorter than herself and nearly as dark as Mai Killian. The woman from Caprial's the other night, she was certain. "Riona Phelan, I presume?" She forced her hands not to make fists.

166

The slender woman inclined her head. She seemed infinitely calm, but her black eyes kindled for an instant, locked with Claire's. "Indeed, cousin. And you are Claire McManus." Her gaze bent around Claire to the figure in the bed. "How are you?" she asked.

"Well enough. Thank you for coming."

"I felt it necessary." She attempted to move around Claire, closer to the bed. Claire stepped in front of her, blocking her path.

Riona's gaze lifted to Claire's. "Are you foolish enough to believe *I* had something to do with this?"

"Can't rule it out," Claire grated.

A flush of anger darkened Riona's narrow features still further. Her lips compressed together in frustration. "Tell your hulking niece my innocence is as obvious as my guilt would be. Is she *nose-blind*?"

Emmett McManus laughed. "No, just inexperienced in our life, cousin. The signs are not obvious to her." To Claire he said. "Your cousin is not our problem." He tapped the end of his nose. "*This* does not lie."

"Okay," Claire replied, stepping reluctantly aside. "I just hope you're right."

With a final glare, Riona grabbed Claire's chair and sat gracefully but somewhat stiffly beside the bed. Claire saw the back of her neck was red and felt mildly pleased.

"I'm sorry this happened," Riona told Emmett. "I'll call Grandfather this evening and inform him."

"No need to trouble the old gentleman," Claire's uncle responded. "I'll be fit in a few days."

Claire moved to Riona's right, where she could see her younger cousin's face. She kept breathing through her nose, trying to bring information on-line through that unfamiliar medium. She *thought* Riona was being sincere, and Uncle Emmett -- far more experienced -- obviously believed so. Certainly Riona

167

was composing herself and marshalling her own thoughts prior to saying a word.

When she finally spoke, Riona did so almost hesitantly. "What we talked about earlier, the ongoing negotiations between myself and Doctor Gregorson, are basically concluded. This other business, the deaths of Soyze dentists, has virtually brought that process to a halt, however." She gestured at Emmett McManus' cast leg. "And now you." She shook her head in exasperation. "There's too much going on here that I don't know about."

"Phone your grandfather," Claire's uncle advised.

"That would be weakness," Riona replied with a tight-lipped half-angry smile. For the first time, Claire felt sympathy for her irritating cousin, if only a little.

"Do it anyway," the injured man said. "He won't think less of you."

"You've never met him," Riona protested, looking even more frustrated.

"I've heard about him since I was small, his many virtues and great skills." He reached out and touched Riona on one hand. "Tap into that fountainhead of knowledge. Neither you nor he will be disappointed."

Riona thought the advice over for a moment, her expression indrawn. Then she sighed, and her features shifted to a kind of chagrin. "All right." She gave a short laugh, bitter-sweet. "I come to comfort you, cousin, and you do more for me than I you."

Uncle Emmett pretended to look modest, brushing off the compliment, and the three of them talked for nearly an hour. As the conversation progressed, Riona emerged as a young gun under the gun. Her own gun, Claire decided, having had some experience with self-inflicted pressure. Grandfather Phelan came across as a wise gentleman who had seen it all and done quite a lot of it. For the first time,

Claire felt an interest in this other side of her family, and no little empathy for her cousin, though she still thought Riona was a snot.

They left her uncle's room together, chatting amiably through hospital hallways and the elevator. When they reached the parking structure, Claire asked, "Think whoever they are will try for me?"

No surprise showed on her cousin's dark features as she stroked her narrow chin. Points for Riona. "That occurred to me, also, while we talked with your uncle. If you had not brought it up, I would have. Since they knew to seek him out, they must know about you."

"And you."

The expression which developed on Riona's face bore some elements of what might be termed a smile, but most resembled their other lives, in the fur. Now, watching her cousin's grim features, Claire wished she'd spent more time in her other form.

"Phelans take their chances," Riona replied coldly. "It's the nature of our business. However, the first two deaths could easily have been done by elements of our people, not some native species, and that could present a problem."

"I hate to show my ignorance, but how many of us are there?"

Riona shrugged. "Who can say? Grandfather knows of others, like your family, who are related, and practice our skill. He has mentioned there are those more distantly related, even those about which we have no knowledge. He also hypothesizes that there must be those of us who know not what they are, who do not practice." As she talked, Riona's black gaze swept the parking garage around them, alert now and probing for potential threat. "I pity those last, who miss the joy."

"I haven't done it for ten years," Claire confessed.

Surprise flickered momentarily in Riona's eyes. She gave a soft grunt, then smiled. "When this is finished, cousin," she said, "I shall endeavor to bring you back to your true life."

"I don't know, Riona," Claire replied. "My fiancée is normal."

One corner of Riona's wide mouth lifted. "Your children will not be. He should be told."

"He knows about our fangs. He saw an X-ray."

Her cousin grunted again, and her smile evened out. "Easier, then. Tell him it's like shopping at Nordstrom. Very addictive."

"Like April Kwong?" Claire asked sweetly, pushing a little, to see Riona's reaction.

There wasn't much, at least externally. Riona went still, then silently studied her from behind lowered lashes. "*Very* good. I misjudged you, cousin. You have true aggression, the best kind. Our blood indeed runs strongly in your veins. Your uncle thought as much, and he was right. Where did you hear about Miz Kwong and myself?"

"Saw you in Caprial's last week when my fiancee and I were out to dinner." Claire cocked her head at her shorter cousin. "Look, is it some Phelan thing, or does everybody in the east talk like you?"

Riona gave a completely unladylike snort, startling Claire. Then she smiled, wide and unaffected for the first time since they'd met. "This is how we speak between ourselves. Since you are one of us, I automatically fell into those archaic speech patterns."

"Makes sense, I guess." Claire's cell phone chose that moment to ring. Irritated, she pulled it out and answered. It was Paul. "Oh, hi. No, he's pretty much okay. Leg broken, a few bruises." As she talked, she watched Riona check out their surroundings for the third or fourth time, and saw her cousin's sleek features reflect some inner decision.

170

"May I speak with him?" Riona asked, turning toward Claire and raising her left hand, smiling again.

Returning her smile, Claire handed Riona the phone.

"Hello. I'm Claire's cousin Riona, and I wanted to hear your voice, so that I might judge if she's chosen wisely." She listened for a few moments, then snickered. "*That* large? I'm *most* happy for her. We must go out some evening, the three of us." Another pause. "Yes, I do have funky canines. Thank you. My pleasure. Here's Claire again."

"You butt," Claire said to Paul, as soon as she had the phone back. "Yeah, like you *didn't* say *that*! Okay, see you at home." She slipped the phone away. "Sorry. He's kind of a smartass."

"He'll be fine with what we are," Riona said, resting one manicured hand on Claire's forearm, her features serious.

"Yeah, probably. I think. We've been together ten years."

Riona reached into her purse and produced a card. "My home phone and cell are on the back. If anything you deem important happens, or merely something puzzling, call me. I have resources." She shook Claire's hand, not releasing it immediately. "And, if we live through all this, I will take you into the forest and show you the life you should have had."

"Okay, it's a deal."

Riona unlocked her rented Nissan Pulsar. "If we can. And remember, call me." She climbed in her car, started it, backed out, and drove away with a short wave.

Her arms folded across her chest, Claire watched her cousin leave, trying to resolve her conflicted feelings. Her overwhelming thought was that the ride -- whatever it might prove to be, and whomever with -- was about to begin.

THIRTY-NINE

Paul felt much of his life was spent waiting for Claire to show up and drop some kind of metaphorical bomb in his lap. Ten seconds through the door, and the action started. This time, make no mistake, the bomb was the sure-nuff real McCoy, but, as always, Claire would detonate it at her own time and place. The thing with her cousin had been interesting, and maybe Paul shouldn't have given what had looked at the restaurant like a sophisticated woman a bad time, but she'd started it.

He listened to Claire's car door close, listened for her steps on the walk, and listened to the key in the lock. Nothing untoward, no excessive haste, no sign of temper. No slamming. Good. Paul didn't need his chops busted just now. Mostly he wanted to know how Claire and Riona had hit it off so well, and why. Claire's antipathy the other night at Caprial's had been strong, and she typically didn't back off from that stance. He quickly composed his opening line after adjusting the filled wine glasses for maximum visibility, took a deep breath and leaned back in his chair.

"Wine's ready," he called out cheerily, before she came into sight from the hallway.

"Oh, spare me your shit, you smartass prick! You embarrassed me in front of my cousin." Glaring at him, she snatched up her wineglass, tilted it up.

"Oh, no," Paul said, grinning at her and shaking his head as he watched her drink. "I don't buy that. You're about a half-step slow coming in the door. When you're really pissed, you flat freakin' *fly*."

Returning his grin as she lowered her wine glass, Claire said, "Think you know me that well, huh?"

"Yeah. Except for the funky canine thing. I need to do some research on genetic anomalies, maybe go through some old circus records. Read the 'Baraboo News Republic.' Stuff like that."

"'Baraboo News Republic?' What's a Baraboo?"

"Baraboo, Wisconsin, the winter home of the Ringling Brothers Circus. The Circus World Museum must have some archives. The local paper probably does, too."

"My, aren't you the amusing fellow?"

"I want to be well-prepared for the wedding and following festivities, in case you've got weirder relatives than Riona out there. You know. The Alligator Boy and the Bearded Lady."

Claire regarded him intently for several moments, her smile and her hard gaze softening. "You're tryin' to make me feel better, aren't you? Because of Uncle Emmett." She reached around behind his neck, pulled him to her, kissed him deeply. "I'm lucky to have you, Pablito."

"And vice-versa. You're amazing. Despite the intensity. And you see right through me." He hugged her.

"What does Coogan think of us getting married?"

Paul chuckled. "He approves completely. Assured me sincerely we'd be very happy. Of course, right after saying that, he told me I should publish an article about your canines."

A wry smile appeared on Claire's blunt features. "Yeah, it always comes back to those damned teeth, doesn't it?"

He kissed her forehead. "Doesn't matter," he said quietly.

"Somebody tried to kill my uncle." The barest hint of worry surfaced in her eyes. "Riona told me to be careful."

"What!"

173

"Yeah. She might be paranoid, but Unc's paranoia kept him alive. He'd armored the engine compartment, put automatic fire extinguishers next to the engine. Otherwise..." Claire drew a forefinger across her throat.

"Jesus. They *bombed* Doctor Spitzley and his wife." He sat down abruptly, regarded her narrowly. "Think there's a connection?"

Claire nodded, not speaking.

"I bet Wismer and Deakins are right on top of this. Somebody working for *another* dental outfit. And this one *lived*."

"They'll talk to my uncle."

"Hell, they'll talk to *you*."

"I suppose. I could sure do worse than having Boothe Deakins looking out for me."

Now Paul laughed outright. "I pity anybody she catches. Won't be enough left to bait a trap with. She absolutely *appalls* Ron, most times. And she's utterly implacable and undeviating."

"Somehow that's comforting."

"Yeah, I guess."

"Look, can we eat in tonight? Watch a DVD or two?"

"Sure. Will there be cuddling?"

"Better than that. The Full Claire."

He laughed again, took her in his arms. "All *right*."

FORTY

Emmett McManus recognized officialdom when he saw it, and every aspect of the two strangers who stepped into his hospital room that evening fairly screamed 'copper.' Since they were somewhat better attired than the Beaverton police and the ATF people who'd visited him earlier, he assumed they were the Portland homicide detectives assigned to the cases there. Claire had mentioned names, Wismer and Deakins.

"Good evening, officers."

The man spoke first. "I'm Lieutenant Wismer, this is Lieutenant Deakins. We'd like a few minutes of your time, if that would be all right."

"Certainly," Mcmanus replied, shaking their hands. Wismer was Paul Tiernan's friend, he recalled, and there were echoes of Paul's intensity in the man's expression. Claire had also spoken highly of Deakins, which likely meant the woman was dangerous in the extreme. "It definitely beats the television, and I'm the only live one you've got."

Wismer winced, but Deakins' smile widened, confirming his first impression.

"We took a look at your car with the ATF guys," she said."You did some nice prep."

"Thank you. I try."

"Why would someone want you dead?"

"I assume because they believe I present a threat to some secret endeavor. Initially, I considered a connection with your Soyze dental homicides, but now I am uncertain."

The next question came from Wismer. "What can you tell us?"

McManus smiled at the younger man. "I refuse to speculate at the moment. This may *not* have anything to do with the Soyze cases, or perhaps the killers are simply moving to the next group. I can tell you that these are not terribly experienced bombers, though their materials are certainly adequate. They should have placed the charge immediately under the passenger compartment."

"That was armored, too," Deakins said, giving him a wolf's grin distressingly like Claire's.

"True, but it would have had more likelihood of success.
Whoever it was didn't *see* the composite-metal panels, or didn't recognize what they saw." He cleared his throat, took a drink of water from the filled glass on his nightstand. "Was the barbecue case also a line-of-sight remote detonator? Because this one must have been."

"Yes," Deakins replied, after a quick glance at her partner.

"Then there has to be a connection. Have the forensics people given you a determination?"

"Not yet," Wismer said, "but I think you're right."

"Fascinating. What will the killers do next, I wonder?"

Wismer frowned. "Good question."

"Motive is not clear to you? Presuming, of course, that you have more information than I."

"You probably have exactly one piece of information less than we do," Deakins said. "Judging from what you've said." As she spoke those last words, her gaze shifted intensity. She watched him tightly, totally focused.

McManus smiled at her, hoping not to let her see he knew *more*, not less, than they did, trying to avoid her trap. "I'm sorry," he replied, feeling his adrenaline spike, knowing his people would sense that subtle alteration in an instant. The lieutenant, fortunately, would not. "I'll certainly let you know, should something more occur to me, or some connection appear."

The two detectives asked a few more questions, then left after giving him their cards. As he manipulated his bedpan, Emmett reflected that his family and their friends had complicated his existence in ways he could not have imagined even twenty-four hours previously. The only bright spot was the obvious mutual delight that Claire and Riona found in their meeting. He placed the bedpan in its designated spot and swung back under the sheets, resolving to relax for the next hour or two, wait for Mai to return, and not worry about Lieutenant Boothe Deakins and her agile mind.

* * * * *

"So, how much does he know?" Wismer asked his partner when they were back in their car. He stuck the key into the ignition, but didn't start the car.

"More'n us," Deakins replied, locking her seatbelt.

"Think he knows who the killers are?"

"No, not now, but I got the impression he had some suspicions." She looked briefly thoughtful, shook her head. "That sounds dumb. He's like Claire. He either knows or he doesn't. The McManuses are not ambiguous people."

"Maybe we need to find out who came to visit him today."

"What, sombody showed up who changed his mind?"

Wismer shrugged. "Well, Claire was there, probably her boss. Who else? Anybody? A bunch? The Jesuit High School Girls' Soccer Team?"

"Claire had to have come from the office. Let's say sometime between four and five. Three-four hours ago."

"We talk to the Beaverton badge who was on duty in front of McManus' door then. He or she'll have seen some ID, at least be able to give us descriptions if not the names. Look into those, background 'em, see what turns up."

"Meow-w-w!"

"Don't start the cat thing with me, Deak."

"Yeah, well, *I* think we're onto something here."

Wismer started the car, backed out of the space. "Don't you wish."

"I'm serious, partner."

"Serious is good. 'Right' is better."

"And desperation is the mother of supposition. Just drive, okay? I'm bushed. We can talk to Beaverton tomorrow."

He steered the car out into the late evening sunset, pointed it toward the freeway. "Tomorrow is another day."

Deakins laughed. "So profound."

"Always."

"You wish."

FORTY-ONE

Howard Taylor Pick had gone through Vietnam to get a college education and go on to dental school. Along that path he learned that good things almost never fell out of the tree of life and landed in your lap. You worked for what you got. You played fair and put your hard nose firmly to the grindstone and life happened. Bad things happened, too, of course, but mostly they didn't happen to the Pick family. He and Hannah and the kids had been fortunate. Howard, Junior, had had a couple of close calls as a helicopter pilot in the Middle East, but he'd walked away with only a few scratches and some good stories. Pick appreciated his son's attitude. No namby-pamby post-traumatic stress crap, just "took us a while, but we got out in one piece," then back to business as usual. A good boy, one his parents could be proud of.

So far as Doctor Pick was concerned, the killing of Soyze dentists merited the same attitude. Care and attention. He watched where he went, what he drove, and who was around. Now, arriving at Oaks Bottom Wildlife Refuge to check the status of a score of Wood duck nesting boxes, he knew nothing was a hundred percent, but blowing up his Chevy Suburban was going to take more punch than poor Jim Spitzley's barbecue, and nobody was going to tip his rig over the side of anything.

The cat thing, that concerned Howard more, but he thought he might have made adequate preparations on that score, too. Hell, he'd be fifty years old on his next birthday. The good Lord shouldn't be calling him home just yet. Besides, what would he do in the eternal realm without Hannah?

He chuckled sardonically at the thought as he climbed out of the Chevy, bringing his telescoping mirror with him. He extended the mirror and walked around the Suburban, checking the wheelwells and undercarriage. When he returned to the rig from his meander, he'd check again, seeing if anything was amiss.

Whistling tunelessly, Howard laid the mirror back on the floorboards, brought out his steel-tipped walking staff, locked the Chevy, and headed on down the main trail from the parking lot. The broad waters of the Willamette sparkled in the early morning sun, a few rowing crews cutting through the silver surface of the river, their wakes shimmering out behind the slender craft.

The occasional runner jogged past the lanky dentist as he proceeded to the first series of nest boxes, set in trees on the river side of the trail system. Pretty sparse foot traffic this early. Howard examined the brown metal circling each tree trunk below the boxes to foil raccoon and other climbing predators. A few tentative scratches, but nothing more. Satisfied, he moved on, back to the main trail.

He enjoyed the Bottom, the teeming riverine wildlife, the kick of being out in nature. Growing up in Preston, Idaho, Howard had joined his father and uncles deer hunting in the Fall, done birds various other times of the year. Even then, he'd liked the chill, frosty mornings and feeling of grass crunching under his boots more than the actual kills.

After Vietnam, he'd never hunted again, but he hiked and bird-watched whenever he could, and his first .22 plinking rifle, his old Remington 30.06, and a pistol or two were still locked up in his study at home. He slapped the heavy belt-pack cinched around his slim waist, feeling the hard outline of the weapon *not* locked up at home, a Smith & Wesson Model 696 revolver. A simple tug-and-grab, and he'd have five .44 slugs available for dispersal. Al Chambers had been his instructor at the school and his friend later, and Howard Taylor Pick was damned if he was going to end up like poor Al.

As he swung off the larger trail onto a lesser path going to the next grouping of boxes, Howard heard a soft thud well behind him, like something had landed on the mulch of the main trail from upslope. He looked back over his shoulder, saw nothing. But he felt the itch. Howard's rep in the 'Nam had been that he might not know where or how, but he *damnsure* knew *when*. His platoon had relied on that consistent instinct, and it had never failed them.

He stood in silence for a minute or two, breathing slowly through his nose, letting his senses absorb the world around him. The itch didn't go away. Something was coming. Smiling to himself, he laid down his staff, carefully pulled the velcro over the revolver's compartment apart, reached inside, gripped the plastic stock, and flicked the safety off.

The big striped cat came then, appearing suddenly in the middle of the narrow path, loping easily. Not accelerating, confident Howard was cornered.

He swung the gun out in one motion, crouched, squeezed one off at the animal's chest. The sound incredibly loud without ear protection. Damn near deafened him.

A hit. Right shoulder. The cat bounced to its right, squalling as it stumbled. Turned as Howard fired again, reversed direction, its gait uneven now, but faster, as fast as thought. And was gone, that quick, a third slug furrowing the trail surface as the striped rump disappeared.

The whole business had taken no more than five seconds.

Howard stood, pistol still up, listening, waiting for the ringing in his ears to subside. His gaze darted from side to side, watching for movement in the undergrowth.

181

He nearly shot the two tall, dark young women who stepped cautiously from the main trail into his field of vision.

"You all right, Doctor Pick?" one asked. The other had her cell phone out. Both carried some kind of short, javelin-looking spears. For a moment, he thought he was seeing double. They appeared identical.

"Yes," Howard answered, taking a deep breath and lowering his weapon. Then he realized he'd been addressed by name. "How'd you know who I am?"

The women continued toward him, the one with the phone walking backward, checking. "We're sort of keeping track of Soyze personnel. You haven't varied your routine, like some of the other docs." She grinned. "Somebody besides us noticed."

"I hit it at least once," Howard replied, grunting in mixed surprise and approval. "Watch where you put your feet. The police'll want to go over this with a fine-toothed comb."

The one with the cell snapped it closed. "They're on their way, Doctor, be here in fifteen minutes or less. Why don't we stay put right where we are until then?"

"Sure," Howard agreed. "Mind telling me who you two are?"

"Our names' Coolidge. Doctor Gregorson knows about us. You'll have to ask him."

"Okay." He found his grin matching hers, the giddy feeling of having survived the threat of death the same as thirty years earlier.

"The cops are gonna be happy with you, Doctor. Their first eye-witness."

"It wasn't a cougar," he said.

"We know. It ran in front of us on its way home."

"Blood on its right shoulder," said the other Coolidge.

A heavy-set, jowly man wearing sweat-soaked lederhosen appeared up at the end of the path, peering nervously at them from under a wide-brimmed white hat. Binoculars hung from his thick neck.

"Nothing happening here, citizen," said the Coolidge who'd phoned the police. "Everything under control. You can move along now."

The fat man nodded, obviously relieved, and disappeared quickly.

"Always wanted to say that," the tall woman said, looking pleased with herself, both sisters laughing.

Howard laughed along with them, barely aware of the note of hysteria in his mirth.

* * * * *

"Guess you two will be up for the citizen's medal of achievement," Boothe Deakins remarked to the Coolidges as the three watched the forensics team scour the path and adjacent brush. Twenty-five feet behind them, Wismer and two uniformed officers were interviewing Howard Pick.

"Like we need the attention," Barbara replied, making a face. Lorna murmured agreement.

"Just kidding," the detective said. "Your privacy is assured by those who benefit from your public-spirited actions. And I don't mind telling you that Carly's idea to put you two on Doctor Pick was so smart I'm in awe."

"You were in awe before," Lorna said.

"Of Carly," Barbara added, grinning, looking pointedly at the lieutenant.

Deakins smiled self-consciously. "Different kind of awe. This was *very* sharp."

"Levi'll be pleased, too," said Lorna. "Pick was a hammer, the man for the job. Just keep us out of the media."

"Speaking of which, you can probably safely split now, before the reporters find their way to the crime tape. Just watch your butts on the way back to your rig. Our kitty had to have a driver, and at some level this was a stalk. They may be pissed."

"Well, duh," Barbara said, rolling her eyes.

Her sister glared at her, punched her lightly on the shoulder. "Hey! You be nice to cousin Boothe."

"Or I'll come to the family reunion," Deakins said, laughing as the Coolidges turned to go.

* * * * *

"I'm not quite bouncing in my chair," Karl Elch said to his two subordinates, in his office with the door shut, a few hours later, "but you *have* elevated my mood. And the the Chief's and the Mayor's." He waved at the sketches of the animal which attacked Howard Pick. "These are amazing."

"And this cat was not either of the two in the previous incidents," Wismer replied.

"We caught Miz Milton at a good point, and she ran the DNA tests within three hours of the incident," his partner said.

Their boss continued to study the drawings. "Built a lot like a cougar, but striped *and* spotted." His gaze lifted. "And your scientist still says this is a human being?"

"Definitely,"

Elch sighed as only a man with a very large nose could, a titanic, almost frightening, rush of air. "When I look for science fiction, I don't want horror. When I do the opposite, there still should be separation. This is both, and I don't like it."

Wismer and Deakins looked at one another for a long moment. "Sir," Deakins said at last, "what we have is a scientific explanation of the situation in

184

which we find ourselves. It's not neat and clean, but it's still homicide. Someone like the Unabomber is out there, sending death in multiple forms at targets. We got lucky. Doctor Pick was more than ready, even more than we thought. We have an eyewitness, and additional evidence."

"That sounded like it should be your line, Ron," the Captain said, looking at Wismer and smiling. He laid the drawings on his desk after giving them one more glance. "Check with the local veterinarians?"

"No," Wismer replied.

"So, this is an extinct species, suddenly returned. The environmentalists are going to scream bloody murder when you put one down."

"Maybe they change back when they're dead," Deakins said, semi-wistfully, "like werewolves in movies."

Wismer cleared his throat. "And they're *not* extinct. Whatever you want to call them, they've been around for millennia, living among us."

"I was thinking maybe there's a village full of them in the Balkans," Elch said, his expression speculative, "out doing their dirty work when the old iron curtain went down and freedom reigned."

"Just how much horror do you read, anyway?" Wismer asked.

"Well, whatever they are," Deakins said, before Elch could reply, "this is their second failure. I dunno about them, but I'd be pissed as hell. They're gonna make a move."

"I hope," her boss replied. He cocked an eyebrow at Deakins. "Got any likely candidates?"

Both detectives shook their heads.

FORTY-TWO

Claire had not played softball regularly since dental school, not like she did basketball, but occasionally on Monday evenings one of her old buddies would have her fill in at practice for someone who couldn't make it. Since she felt dentistry was entirely too predictable, and softball not, she was always eager to go. She'd grab her glove and bat and head out the door.

She reminded herself as she unlocked her front door and opened it, that in August she'd be in Paul's place with him, with a different fading sunset limning the world with darkening tones of orange sepia.

She stepped inside, closed and locked the door behind her, then opened the little entry closet where she kept her jackets and sports equipment. She tossed her glove in the closet, but had not quite released the bat when movement registered down the hall to her right.

That small, fortuitous act saved her life.

Claire shifted her grip on the bat, gripped it tightly in both hands. She turned, saw the beast coming slowly toward her, fangs barred, its long tail switching.

"Now you die, cousin," it said in a slurred, rough *certain* voice. "You cannot change quickly enough."

It sprang, claws wide. Claire swung, feet planted and her shoulders solidly behind the blow.

The thick part of the bat caught the animal at the base of the neck, knocking it into the wall. As it fell, spread claws ripped diagonally left and down Claire's neck and across her upper torso, tearing through her T-shirt and bra and knocking her backward. Blood sprayed, fanning over her face, nearly blinding her.

On its right side, the cat lashed out at her legs, raking her left thigh. Barely able to see though the blood, but filled with cold rage, Claire slammed the bat down into its ribs, once, twice, three times. It struggled to regain its feet on the tile floor, thrashing at her, connecting more often than not.

"Having *fun*, are we, *Cousin*!" Claire shouted, knocking a front leg out from under the beast, seeing it beginning to panic now, her mostly able to evade the flailing claws.

But she was bleeding heavily. Sooner or later -- probably sooner -- she would slip on the blood-slickened floor and go down, and he'd be on her with a vengeance, royally pissed. She needed a solid head-shot. A few cracked ribs and bruised forelegs were not going to discourage her assailant completely.

She worked him closer to the corner by the front door, dodging away, smashing him down, smelling the beginning of desperation. She stepped aside enough to give him the glimpse of a way out. His gaze darted toward the kitchen, he slid his back legs against the front door, and took a wild swipe at Claire with his right front paw. Claire leaned away from the blow as he turned to run, then moved in with a long-arced swing that caught him exactly at the base of his skull. Knocked him flat.

But not out, just out of fight. He regained his unsteady feet and scrambled rapidly toward the back of the apartment. Claire half-leaned, half-fell against the wall as she watched him go. She thought about throwing the bat at his retreating striped butt, but settled for just trying to keep her feet. Barely managed that, using the bat for a crutch as she searched the tile for her cell-phone, knocked from her torn front pocket. Blood ran sluggishly down her forearms and dribbled to the floor in clotting strings.

The cell turned up in the less-gory corner. Claire folded the cover back and punched Paul's programmed number with a shaking forefinger, trying to quiet her heaving chest and the weakness in her knees while she waited for him to pick up.

"Hi, you," he said.

"*You* need to get over here. Right now. I'm fairly close to being really hurt."

"*What?*"

Claire took a deep breath, steadying her voice, pushing away the blackness at the edge of her vision. "I'm not kidding. One of my relatives stopped by. Tried to kill me. I'll be okay, but I'm a mess. The entryway is worse. Use your key to get in. Now."

"On my way." The line went dead.

It was hard to smile with a split lip, but Claire tried as she stuck the phone in the unripped pocket of her shorts. Her right eye was swollen nearly closed, she felt a pair of deep gashes on her right cheek, and she didn't want to look down at herself. At least there was no carpet between her and the refrigerator. Clean-up wouldn't be too bad.

And she had won.

She walked slowly to the kitchen, still supporting herself with the bat, pausing whenever her vision began to tunnel down again. Leaning against the counter by the refrigerator, Claire opened the freezer compartment, removed a package of ground chuck, stuck the whole thing in her microwave, and set it for ten minutes on defrost.

Then she went unsteadily over to the opened sliding door leading onto the deck and shut and locked it. She'd been stupid to leave it unlocked after what Riona had said at the hospital. A twenty-foot drop to uneven sloping ground had seemed a stretch as an entry route. It hadn't been for whoever had come for her.

And who had that been? Not Riona. Uncle Emmett had eliminated that possibility. Besides, her attacker had been male. Riona's brothers? Riona would know in a heartbeat, if the subject of the attack on Claire came up in conversation. In any event, why would one of them come after Claire if the attacks on the Mormons had screwed up whatever was going on with Sozye? That was important to the Phelans, the reason they were in town. There had to be money involved, lots of it.

Not her main problem at the moment. Paul would be here within minutes. There would be no avoiding both Claire's condition and her family's secret. Provided he made it past the entryway without throwing up or fainting. Or both. She sighed as she reopened the fridge, brought out a gallon jug of electrolyte mix, and poured a big glass. She'd hoped to put this off until nearer the wedding.

At least she'd quit bleeding. Her legs were cut to ribbons, that first clawed blow had damned near ripped off her face and her left breast, and only the revelation of what she was would leave her unscarred. Sighing again, Claire emptied her glass and poured another. Her hands had stopped shaking, that shocky feeling had disappeared, but the pain, mostly kept at bay by her adrenaline rush, had arrived in spades. She let herself slide down to the floor, biting her lower lip and groaning as movement reopened fresh wounds.

C'mon, lover, Claire thought. *I need to get this over with.*

* * * * *

The entryway had been horrific, blood everywhere -- *Claire's blood* -- but the sight of the damage done to Claire herself nearly took Paul to his knees, gagging. Swallowing bile, unable to look away from the most important person in his world, he forced words out. "Did you call 911?"

She shook her head, eyes narrowed with pain even from that small movement. "I didn't, and you don't."

"Claire! Jesus, you're *hurt*!" He started for the phone on the counter.

"*No!*"

"Are you fucking *nuts*? You need help!"

"No. I'll be okay. Get the meat out of the microwave. Put it on the floor." She began stripping off her shredded T-shirt, wincing with each movement. "You're about to get the straight scoop on those funky canines, lover."

With her shirt and bra off, the deep gouges down her face, neck, and over her chest and stomach were completely revealed. Her left breast was just so much raw flesh, oozing blood. Paul averted his gaze, feeling his stomach rebel again. "Oh, *Claire*," he said, voice trembling.

"I know. Get the meat."

"Okay." He unwrapped the steaming package and dumped the meat on the floor.

Claire slid her legs out of her torn shorts, blood-soaked panties, and shoes. "Oh, boy," she said, and took a long, deep breath. "It's been a while. Here goes."

At first, Paul couldn't see anything happening, then Claire's features began to shift as her face reconfigured. She dropped to all fours. Her back legs shortened. A tail extended out from the rear of her hips. Her shoulders narrowed, chest deepened, and her breasts disappeared. As her face changed, her jaws remodeled, and the huge fangs he'd seen on the panograph protruded from her gum tissue, wet and gleaming. Without intending to, Paul stepped back, his breath caught in his throat.

Fur sprouted, beginning on Claire's head and flowing rearward over the rest of her body. Stripes interspersed with spots appeared as the fur thickened.

Another minute of surface twitches and subtle changes, and a cat raised its head and looked at him. Claws clicked on the kitchen tile.

"Ahhh. The *pain* is gone," she said, her voice strange against her altered palate. She shook herself and seemed to grin at him, unchanged eyes shining in a cat's face. "A collar would be *cheaper* than a wedding gown, lover."

Paul fumbled for a chair, sank onto it, his knees giving out. He couldn't take his eyes off those *fangs*. "Holy shit," he said weakly.

"Give me a minute here," Claire said, and bent down to the meat, bolting it in great mouthfuls, her throat pulsing as she swallowed. She licked the tiles clean, then raised her head, cocking it at him. "Now you know," she said.

Paul nodded, still staring at her. "This is what... *killed*...Duncan and Doctor Chambers?"

"Yeah. Not me. Not Riona. Somebody else. But there's no question. It was one of us. Or more than one."

"This is what Ron and Boothe were asking about the time they came to the office. The tooth thing. Only they couldn't tell me."

Her round head tilted the opposite way. "Tell *me*."

Paul gave her a short explanation, then said, "They must've had fur samples. Someone did a full genetic analysis."

"Someone who recognized the human gene complement." Her rough, pink tongue rasped around one long canine. "So they know they're looking for some kind of big carnivore. Oh, that's *cute*." She looked out through the balcony windows, into the growing darkness of the forest beyond. Her ears pricked up, swiveled. "That damned Boothe! She'd believe in a heartbeat. Then convince Ron."

191

Looking back at Paul, Claire shook her head and turned the underside of her right paw up. She licked it, then ran it over her head and face before licking it again. Just like a cat. He felt his mouth fall open. She laughed, seeing his reaction. "I'd forgotten how good this feels, how *natural* it seems. In the fur."

"That's what you call it? 'In the fur?'"

"Yeah."

"Can you do it from birth?"

"Yeah. My dad and Uncle Emmett both did. So did Mom, but a lot of us -- like me -- wait until puberty. The whole hormone thing seems to make it easier."

"And the kids..?"

"Oh, yeah. Any and all. I'm a double homozygous dominant." That eerie grin reappeared. "Potty box is cheaper than diapers, too." She continued washing, licking her shoulders and front legs, removing the remaining blood.

Paul gestured weakly at her. "When you change back, will you be healed?"

"Completely." Still grinning, she asked, "Is this making you jumpy, lover? Want me to change back now?"

He leaned forward, rested his elbows on his knees, and studied her. "No, I'm just glad you're okay. And you're *beautiful* this way. Kind of like a sturdier cheetah."

She paused in her cleaning, cocked her head again. "Lick you all over?"

His burst of laughter surprised him. "Nice your sense of humor still works," he replied, his guffaw fading to a chuckle.

"Speaking of which, probably should get to work on the floor and the walls. So I'll hafta change back, grow hands, help you scrub everything down. Then I'm gonna call Uncle Emmett." She rose onto all fours,

walked over to him, stuck her nose into his crotch, then raised her inquiring gaze to his. "You sure?"
"Claire!"

FORTY-THREE

There are entirely too many good-looking women involved in this case, Boothe Deakins thought, as she watched Riona Phelan enter the trendy little coffee shop where they'd agreed to meet. She wasn't the only one watching Riona, either. That unselfconscious sleek look drew the eyes of half the people in the place, men and women alike. The lieutenant noted no signs of makeup on Riona's narrow features as the younger woman approached her table with long, graceful strides, but her dark hair gleamed, the thick eyebrows had been artfully plucked, and her slacks and jacket impeccably tailored. She smiled at Deakins.

Deakins stood, smiling back, and saw a certain wariness appear on a face which resembled Emmett McManus more than a little, though the expression could as easily be Claire's. "I guess I'm not hard to spot," she said, letting her smile slide toward rueful, extending her right hand to Riona.

Riona smiled back with very white teeth which fit her face perfectly. They shook hands, two tall, slender, strong women. Not hard, not testing their strength, but sizing each other up.

"You're very distinctive," Riona agreed, her smile softer for the moment, as they sat down. "Your hair is quite lovely."

Compliments about her appearance were not something the policewoman was accustomed to. "Thanks, and I can see the McManuses don't have any bad-looking relatives. Not that we're here to check out either each other or our fashion senses." Deakins nodded to the waitress, who headed swiftly in their direction. "They have great scones here, if you're hungry." Try to be charming, she told herself. This is

Claire's cousin, after all, and from all indications one hardass babe.

"How can I help you?" Riona asked after the waitress had come and gone.

"You visited Emmett McManus in the hospital the evening of the attempted homicide. He was quite reserved with us, and may have been more forthcoming with you. Did he say anything to you that he might not have shared with us, some further thoughts that you might feel could be significant?" Deakins let her smile widen. "Don't violate any confidences, please."

"Neither of us believes I will tell you anything of which you are not already aware, Lieutenant. You suggested this meeting because you wanted to see me for yourself, to judge where on earth I might fit in with these mysterious events. If at all." If her words held a touch of frost, Riona's smile did not. "Don't attempt to be the 'good cop' with me."

"I left the good cop back at headquarters doing paperwork," Deakins replied, grinning. "Mister McManus knows more than he's telling us, even if he calls it speculation."

"You are doubtless correct. But we spent no time alone. When I arrived, his niece Claire was with him. Mostly we spoke of family, since Claire and I had never met. She and I left together, talked all the way to the parking structure. She seemed very nice."

Deakins snorted, unable to stop herself. "Interesting concept, a *nice* Claire."

Riona's smile widened. "I meant by the standards of our family, of course."

"I think I know how that must be," the lieutenant replied, nearly snorting again. She considered Riona for a moment. "You'd never met Claire, so you're from out of town. Here on business?"

"Yes. Phelan Associates researches and locates missing, lost, or stolen items. My brothers and I are negotiating the secondary sale of some recovered documents."

"Can you tell me with whom?"

"We're acting as agents for Doctor Lu at Considerate Care, negotiating with Soyze Dental Associates. And please tell no unnecessary person. I am violating company confidentiality telling you even this much, Lieutenant."

"I appreciate that," Deakins replied, hearing silent alarms going off in her head. This *had* to be the connection in the homicides. "How much longer will you be in the area?"

Riona shrugged, exasperation briefly crossing her features. "The deaths of Soyze dentists have slowed the process considerably. To say that our time here is dependent upon the successful conclusion of your investigation would not be without basis. My grandfather, the head of our company, has stated two more weeks, and then we return to the east. Already my brothers chafe at the delay, hating to work at a distance, spending hours hunched over their laptops and fax machines."

For a cousin of Claire's, the detective thought, Riona was being awfully informative, though the Phelans must work with official authorities frequently. "Let me share something I shouldn't, then," Deakins said. "We believe all the deaths are connected, besides their common workplace. The first two were some kind of large cat, as the papers have reported. Presumably a cougar or cougars, or so we thought initially." She leaned toward the darker woman, lowered her voice. "There was a *third* cat attack a few days ago. Unsuccessful. The newspapers reported it as a large, feral, domestic animal, but it wasn't. We had eyewitnesses."

Riona's gaze narrowed. She ran her right hand through her short hair. "And..."

"And it wasn't a cougar." She watched Riona intently, hoping for a reaction, thought she had her hooked, and saw an infinitesimal widening of pupils. *Maybe something.* Maybe not. On to the next point, keeping her voice dead calm. "The dentist wounded it."

Riona's gasp was inaudible, but Deakins *saw* her chest and throat tighten for a split-second, and felt satisfaction surge through her own body. A definite hit.

"But it escaped?" Riona asked, her voice absolutely steady. Her hand swept reflexively through her hair again.

"Yeah," Deakins replied, "but whoever's running it got stupid. We have fur and blood samples. We can ID it." She shrugged, smiling evilly. "Maybe next time we'll have a specimen to examine."

The arrival of the scones and their coffee prevented any verbal response by Riona, but as soon as she'd taken two sips of coffee, she asked, "How well do you know Claire?"

"I've known her for nearly two years. I met her when my partner and I were teamed up. Lieutenant Wismer and her fiance' are childhood buddies. Claire's a very tough, capable lady." She took a bite of scone, chewed thoughtfully. "*You* remind me of Claire."

Riona let out a burst of laughter that caught the attention of everyone near their table. "I hope that's a compliment." She started on her own pastry.

"Oh, definitely. I just wish Claire's uncle had said something that would help us. Whoever's running the cats are the same people who went after him."

Another tiny reaction. "*Cats*?" Riona asked. "There's more than *one*?"

"We have three individual animals, two male, one female. Spots and stripes, our witnesses stated. Our mammalologist was uncertain as to exact species, but it apparently looked like a hefty cheetah."

"Have you talked to Claire about this?"

197

"No. Why would I do that? How could *she* help us?"

"I can't tell you that now. Call her this evening. I will have spoken with her by then." The last two bites of scone disappeared into Riona's mouth. Her expression as she wiped crumbs off her lips seemed quite satisfied, as though she'd reached some inner decision of true importance. Or maybe something had fallen into place.

"Okay," Deakins replied, trying to make the connection between Emmett McManus, Claire, and this woman whom she was absolutely *certain* knew what the deal was with the cats. It was more than just family.

"In the meantime," Riona said, standing, "I shall speak with my grandfather. Claire will inform you of his decision. I have worked too long and hard on this assignment to have it yanked away."

"Okay." *Things were progressing rapidly,* Deakins thought as she rose to her feet, *but in what direction?*

The two woman shook hands again as they exchanged goodbyes. Riona gave the detective a large conspiratorial wink, and walked gracefully out of the coffee shop, another round of turned heads trailing in her wake.

Interesting, Deakins thought, bringing out her cell phone and dialing her partner. After a brief conversation, she put the phone away and unfolded a small plastic evidence bag from another pocket. Into the bag she carefully placed the half-dozen or so individual hairs that had fallen to the table top and floor when Riona Phelan brushed her hand over her scalp. The *real* reason the detective had asked for this meeting. Rose Milton had agreed to quickly test any additional biological evidence that turned up, and Deakins would call her from the station. By this evening, they would have some answers.

The lieutenant was nearly whistling as she headed back to headquarters.

FORTY-FOUR

"Would either of you like another glass of wine?" Paul asked Riona and Claire. The three of them sat on his balcony, nibbling on nachos and salsa, Paul nervous and the women introspective and quiet, something Claire almost never was.

"Please don't feel you have to be the attentive host, Paul," Riona replied, laughing softly, her dark eyes dancing.

"Hit me," Claire said flatly, pointing at her glass. All three were barefoot in shorts and T-shirts, enjoying the warm July evening air. The concrete surface under Paul's feet still held the day's heat as he went to fetch their second bottle, listening to the conversation behind him.

"Alcohol slows the shift," Riona warned Claire.

"Tough. I need some serious fortitude. I'm going to be naked as a jaybird in front of two cops."

Riona shrugged, unimpressed. "They are your friends."

"That makes it worse."

"Wis'll be embarrassed," Paul said, reappearing with the wine, filling his and Claire's glasses.

"Lieutenant Deakins will not," Riona said matter-of-factly. Her gaze lingered on the wine bottle.

"You sure you don't want some?" Paul asked, holding up the bottle.

Riona waved it off. "Even I admit to some reservation. "We are taught from birth not to give ourselves away."

Paul looked at his watch. "Almost seven. We should probably go in and shut the drapes. They'll be right on time."

They went inside, bringing their glasses, Paul carrying the half-full wine bottle. He closed the drapes, then joined the two women at his dining room table. The doorbell rang just as his butt hit the chair.

"Showtime!" he said, smiling at them, rewarded with identical expressions of reluctant admission.

"We go together, cousin," Riona said, resting her right hand on Claire's left shoulder as Paul headed for the door. He heard Claire grunt in reply.

"Drinks are on the house," he said to Wismer and Deakins as they entered, noting that both officers seemed preoccupied and more serious than usual. Ron managed a micro-smile after saying hello, and Boothe even less. Deakins carried a yellow plastic bag, and through its semi-transluscent surface, Paul thought he saw the word 'evidence.'

"Before we start with your deal, I've got some questions for Claire's cousin," Boothe said. "That all right?"

"Sure, if it's okay with her," Paul replied. "Right this way."

When Claire and Riona stood as the trio entered the dining room, for the first time Paul truly saw their kinship, their movements and expressions so perfectly mirrored one another. Claire might be taller, more muscular, and fair, and Riona dark and panther-slim, but anyone would see them as related. Maybe it was their shared lycanthropy, a jarring thought in itself, if entirely logical. He made a mental note to throw out the baggie with Claire's hair in it.

When the greetings and introductions were done, Boothe set her bag on the table. "We have some evidence from the first homicide -- Duncan -- that the media were never shown or told about." She lifted a pair of running shoes, socks, shorts, sports bra and T-shirt from the bag, then looked pointedly at Riona. "Any of these items look familiar?"

If Paul had blinked, he would have missed Riona's reaction, a split-second of recognition and realization before a knowing smile moved onto her features. "They're all mine," she said. "I left them in

201

Philadelphia, and purchased new here at Nike Town. I believe I understand what has been going on. Plus I also know that DNA tests were run on whatever samples were taken from the murder scenes. You know what Claire and I are."

Ron spoke for the first time. "Claire, how's your nose? Is your cousin telling the truth?"

Riona laughed. "*Very* bright, Lieutenant! Tell him, Claire."

After giving Riona a sharp glance, Claire inhaled, seemed to hold the breath for a moment, then said, "Yes."

Both detectives appeared to visibly relax, though it was hard for Paul to tell with Boothe.

"Guess we won't need that search warrant for your place, after all, Miz Phelan," Ron said, relaxing still further.

"Don't be a fool, Lieutenant," Riona replied. "Claire and I could be in league. Co-criminals."

"We considered the clothes a plant after the second homicide," Boothe said, shaking her head. "It was just too obvious. And we knew they were yours after I recovered a few hairs at the coffee shop this morning."

Riona nodded knowingly. "Ah, I see. Very clever."

"Does this mean we don't have to strip?" Claire asked.

Now Ron looked pained, embarrassed. "Actually, we'd like a few photographs of your other selves to give us more background." Boothe, Paul noticed, did not share her partner's reluctance to see Claire and Riona in the human altogether.

"You can change in the bedroom," Paul said, thinking *that* was a new meaning for the word.

"And quickly," Riona put in. "I need to call my Grandfather soon. He goes to bed after 'Nightline.'" She rose to her feet, extending her right hand to Claire.

"Come, cousin. I shall show you some shortcuts to the fur."

* * * * *

Even as kids, Paul had found Ron unflappable, and he admitted that most people would have been taken aback by the sight of Claire and Riona in their other forms, but his friend seemed royally stunned, a real surprise. Boothe was almost clinically interested, particularly while she took the photographs. Ron merely watched during the process, his gaze troubled and his hands clasped in his lap.

Both darker and more gracile than Claire, Riona looked much more like a modern cheetah, beautiful and elegant. It was easy to picture the pair under a tree on the veldt, sitting out the heat of the day or waiting for prey, passing the time grooming one another. Or perhaps nursing their cubs. *His* cubs, too, in Claire's case, Paul reminded himself. He pushed the thought away. *Don't go there.* Yet.

"It's hard to imagine something that lovely killing for pleasure," Ron said when the two women had padded off to the bedroom. He looked far less troubled with them gone.

"We'll see what Riona has to say when she's talked to her grandfather," Paul replied, looking over at Boothe, who'd shot a full roll of thirty-six, and appeared very pleased with herself as she replaced her camera in its pack.

"Me," she said happily, "I'm tryin' to decide whether to go with the *National Geographic* or the *National Enquirer.* "What do you guys think?"

Ron lifted one weary eyebrow at his partner. "I think I'm not going to be reading any bedtime stories with cats in them to the kids anytime soon." He regarded Paul seriously. "This gonna affect your relationship with Claire?"

"Well, I've seen her nude before."

"And you didn't see Byron Duncan or Al Chambers after one of these things got done with them."

"Wis..." Deakins cautioned. "It wasn't Riona or Claire who did that."

"Yeah, I know. It's just kind of overwhelming. I thought I'd seen about half of everything. People killing babies, kids, their families, themselves, total strangers even. Frigging gang shit. Drive-bys. Snipers. This ratchets it up one more notch for me. And it's *weird*!"

Boothe looked at her partner with sympathy. "Well, *I'm* weird, too, and you put up with me. This is part of the job, just a new flavor. We find 'em, we take 'em down."

"Riona is your ticket," Paul said. "Her grandfather started the company, most of their people out in the field are like her and Claire. Believe me, he's the key. And he's *not* the problem."

"No, he's the solution," Riona said, as she and Claire re-entered the room, dressed again, "and he'll be here the end of the week." She sat down heavily. "Phelan Associates employs fifteen of our kind, all Phelan relatives. Three of them are presently on vacation. My brothers have been rather distant since their month-long trip to Ireland last year. Grandfather fears an insurrection is brewing. 'A palace coup,' he calls it. He is uncertain as to the number of individuals involved, how many are ours and how many are from the Old Country. He is *quite* certain that they have been honing their skills on Soyze dentists."

"But *bombs*?" Ron asked.

"Easy enough to find bomb experts in Ireland," Paul replied.

"They aspire to well-rounded evil," Riona said.

"And they set you up to take the fall," Claire added, and Boothe nodded grimly.

Riona sighed, stood. "I have what they want in my purse, the key, quite literally." She went over to the kitchen counter, reached in her purse and returned with a small object in a baggie. "The reason for our being here, the thing that we sold to Benny Lu, who allows us to broker it to Hyrum Gregorson, are the first one hundred sixteen pages of the Book of Mormon. This safe deposit box contains that treasure." She handed it to Boothe Deakins. "The Bank of America on Southeast Belmont."

"Why are you giving it to us?" Boothe asked.

"Because it will be safe with you, and the police can recover it if needs be. You see, Grandfather feels their next move will be to come for me."

Boothe's eyes widened momentarily. "Your *brothers*?"

Riona nodded, and her smile would have frozen the Devil's heart. "Yes. My *dead* brothers."

FORTY-FIVE

April Kwong didn't see the blow that bounced her off the entry wall of Riona's rented condo. At first, she didn't even realize someone had struck her. She lay gasping on her back on the carpeted floor, still clutching an insulated bag of Chinese take-out, and blinked up at the four men towering over her. She shook her head to clear it, and repressed a shudder, seeing Phelan bloodlines in all four faces.

One squatted down beside her, his dark features coldly pleased. He gripped April's chin in strong fingers. "Hello, little rice eater. My name is Lorcan Cole. We were awaiting my friend Senan's sister, but I believe that you will serve to wile away the time until she arrives." He pulled April easily to her unsteady feet, still gripping her face, then removed the bag of take-out from her unresisting hand and gave it to one of the others.

"Patrick," he said softly. "Here's something for you to play with. You've been complaining about the recent dearth of meaningful exercise." To her right, April heard something like a hopeful growl, deep and menacing.

Her wits mostly returned, she kicked Lorcan Cole in the left shin as hard as she could.

With an angry roar, he lifted her overhead by her neck and shook her violently. "Little slut!" he shouted, "you will *not* resist us!" He pivoted and threw April against the wall. Her world went grey, and she slid bonelessly back to the carpet, tasting blood in her mouth. Swallowing, nearly choking, she managed to lift her head enough to see the source of the growl, and immediately wished she hadn't.

Blue eyes set in broad, furred, striped features stared into hers, massive shoulders beyond. The light of anticipation showed clearly in the depths of that gaze, and his pink tongue caressed one long fang. Terrified, April cried out and tried to get to her hands and knees and crawl backward away from the advancing beast, but Cole stepped on her lower back, pinning her to the floor.

"Be very afraid, Miz Kwong," he said to the struggling woman. "Patrick is known for his enthusiasm for sport." He chuckled. "From your lower vantage point, I'm sure you see what sort of sport I mean."

April did. From between the creature's rear legs hung a long, glistening penis that had to be close to nine inches in length. As she watched in growing horror, a single purlescent drop appeared at its tip.

Whimpering in terror, April gathered her breath to scream. Cole kicked her in the back of her head. Her right cheek hit the carpet, and the world went grey again.

"Shame on you, Miz Kwong," her captor scolded. April heard him as if from a distance, her senses barely functioning. "There can be no noise." He snapped his fingers. "Gag her and carry her upstairs. Let Patrick play with her until Miz Phelan arrives. He does so enjoy a new toy, Miz Kwong. You can be something akin to a catnip mouse."

April tried to scream as they stripped and gagged her, but they were too quick, and she could only grunt and thrash helplessly while they dragged her up the stairs, her butt and legs thudding on each tread.

Patrick followed closely, his rough tongue rasping her lower legs and feet.

"You seem to have truly caught his fancy, Miz Kwong," Cole said, chuckling again from behind the big cat. "You can warm him up for the next course. He won't rape you, however, That heady pleasure shall be reserved for your foolish lover, Miz Phelan, who stands in our way."

His low laughter turned more sinister. "For a bit longer only, however."

FORTY-SIX

After seeing April's Honda out front, the smell of noodles, pork and chicken laced with Asian spices came as no surprise to Riona. The underlying odor of one of her brothers and three -- no *four*, one was in the fur -- strangers put her on high alert. She needed to avoid death until tomorrow, when her grandfather would arrive from the east. *One old man*, she thought, *riding to our rescue*, and found that both amusing and comforting.

Still, her hands were steady as she hung her raincoat in the hall closet -- there had been showers today -- took a deep breath, and walked into her living room. Senan and three others awaited her, all wearing dark warmups. One, of lesser height for her kind, stood and smiled in welcome.

"My name is Lorcan Cole..," he began, but Riona cut him off.

"Where is April Kwong?"

"Upstairs," Cole replied, recovering quickly. His smile shifted to suggestive. "She has been quite busy, but from the absence of thumps recently, may be taking a breather."

"Pray she is not truly harmed, Mister Cole," Riona said, cocking her head at him, giving him a cool smile. "'Lorcan,' 'Little Fierce One.' You *do* appear to be the runt of the litter."

Cole's features blanched with anger.

"No matter," Riona continued, dismissing Cole and turning to her brother. "Where is Sitric?" He looked away, unable to meet her gaze. "Ah," she said acidly, draping her blazer over the back of a dining room chair. "*One* of you maintained a spine. Grandfather will be less disappointed."

"Where is the *key*?" Cole asked, telling her why she was still standing, and still somewhat in control of the situation.

"He'll be here tomorrow. My Grandfather, that is."

"Where is the key?" He stepped two paces toward her.

Riona arched a brow at him. "You seem fixated, little cousin, an unhealthy thing. The police have it. I gave it to them for safe-keeping, in anticipation of this meeting."

Cole goggled at her, momentarily speechless, completely taken aback. The other three shifted uneasily in their seats. Senan still wouldn't look at his sister.

"Which of you attacked Claire McManus?" Riona asked, changing the subject again. "I understand she beat the holy shite out of whoever it was." She crossed her arms over her chest, addressing them all. "It's beginning to come apart for you, isn't it? You failed with Claire and her uncle, then Doctor Pick proved more than ready for your efforts. A *wonderful* man. Now I have removed the safety deposit box key from the playing board."

"You're *lying* about the key," Cole said.

Riona reached into her purse, brought out Deakins' card and held it up. "You can call this officer, verify the truth of my statement." She faced her opponent from six feet away, and flipped the card to him. "The police know all about us, Mister Cole. They knew *before* Claire and I showed them. They did genetic testing, you see, discovered our dual nature. And they *believed*." She kicked off her shoes.

"Take her!" Cole shrieked, throwing Deakins' card to the carpet. The two unnamed ones sprang to their feet. Senan remained seated.

"Revenge is all you have left," Riona finished, as they grasped her arms.

Cole stuck his face close to hers. "Upstairs, our friend Patrick has been knocking your pet rice monkey about. Shall we go see what's left? Perhaps he has rested enough to do the same for you, adding something of a more intimate -- and penetrating -- nature."

Riona shrugged, regarding him levelly. "Perhaps. Then what will he do, should he survive me? Go back to boning you in the arse?"

Cole hit her hard, across the face.

Riona shook her head to clear her vision, then gave him a fierce bloody-lipped smile. "Best kill me now, Mister Cole, or I will be your death, I promise you."

Breathing deeply, visibly restraining himself, Cole said only, "Take her to Patrick."

When she first saw April, curled into a bruised and bloody foetal ball in a corner by the bed, Riona thought her friend was dead. April's eyes, half-open and apparently unseeing, remained as unresponsive as the rest of her when Riona called her name. "Just resting," Cole assured her cheerfully as Riona removed her garments and they tied her securely to the bed. She hadn't replied, hadn't fought back. Let him think he was in charge again.

Now, later, with the enormous Patrick back in human form and downstairs with the others, Riona could hear April's shallow breathing, even though she couldn't see the beaten woman. Riona felt grief and guilt. If not for Riona, April would have been spared the horror of Patrick. If not for April, Riona would have suffered more, though her hips ached and her raw crotch burned from multiple violations. Testing her bounds, she promised herself that Patrick would be the first among them to die.

Large as he was, she admitted that might take some doing, and first she had to get free. The cunning elastic restraints would adapt if she changed while

211

spread-eagled on the bed, keeping her locked in a position less comfortable that her current one, and still not free.

As she tried to think her way out, Riona heard Cole, Senan, and the other two prepare to leave the condo. Cole's final words to Patrick left no doubt that the big man would stay to guard them, though he remained downstairs after the front door shut and Riona heard a car start up outside.

She listened carefully, scarcely breathing. A toilet flushed below, and the faint tinkling of bottles floated up the stairs. Patrick must be thirsty. This would be her best chance. "April?" she said softly, tilting her head toward the unseen woman. There was no verbal response, but Riona thought she heard a soft stirring. "April?" she repeated.

The slightest querulous murmur came from the floor.

"April?" Riona said again, keeping her voice low.

"Ri..on..a."

"April, can you get to the bed?"

Silence, then,"Bed?"

"Patrick's gone, April. *I'm* on the bed."

Movement. A few seconds passed, then a hand appeared on the edge of the sheets. Another hand, and April's dazed, bloody features slowly raised into view.

"Oh, April!"

A parody of a smile appeared on April's face. Her right hand, crusted with blood, reached out and stroked Riona's right cheek.

"I need to get free. There're scissors in the bathroom, April. Can you get them?"

A struggle for comprehension warred on April's battered face. She looked toward the bathroom door, gave a bare nod.

"Be *very* quiet April. Patrick's in the kitchen."

Another nod, and April disappeared. Even straining, Riona scarcely heard her progress into the bathroom. Minutes passed. Riona thought she heard a drawer open and close, and the occasional sounds from the kitchen below told her Patrick still occupied himself with his drinking. She willed him not to hear, picturing a large, blond Irishman seated in her kitchen, with a beer in his hand and smug, satisfied smile on his face.

The *other* image, the one of Riona in the fur meeting Patrick on the stairs, that one could wait another few minutes. She readied herself for the change, pushing away the pain in the lower part of her body, negating her rape.

April's sweat-sheened face reappeared over the edge of the bed, her breath coming rapidly. Her left hand clutched the orange-handled scissors.

"Good, April, good," Riona said, wiggling her right wrist. "Now, can you cut it?"

Her lower lip clenched between her front teeth, April took the scissors in both hands and began to gnaw through the elastic. The material was tough, April's sweaty hands shook with the effort, but the elastic slowly parted, then let go with a loud snap.

Less than five seconds after the sharp sound, Riona heard a chair scrape back from the kitchen table, followed by barefoot steps on the floor. She grabbed the scissors from April, and swiftly sliced through the remaining restraints.

"Get down on the floor, April, under the bed if you can." Riona hurriedly broke the scissors in half, tossed the halves to April. "If he gets by me, use these."

She rose to her feet on the bed, changing, feeling her fangs move into place, her claws extend. Her grandfather had taught her speed. She needed every bit of that now.

213

Patrick had sprinted halfway up the stairs when Riona launched onto his broad chest, took him over backward, and tore out his throat.

In this case, she reflected, as she finished, revenge was not a dish best served *cold*. But it *was* sweet.

FORTY-SEVEN

"Jesus F. Christ," Wismer said, looking down at the body of the huge, blond man lying at the base of the stairs. The corpse of the late Patrick Mulvey, wearing only bloody boxer shorts, lay face-up, shoulders on the floor, bent legs extended up the stairs. The front of his neck was ruined.

"I restrained myself," Riona Phelan said, her delivery as parched as her smile. "For your sakes," she added, tugging her white bathrobe tighter around her lean body.

Deakins held up an evidence baggie with a blood-smeared half-scissors inside. "Here's the defensive weapon."

Her partner looked around, then let his voice drop. "Did you..?" he asked Riona.

She nodded. "Yes. He practically killed April. She will not recover soon. He *raped* me repeatedly. Besides, this was easier, and infinitely more satisfying. He saw his death coming in a certain, familiar way."

"I didn't think your...people...would be this large," Wismer said, his gaze returning to the deceased Patrick.

"Nor I," Riona agreed. "Had he been in the fur, this would have been a battle I might not have won. He was appallingly strong. Interestingly, their leader, one Lorcan Cole, is at the other end of our spectrum. Small and pugnacious."

"Lorcan Cole," Deakins said. "Probably should check with the feds, see if he has any paperwork beyond an Irish passport. Not that it matters much, not like he's taking flying lessons." She looked at Riona. "Any idea how many of them there are?"

"More than ten, fewer than twenty. My brother Sitric apparently disagreed with their methods and paid the final price, but no mention was made of other objections."

"They *killed* your brother?" Wismer asked incredulously.

"Yes, and Senan would not look me in the eye, so his shame may render him less effective." She regarded the two detectives levelly. "Understand that *both* my brothers have to die. Traitors are not tolerated in our society. Senan will perish under the claws and fangs of either Grandfather or myself. But, should I survive the next few days, I will still grieve for my brothers at the end."

"I'm sorry," Deakins said.

Riona shook her head. "Do not be. Save your pity for poor April, who was a true innocent in this. And spare no pity for Lorcan Cole and his minions." She savagely prodded the corpse lying between them with one foot, smiling her liquid oxygen smile. "Particularly this brutal offal."

"Captain just pulled up outside," one of the evidence people called down the hallway, altogether too cheerfully.

"Oh, boy," Wismer said. "Here we go."

"I will be glad to handle the explanations," Riona offered, and Deakins snorted.

Wismer regarded her seriously. "That might work. What d'ya you think, Deak?"

His partner considered for a moment, then grinned. "Sure. Catgirl wins the toss." Riona gave her a wry smile and a spare bow.

They waited in silence as Elch made his way into the front hallway of the condo. He paused briefly with a pair of technicians before arriving at the base of the stairs. "Miz Phelan, I presume?" he asked, after greeting the lieutenants.

Riona nodded as they shook hands. "Yes. A pleasure."

216

Looking even more Lincolnesque than usual, Elch squatted beside the over-sized corpse. He glanced up at Riona after a cursory examination of the late Patrick. "This one of 'em?"

"Yes."

"Are you..?"

Her bright smile lit up her dark features. "Yes." She laughed. "I believe you have seen one of my old running outfits."

Elch smiled back at her as he straightened up to his feet. "You're taking this well, young lady, considering what you must've been through."

Riona's smile vanished abruptly. "I have taken the first step on a trail of revenge, Mister Elch. That is all. One of my brothers is dead, another has shamed our family, my friend has been cruelly beaten for sport, and some fine people are dead because a group of young fools craved power."

The Captain's gaze shifted to Deakins. "Miz Phelan seems to have a familiar attitude. You two bonded yet?"

For once, Wismer saw his partner look uneasy. "Riona was *raped*, Sir," she said quietly.

Elch went completely still. His large, hazel eyes misted for a moment. He blinked twice, frowned. "I apologize, Miz Phelan. I didn't mean to appear flip."

"No offence, Mister Elch. I understand police flatliner humor, along with the necessity in your position to be politically correct." Riona lowered her voice and regarded the tall man very intently. "Let me place this in perspective for you, however. I killed this man. I enjoyed every second of it, and I wish I could bring him back to life so I could do it again. Does that clarify the issue?"

A slow, rather uncomfortable smile formed on Elch's long, craggy features. "I believe it does, Miz Phelan. I believe it does."

217

Riona nodded sharply. "Good. Then you will understand when I tell you that there is a reason why there is blood on his shorts."

Without looking down at the sprawled corpse, the Captain merely asked, "Something the medical examiner might notice?"

"One can hope," Riona replied, with a malicious grin.

"I suppose I can skip the standard offer of grief and trauma counseling, then," Elch said, sighing. He turned to Wismer and Deakins. "Have you requested Miz Phelan's aid in the homicide investigations?"

"Wouldn't that be outside our policy guidelines?" Deakins asked. A subdued note of quick and eager hope surfaced in her voice, however, Wismer noted, and he knew it had to do with Boothe and Riona being on the same page in the big book of life and death.

"My Grandfather will be here tomorrow evening," Riona said. "He's the head of our company. Perhaps we should seek his advice on how to deal with our problem."

The Captain studied the corpse on the floor again. "Miz Phelan, you seem to have figured out at least part of the answer on your own."

Riona permitted herself a tiny smile. Seeing it, Wismer shuddered internally. The ride was about to begin.

* * * * *

Benny Lu paused at the edge of the well-lit Providence Hospital parking lot, and took several deep breaths, trying to use the familiar normalcy of the rows of cars to compose himself after visiting April Kwong. The absolute horror of what had been done to her still nearly overwhelmed him. In her hospital room, watching the heavily-sedated and unconscious April

218

lying in her bed, Lu couldn't speak, and had barely kept from sobbing aloud in anguish.

He made his way slowly across the lot toward his Mercedes, automatically thumbing the door-lock remote as he approached the car. The normally-irritating beep was strangely consoling now.

As he reached down to open the door, Lu heard the whir of a descending car window behind him.

"Riona Phelan's boyfriend did this thing," came the British-accented voice. "Then she killed him to keep him silent."

Lu forced himself to turn around. He wanted to get into his car and drive away, away from the senselessness of April's violation, away from any conversation with another human being. But instead he faced the compact, swarthy man seated in a rental KIA and asked, "What did you say?"

"She's also stolen the safe deposit key. She means to have both your money and the manuscript for herself."

The Considerate Care owner felt his heart speed up, his shoulders bunch with growing anger. "Who are you?"

"My name is Lorcan Cole."

FORTY-EIGHT

"This has not been a good evening," Wismer said, as he and Boothe stood looking up at the slightly-swaying body of Senan Phelan hanging from a bulky stringer near the vaulted ceiling of the Phelan brothers' rental. "He could have helped us."

"Maybe *he* had help," Deakins suggested, watching the slowly-turning corpse as she tapped the speed-dial on her cell-phone, calling the answering service for the Coroner's office. "The meatwagoneers are gonna love us tonight. Too bad we didn't get the search warrant a coupla hours quicker. We would have been here sooner."

Wismer sighed, massaging the back of his neck with his right hand. "Yeah, but he could have been hanging here from shortly after he left Riona's with the others." He glanced around the apartment. "But according to Riona, both her brothers used laptops. So if his is here, then we may have a suicide. If it's not here, and it's not in his rental car, then we have another homicide."

After speaking briefly with the answering service, his partner tucked away her cell and contemplated the slack body. "Elementary, my dear Wismer," she said. "Probably we should look around before the crowds arrive, then. Just in case."

Less than three minutes later, the detectives discovered a Compac laptop on a small desk in what had likely been intended by the place's builder as the third bedroom. Deakins eyed it speculatively. "This may give us some good info, Ronald."

"We should have Riona get into it. She'd be more familiar with their company's stuff, be able to ferret out what doesn't belong."

"Good thinking." She bent over and examined the surface of the device. "Maybe it's not his, though. Don't see any claw marks. No chewed places, either."

Wismer tried not to laugh, failed. "Don't start, okay?"

* * * * *

At close to Midnight, a full day ahead of him tomorrow and unable to sleep, Benny Lu sat in his study and contemplated Lorcan Cole's explanation of events leading up to what happened to April Kwong. He could find nothing false with any of what he'd been told. He regarded his half-filled glass of Port and tried to think more clearly.

He mustn't let his grief and compassion for April overwhelm his rational mind. Cole had been clearly agitated during their conversation, had intimated he feared for his own life, and his explanation held together on its surface, yet Lu felt reluctant to trust the man. Still, he had little choice, if anything was to be salvaged from the situation.

He took a swallow of Port, happy for the partial insulation of alcohol. If only he had a contact somewhere in the police bureau, could discover if Riona Phelan was in custody, or had fled into the night with both his money and the Mormon document. He shook his head, took another drink. The Phelans had seemed so reliable, so stolid. Had he been a fool to trust them? It certainly hadn't seemed so at the time, and the company had checked out at every level he could find to check. He'd call Philadelphia in the morning, see if he could discover if they'd heard anything from Riona. He was tempted to dial her cell phone, but if she answered, what would he say? No, Lorcan Cole was probably telling the truth, or most of it. Perhaps when April awakened from her protective coma, she could shed some light on the situation. He hoped so. Though not knowing was nowhere near as awful as what had happened to her, he hated uncertainty. Sighing, sick at heart, he turned off his desk lamp, locked the door to his study, and trudged slowly upstairs to bed.

* * * * *

Several miles to the west, just on the other side of the Willamette River, Riona Phelan looked around Boothe Deakins' spare bedroom and nodded approval. A Murphy bed had been tilted down to the floor after Boothe cleared a space for it and brought out fresh sheets. "This is very kind of you, Lieutenant."

Deakins snorted. "It only makes sense. You're not only the closest thing to a witness we have, you may be able to find something in that laptop that'll leverage the case. So you're doubly important, particularly until we can interview April Kwong."

"Is she going to be safe?" Riona asked.

"Oh, yeah," Deakins replied, chuckling. "Don't believe everything you see in the movies. We've got two officers with her, and the only visitor they've let in so far was her employer, Doctor Lu. Not that anyone else has tried. The only other civilian who'll be allowed to see her, besides hospital staff, is you."

"So I sit here tomorrow, in between seeing April, and manipulate Senan's computer until we go to meet my grandfather? Is that correct?"

"Yeah, pretty much. I'll check in every so often, see if you've found anything important -- like names -- then pick you up to meet the plane. He's due in at eight in the evening?"

"Yes."

"Ron is at the bank now, with two carloads of back-up, picking up the papers, so we're close to nailing down what we can. For now."

"Who will go with us to PDX?"

222

"Besides the dozen or so unobtrusive plainclothes security who'll be in place before we arrive? You, me, Ron, Claire McManus, and her uncle. A couple of unmarks escorting us to and from PDX, but they won't go in with us."

Riona smiled in what Boothe hoped was appreciation. "Cole knows Grandfather is coming. He may make a move."

"Everyone, including PDX Security, will have Cole's description. He shows, we'll do our best to nail him. Problem is, he's the only one we *have* a description on. Claire, her uncle, and you are our olfactory back-up. You smell anyone funny, we take 'em down."

"Good thinking. You're quite bright, Lieutenant."

Deakins shrugged. "Don't give me all the credit. The Captain's no fool. Neither is Ron."

"But I'm *your* responsibility. *You're* protecting me."

"Hey, I run the babe shelter."

Riona curled a lip in a half-smile. "What a *wonderful* expression."

"*And* I cook breakfast."

"One can only hope."

FORTY-NINE

Even though she knew that things could get really sticky in the next couple hours, Claire found herself awaiting Magnus Phelan's arrival at PDX with rising excitement. Uncle Emmett stood quietly, gaze forward and hands folded in front of him. Boothe and Ron looked everywhere except the concourse arrival corridor on the other side of Security. Only Claire's sensitive nose told her Riona's anticipatory mood matched hers.

Riona had spent much of the previous night and a large portion of today trekking through her dead brother's laptop, searching for names and information. She had established a pattern of activity going back nearly a year, and, more importantly, there were names Riona didn't recognize, except for Lorcan Cole and the late Patrick Mulvey. The police were running checks on them all, even going so far as to make inquiries of Interpol and the Irish Gardai. If all the names were Cole's allies, there were fifteen or sixteen remaining, including Cole himself.

Suddenly Riona laughed. "I see him."

There was quite a crowd coming off the plane. Apparently the stop at Denver had nearly filled it. Claire stood on her tiptoes and craned her neck for a better view. "Older gentleman, white at the temples?"

"Slim and elegant, with a touch of Cary Grant," Riona added, still laughing. "Or so *he* says."

"He has a woman with him?"

"Oh, yes. Someone on the plane, I suppose. He calls it his 'hopeless attraction for the opposite sex.' Women gravitate to him. He seems unable to do anything about it. Grandmother just shrugs."

Animal Magnetism, Claire thought wryly. Magnus Phelan looked at least twenty years younger than his purported age. Wearing a beautifully-tailored dark suit, not a black or white hair out of place, he might well have stepped from the pages of some mens' fashion spread in *GQ* or *Esquire*. "He looks like you," Claire told Riona, as the couple approached.

"And my grandmother," Emmett McManus put in. "But they *were* brother and sister." As he spoke, Boothe and Ron stepped unobtrusively away, keeping out of the happy family setting.

Riona's grandfather stopped some distance away, talking with the attractive fortyish woman who'd accompanied him off the plane. They exchanged cards and shook hands briefly, smiling their farewells, very proper business people. Then, as the woman walked off, Magnus Phelan came and stood in front of them, his eyes only for Riona.

"I am so sorry about your brothers, my dear," he said softly in a mellow lilting baritone, setting his briefcase on the concourse floor next to his wheeled carry-on. He took Riona in his arms, and, watching them hold one another, Claire felt a lump form in her throat.

"Now I see why my grandmother always spoke well of her younger brother," Uncle Emmett observed to Claire.

Before Claire could answer, the Phelans released each other, and Magnus grabbed her uncle's hand. "Emmett, my boy! At last! Such a pleasure. I remember talking to you one Christmas. You'd just gotten a new train set."

"I still have it," her uncle replied, with a reserved smile.

Magnus clapped him on the shoulder. "A true Phelan! *Never* let anything go."

Next the old man -- though no one would think him that -- turned to Claire, his hand out. His nearly black eyes -- so much like Riona's -- became even more sincere. "Hello, Claire. Riona has spoken most highly of you." His brogue and smile seemed to deepen with each word.

"Thank you, sir," Claire said, smiling back as they shook hands. "A pleasure."

The dark gaze hardened. "We will kill them all, you know. Every blessed one. If I can, I will finish Cole -- a traitor to our blood -- myself." He carefully looked Claire up and down. "Riona mentioned you were attacked in your home. No residual effects?"

"No, sir," Claire replied, shaking her head and letting her proper smile turn into a grin. "I had a baseball bat."

Grasping both her hands in his, Magnus Phelan laughed warmly, a rich sound which seemed as though, if necessary, it could change everything and make the world right. "Good girl!" he exclaimed.

Beside Claire, Riona bit back a giggle. Claire was certain she heard a note of relief in the giggle, and understood completely. She felt a touch of the same elation.

"It would be good if a few of them remained mobile enough to be witnesses to what's gone on," Boothe put in, as she and Ron rejoined the quartet and introduced themselves.

"Depending upon circumstances," the old man assured them. His voice changed, became almost a growl, and his eyes flashed. "Cole, however, is mine, unless Riona finds him first."

Riona inclined her head. "He is yours, Grandfather."

"We really need to get going, folks," Ron said. "The key to keeping this arrangement clean is to keep it moving. Standing still is not the hot ticket when someone is looking to take you down."

"Right you are, Lieutenant," Magnus Phelan said, recovering his carry-on and briefcase. He gave them a totally urbane and innocuous smile, took Riona's arm and gestured toward the front of the terminal, then winked at Claire over his granddaughter's shoulder. *What a charmer!* she thought. Hard to imagine him ripping out someone's throat.

But she knew that was simply a matter of time and circumstance.

* * * * *

After leaving Airport Way, the main route to the PDX Terminal, both Ron and Boothe grew more focused and silent. Ron drove, Claire sat on his right. The others occupied the middle and rear seats. The mini-van provided by the tactical arm of the Police Bureau was heavily-armored, at least against conventional small arms. Both detectives felt that any strike from Cole's forces would almost certainly come on I-84 West going into downtown Portland.

"How much do we know about these people?" Magnus Phelan asked.

"Cole and three others are suspected to be chummy with members of the Real IRA," Boothe replied from behind him, never taking her gaze off the freeway. "The remainder are either ex-provos or 'known associates' of unredeemed Sinn Fein bad guys." As she spoke, she took a headset out of a small nylon pack, plugged a connecting cord into an outlet in front of her, then hooked another line to an overhead socket. "Low-level bombers and such?" Uncle Emmett asked.

Boothe nodded as she fiddled with the headset controls. "Exactly. They muled the stuff and made the bombs, which were then apparently passed on to the actual bombers. The Gardai couldn't rule out the occasional foray into placement, however, for at least two of them."

Ron swung the van west onto I-84, keeping in the right lane, and Claire noticed his grim expression deepen.

228

"Where're our escorts?" she asked him, feeling her pulse rate rise with the possibility of danger.

"Maroon Caprice seven cars in back of us, just behind the UPS truck. Blue Saturn in the curve up ahead."

In the rear, Boothe spoke into her headset, presumably to the Caprice and the Saturn. Listening to her, Claire watched the Saturn, a hundred yards in front of them. Overhead, two bright red ultralight aircraft appeared, visible through the upper half of the windshield, cheery droning mechanical dragonflies forging steadily ahead of the slower freeway traffic.

Suddenly, Boothe's voice became more urgent. "Same rig? You're sure? Good job, Carly! You know what to do." Then she addressed them all. "Listen up, people. They're back a ways, but coming up fast in the center lane. Orange Volkswagen van, same one that finished Doctor Lockwood."

Claire turned in time to see the body of the UPS truck explode in a fireball. Time seemed to slow as the wild-eyed driver stood on the brakes and fought to keep the heavy vehicle in its lane. Smoke filled the freeway, cars skidding through the dark clouds. Flaming parcels fell from the ruptured truck, tumbling diagonally across the pavement.

Not taking his eyes off the light traffic in front of them, speeding up slightly, Ron asked, "RPG?"

"Oh, yeah," Boothe replied, then spoke to the rest of them. "We do *not* have any protection against this ordnance, folks. Even an indirect hit will open us up like a can of beans struck by an M-16 round. Which may not happen. They'll want Riona and Mister Phelan alive, try to make us give 'em up." She reached down in front of her, began fiddling with something, and Claire heard several zippers. "Open the top, Ronald."

Well behind them now, the UPS truck had slewed to a stop, canted against the freeway wall.

229

Claire could see the driver, still inside the vehicle, spraying foam into the rear compartment. Then smoke billowed over the rig, obscuring her view. An instant later, an orange Volkswagen van, its right side door open, shot out from the cloud, a quarter-mile or more to their rear.

Boothe stood, crouched, cradling a charcoal grey assault rifle in her freckled hands. "Hold it steady, Ronald. I need a stable platform." She straightened up, her head and shoulders out of the sunroof opening.

"Lean forward, folks," Ron cautioned, "just in case." He didn't smile, all business. Claire wondered if he was thinking about Margie and the kids.

The trio in the middle seat obeyed, but Claire couldn't stop watching the chaos behind them, though she did hunker down a bit and hold onto the back of her seat. The few cars which had managed to avoid each other and the UPS debris flew past them and the advancing Volkswagen in the other lanes, bent on escaping. "What's an RPG?" Claire asked Ron.

"Rocket Propelled Grenade. RPG-7. Russian manufacture. Everybody's got 'em. The Somalis used 'em in Mogadishu. Penetrate up to six hundred millimeters of steel."

Dentistry being a metric profession, Claire did the math. "That's nearly two feet!"

Bent over the wheel, Ron nodded grimly. "Go through this expensive cheeseball like nothin'."

"Steady!" Boothe yelled from above, and fired.
A body rolled out the open door of the Volkswagen, flopping across the pavement. Claire saw movement within the orange van, the end of some kind of tube quickly pulled back inside.

"Shit," Boothe said. "One of the other guys grabbed the launcher." She fired twice more, starring the VW's windshield. "Armored," she said in disgust, as the Volkswagen dropped back slightly and moved into their lane.

230

At that point, they were fast approaching the 58th Avenue entrance, on their right. Ron was on his radio to their escorts and the dispatcher, listening carefully and muttering mild curses. "Our rear escort is stuck. S.W.A.T. ground teams can't get to us, not that they could do much. Freeway's clogged, except in front of us. Effective range on the launcher on a moving target is three hundred meters, unless they get lucky. The Saturn is dropping back to us."

Someone appeared in the VW's sunroof opening and began firing. Rounds spanged off the police van. To Claire's surprise, Boothe didn't duck down much, but calmly returned fire. On her second or third shot, their assailant threw up his arms and fell back into the vehicle. "Three to go," she announced cheerfully. Then, to Ron: "Hold 'er right at fifty."

"Can we sit up now?" Magnus Phelan asked. "Huddled down would seem to offer no true protection."

"Sure," Ron replied. "Sorry."

"Would you trust me with your automatic, Lieutenant?" Uncle Emmett asked. "While you drive?"

"Good idea." Reaching under the lapels of his jacket, Ron passed his weapon back to Claire's uncle, who held it in his lap after a brief inspection. He seemed happier, as opposed to Riona and her grandfather's obvious frustration, predators denied the prey they craved.

A large refrigerated tractor-trailer rig appeared ahead in their lane, 'Spokane Poultry' lettered prominently on its rear. Simultaneously, the Volkswagen's side door slid closed and it sped left across two lanes. The door opened again for several seconds, and the RPG launcher poked out. With a flash and a cloud of blue-grey smoke, the little rocket blew open the rear doors of the poultry trailer.

231

Frozen turkeys spilled from torn shipping boxes and out the ruptured doors, toppling onto the freeway and skating over its surface like huge, misshapen, beige hockey pucks. Within seconds, the freeway was awash in pinballing poultry. Claire couldn't believe her eyes. A waterfall of hard-frozen birds continued to tumble from the trailer, some rebounding three or four feet into the air like enormous superballs.

"Oh, Christ!" Ron said in disgust, slowing and lightly braking the mini-van as he tried to avoid cramming twenty-pound frozen carcasses underneath its chassis. From above, Boothe put a few more rounds into the Volkswagen. A turkey bounced off their windshield, flew over the concrete retaining wall and disappeared. Ron rammed a pair of birds, sending them skittering away.

The freeway in front of them now resembled a giant pool table, turkeys crisscrossing the space between the bordering walls in ever-increasing numbers. The Volkswagen held steady a hundred yards behind them, its higher ground clearance letting it pass over the sliding birds with minimum veering. Above, the ultralights had turned around, were now lower and coming back, a half-mile to the west, apparently drawn by the chaos on the freeway. Behind them, Claire saw a black and yellow news helicopter rise above an overpass and slick in their direction.

Boothe began firing again. "What're they doing back there?" Ron yelled at her.

"Nothin'. Holdin' steady."

In the air, the news chopper was rapidly overhauling the ultralights, but staying well above them.

Their van tried to roll over a pair of birds, slammed sideways into the concrete wall. "*Fuck*!" Ron shouted, fighting the steering wheel as sparks erupted less than a foot from Claire's right shoulder. "Get back inside, Boothe! Buckle the hell up!"

Boothe slid down and grabbed her belt, getting it locked in place just as Ron swerved into the middle lane, tires squealing. "We're about done here, folks," he said, stamping the brakes twice, his jaws clamped together. Another turkey impact nearly tore the wheel out of his hands. The van rocked and slowed further, jouncing through the frozen flock.

Claire glanced at Boothe, who had her headset back in place and spoke calmly into it. The Volkswagen had closed to within fifty yards, steadily gaining in spite of its own evasive actions. *We are so screwed*, Claire thought, gulping down panic and clutching at the grab handle above her head.

She felt a particularly stout bird wedge itself under the police van. The rear of the vehicle began to come around, despite Ron's determined efforts to correct the motion. They intercepted more turkeys. Tires skidded and bucked, finally bringing them to a shuddering, diagonal stop in the right-hand lane.

The Volkswagen stopped thirty feet away, its side door now fully open. Three men smiled grimly out at them, only their teeth really visible in the shadowed interior. Another sat propped up against the rear seat, bandaged and blood-covered, either unconscious or dead.

In the following silence, the scene took on an almost surreal, slow-motion quality. The man carrying the RPG jumped out, went to one knee and leveled the launcher at the police van. One of his companions stepped to his side, arms crossed over his chest, and said in a loud, angry voice: "Give us the Phelans, or you all die."

"Fuck you, cat-boy!" Boothe shouted back, calmly snapping a filled magazine into her rifle, starting to get to her feet again.

Magnus Phelan unbuckled his belt, his intent obvious. "Riona..." he began to say.

A sound like incredibly amplified ripping canvas washed over them, drowning out his next words. The Volkswagen bucked, lurched, and sagged. The two men facing them seemed to instantly come apart into bloody tatters. The RPG discharged. Its rocket flashed up at a forty-five degree angle and kebobbed the hovering news helicopter. Like a movie special effect, the little aircraft exploded into a ball of orange flame. Its tail section spiraled down onto the MAX tracks paralleling the freeway, while flaming debris from the disintegrating main body rained down on the hillside beyond, setting the dry grass afire.

Then it was quiet, except for the brief four-stroke roar of the ultralights as they swooped low over the freeway before climbing into the darkening skies to the east. Claire sat with her mouth open, watching the grass fire from the helicopter spread up the hillside. *She had just seen at least six people die.*

Ron turned to Boothe as the small crimson planes disappeared. "What the hell *was* that?"

"The Mormon Air Force. MG-3 machine guns," she replied, grinning at him. "Armor-piercing rounds." She regarded what was left of their four opponents and their vehicle. Tongues of flame licked over the rear of the Volkswagen. "Seemed to work okay."

"Yeah," Ron agreed, with a long sigh, "just not for the news people." Still, his shoulders sagged with relief. He pointed down the freeway. "Here come the S.W.A.T. guys."

Boothe's grin widened. "Can the Cap be far behind?"

Claire tore her gaze from the expanding hillside conflagration, and watched the dull black armored truck swing around the turkey trailer, two hundred yards away. It rolled slowly through the sea of frozen fowl. Then she turned to Riona and her grandfather. "Are you two okay?"

Both nodded wordlessly, identical feral smiles on their narrow features, denied revenge but glad to be alive.

Uncle Emmett returned Ron's automatic, his own smile only a few degrees less dangerous-looking than the Phelans', and directed at Boothe. "Lieutenants, I can truthfully say I believe I now understand the term, 'Rogue Cop.'"

Boothe's angular features, already flushed, turned even redder.

FIFTY

Karl Elch shook his head as he gazed out the windows of the over-loaded police helicopter as it lifted sluggishly off the freeway. Fire crews on the hillside had nearly extinguished the grass fire, and ambulance crews waited to bag the immolated bodies of the news people. "I wouldn't have thought as many people stuck in the eastbound lanes would have climbed over the divider to grab those turkeys as they did."

"Did you want a couple, Sir?" Ron asked, seated by his boss. "If I'd known..."

Sitting at the rear of the passenger cabin beside Riona, Claire stifled a giggle, earning a warning glance from Boothe.

"You are *not* out of the frying pan on this one, Lieutenant Wismer," their boss replied sternly. He turned his baleful gaze to Boothe. "And you, young lady. Only the astonishingly low carnage level -- except for the news chopper, a few minor wounds, and lots of stress -- plus the current presence of civilian witnesses prevents me from yelling at you until I burst a blood vessel."

"Lieutenant Deakins proved most resourceful, Captain Elch," Magnus Phelan said. "Had she not, you and the pilot would be alone in this craft."

Elch looked even grimmer. "Don't remind me. Dozens of those eastbound lane people will at least *think* they saw two private aircraft strafe the freeway. The media will have a field day."

Resting a well-manicured hand on Elch's bony shoulder, Phelan awarded the younger man an indulgent smile. "You realize that those mysterious craft are by now almost certainly dismantled and hidden well away from prying eyes?"

"Where'd they come from, anyway?" the Captain asked Boothe.

"Private airfield out by Sandy. Like Mister Phelan said, at this point they're on their way over the Mount Hood highway inside a large produce truck. Their crews are riding their bicycles back into east Portland."

"Where'd they get the ordnance?"

"A friendly NATO country." Her grey eyes twinkled as she said the last word. "Turkey."

Elch rubbed his big right hand over his long features, his expression thoughtful. "*Jesu Christi*!" He held up his other hand. "And I don't think I want to know anything more just now, thank you very much. Albright is going to fill his britches, and the Mayor is going to pee his pants."

Magnus Phelan's expression grew calculating. "If there were sixteen of them, there are now twelve, assuming the one who fell onto the freeway in the initial exchange escaped. Should he be true to his blood, Cole will take this personally. We have the bait -- the document. Now we have only to determine placement and circumstance of defense. Make no mistake, Mister Elch, these are resourceful gentlemen, but they will come to us if we make the situation attractive enough. They cannot do otherwise. They gambled and lost. Cole will want his revenge."

Elch's thoughtful expression didn't change. "You're sure of this?"

"Of course. Whatever else they might be, these are, first and foremost, Irishmen." His smile would not have looked out-of-place on a wolf. "We need only formulate a good plan. They will come."

"All right!" Boothe Deakins said softly, her expression mirroring Magnus Phelan's exactly.

* * * * *

"I heard some sort of heavier automatic weapon," said the dirty, disheveled man slumped in a chair in Lorcan Cole's kitchen. Nine men and two women surrounded him, their faces mostly alloyed equally with anger and curiosity.

Cole forced himself to be calm, but he wanted to kill someone, preferably Magnus Phelan, his nasty granddaughter, or that damned bitch cop. All three would be best. A mission with good chance of success had gone into the loo, they had lost four men, and their quarry remained free. "Before or after the RPG took down the helicopter, Liam?"

"Before, I'm certain," Liam replied, accepting an opened can of beer from one of the others. He took a long, appreciative swallow, smacked his lips. "Yeah, for sure. Seconds only, though. It was right after that carload of nuns nearly rode me down. There I was, crawling to safety -- badly wounded, mind you -- and they just barely missed me."

A tall, thin man named Ramsey clucked sympathetically and shook his head. "Ah, I'm sure they meant nothing by it, Liam. Holy women, after all."

Cole ignored the nun issue, and instead took Boothe Deakins' card from a pocket and studied it. "She had some asset of which we were unaware. Pity the news people only transmitted a few seconds of pictures before their fiery demise. We can do a search, find where this woman lives..." He turned to Liam. "She *shot* you. Would you like to have a go at her?"

The seated man's dark gaze kindled as he sipped his beer. "Aye, and the sooner the better. Find her, and I'll take a lad or two over to visit."

"Twenty-four hours, then," Cole replied. "Butcher this bitch first, then determine how to get at the Phelans."

"What about the document?" asked Ramsey.

238

"After the Phelans, we find an Irish copper we can lever. Threaten his family or somesuch." He straightened up, replaced the card in his pocket, and addressed them all. "Can I assume you find that agreeable?"

Eleven throats growled assent.

* * * * *

Other than his connection with Claire, and through her with the Phelans, Paul had no idea why he sat in the Kenneth R. Cantwell Memorial Lecture Room. He was small potatoes in a place filled with Dental School Department heads and prominent leaders of the local dental community, not to mention the Dean himself, plus the Chief of Police. He felt more than a little intimidated, though Claire's hand on his helped.

The Mayor and Chief Albright had just breezed out the door, accompanied by a trio of acolytes and advisors -- all of whom towered over the diminutive politician -- the Mayor's final words something to the effect that he wanted no tarnish on the city's image, but he would accept whatever plan those in the room agreed on. Also, he hadn't actually been here, in case anyone should ask.

Paul found he basically felt the same as the Mayor, but now Karl Elch had taken the podium, clasping its edges in his big hands and smiling out at a group of men and women who comprised the brains, bones, sinew, and musculature of Oregon dentistry. The Captain was famed for his people skills, had managed to stay afloat in the shifting crap-shoot of Portland politics, and he knew how to turn on his multi-ethnic charm.

Flanked by the Dean, Magnus Phelan, and Quintus Jackson, the African-American ex-football player who served as Director of Clinics, Elch began to

239

speak: "I'm sure you've all read the hand-out carefully, and understand the situation as completely as we do. Members of your profession have been murdered, the perpetrators have not been apprehended, and, while we have the names of a small number of foreign nationals who are likely responsible, the deaths may continue. The Dean has suggested that a trap be set here at the school, that the killers be drawn in and dealt with. I assure you we have the bait." He paused, let his gaze sweep over the group, as if accepting questions. The crowd, more than two dozen of them, remained silent, watching Elch, all apparently of one mind. The handout must have been more convincing than Paul thought.

In the silence, Dean Dorfman stood up and walked to Elch's side, spoke into the microphone. "Who will volunteer for duty here tomorrow night?"

Every hand in the room shot up, though Claire's was much faster than Paul's, and Paul's clearest memory of that moment would always be the look of smug satisfaction on the face of Boothe Deakins, leaning against the wall on one side of the lecture room.

The shit. The fan. Together at last.

FIFTY-ONE

Benny Lu hung up the phone, his hand and mind scarcely registering the sound of the contact between the receiver and the base. The Friday afternoon noise of his staff in the area beyond his private office seemed similarly to recede as he contemplated the information Hyrum Gregorson had just given him.

The Mormon document was at the Dental School! Gregorson had no idea of the whys and wherefores, but the Dean had called him and discussed the matter, then asked him to contact his counterpart at Considerate Care. "Technically, Doctor Lu, the document is yours," Gregorson had stated, "so I am somewhat puzzled that they contacted me first. But the Dean seemed uncertain as to the ownership of the papers."

"You could be expected to have a larger moral stake in their disposition than myself," Lu had replied, truthfully enough. Gregorson had merely chuckled and thanked him for the thought, then hung up after saying goodbye.

Lu sat and mentally examined the situation. Cole had said the Phelans had taken the documents, which made perfect sense, if one assumed that the Phelans might be so inclined. Certainly Cole did not have the missing pages, Lu also did not, and now he knew that Gregorson did not. Also, Gregorson had expressed puzzlement as to how the pages arrived at the school. Imagining a circumstance in which the Phelans took the Book of Mormon document to the Dental School defied logic. None of the three ever mentioned any connection with the profession, and when he'd finally gotten up enough nerve to phone Riona Phelan, he'd only gotten her answering machine.

He thought a bit longer, finally deciding a possible answer would not come until April Kwong was taken off meds and awakened, which was to take place in late afternoon tomorrow -- Saturday. He would be there tomorrow evening, he would listen closely, and perhaps he would acquire knowledge he did not now have.

In the meantime, he called Lorcan Cole.

* * * * *

"The focking papers are in the Dental School!" Lorcan Cole announced to his assembled companions. Three hours had passed since he called this meeting. Ramsey and one of the others had been up to the School already. Cole took a last swallow of Guinness and sat the emptied bottle on a coffee table nearly covered with other empties. "What's the news, Cathal?" he asked Ramsey.

"The school's large, eight floors. Dean's office at the top, a sort of penthouse. Place closes at noon on Saturdays, so far as patients being seen. Some of the students might stay on for another hour or two studying, but basically the place empties out at mid-day."

Cole nodded, uncapped another beer. "So there's likely to be some security, but otherwise the building'll be deserted. That's good. Do we blow the front door down, then?"

Being a break-and-enter man who had no love for explosives, Ramsey looked momentarily aghast, then took a deep breath before replying. "There's a tunnel over from the lower levels of the Medical School. Enters on the fifth floor. There's our way in. We fox the alarms, tie up the watchman, ransack the Dean's office."

"And if it isn't there?"

"Then we go out the way we come in, and write it off."

Cole thought for a moment. "Fair enough. We've lost four to bad luck..."

"And that smart bitch copper," Liam put in.

"Ah, yeah," Cole replied. He smiled at them all. "But you've got her address. She'll be off the playing pitch by sunrise tomorrow."

"Sooner'n that," Liam said. "Me, Jimmy, and Eileen'll be payin' a wee visit tonight, a coupla hours past sunset. We'll punt in off the river."

"Sounds grand," Cole said, his tight smile widening as he took a swallow of his fresh beer. "Bring me back a bit of her spleen."

FIFTY-TWO

"The breeze off the river is very pleasant," Riona said, looking down at the water gleaming in the darkness below. She curled her tail around her haunches and settled her chin on her folded paws to complete the picture of a contented cat.

Claire regarded her beautiful cousin for a moment, then smiled, if exposing her fangs could be called a smile. The two women -- in their feline forms -- sprawled atop Boothe Deakins' roof, awaiting possible retaliation against Boothe for the events on the freeway. Claire had doubted any sort of direct revenge, but when Riona explained she had taunted Lorcan Cole with Boothe's business card, the possibility had suddenly seemed more likely. In an electronically-connected world, almost anyone could be found.

Now, an hour-and-a-half after sunset, the tile roof still held heat from the warm day, and Claire felt slightly drowsy. "I could take a nap," she said, stretching and yawning, exposing her fangs again. Her extended claws skritched on the tile.

Riona chuckled, a sort of purring growl. "Be wary and alert, my large cousin. We are only three, though Boothe Deakins possesses an arsenal of vast magnitude."

"No kidding. I'd never seen an AK-47 before."

"She prefers her pair of silenced automatics, I notice, for this evening's activity," Riona replied, curling up next to Claire.

"A regular Tomb Raider."

Riona chuckled again. "More like a 'Womb Raider,' I think."

"C'mon! I've met her *boy*friend."

The expression of condescending superiority which came so easily to cats appeared on Riona's

244

furred features. "It takes one to know one, my dear Claire."

Claire nodded. "That's right. April Kwong."

Her cousin's gaze kindled. "Poor April, beaten horribly for knowing me." Her murderous claws unsheathed, and her husky voice seemed to well up from deeper in her throat. "I will kill as many as possible."

"The cops'll probably want one or two for questioning."

"Then they will need good fortune."

"Incidentally, why are we on the river side of the roof?

If they come in through the parking lot, we won't be able to see them."

"Then they will have to go through the front door or the garage, activate Lieutenant Deakins' motion detectors, and be subject to her lethal weaponry." She reached up with one claw to pluck something from between a canine and lateral incisor. "Also, Grandfather feels that, being Irish, they may come in off the water. A traditional means of secret access."

"Your grandfather's quite a guy," Claire replied.

"You will think so, should you see him in action tomorrow night. He is quite skilled."

"At his age."

"Death incarnate, and age makes little difference."

As Riona finished speaking, a dark Zodiac-type inflatable left the edge of a dimly-lit marina on the far side of the Willamette. The two women watched as the little craft moved silently out into the main current and began to slant against the water's flow toward the small-boat moorings on their side of the river.

"Lie as flat as possible," Riona advised softly. "We are no longer backlit by the sunset, but we must be cautious."

"Maybe it's just kids doing a sneak. A little summer adventure."

Her cousin peered into the darkness. "They are adults wearing dark clothing."

"College-age Goths."

"No. The wind has shifted to the east. I can smell them now. They are our sort."

"They won't be able to smell *us*."

Riona made a small sound of approval. "You are
learning, cousin."

"What exactly do I do?"

"With your size and weight, falling on one of them from this height should suffice. One or more will go in the front. Whoever remains will try the rear, off the deck below us."

"Two in the front might be too many for Boothe."

"She has two Claymoores in the garage. I watched her wire them. The windows are solidly barred. Only the front door is truly available, and she has cameras everywhere."

"I hope she's ready."

"Never otherwise, I suspect."

Out on the water, the little rubber vessel passed the river's midway point. Claire felt her pulse rate rise in anticipation.

* * * * *

Cycling between her observation cameras on her laptop, Boothe saw Riona and Claire plaster themselves to the roof surface, saw their ears tip forward, and knew Riona had seen something. *Good*, she thought, checking the position of the six-by-six mirror facing her front door at a 45-degree angle.

Anyone coming into the entryway would see a bathrobe-wearing Boothe seated in a leather chair, reading a magazine, seemingly directly in front of the door. Boothe actually sat ninety degrees away from where she appeared to be, behind a heavy panel of *Augard-V* bullet-resistant glass. She figured it would take two-to-three seconds for a gunman to realize he or she was firing into a mirror, and the *Augard-V* would negate at least some of the next fusillade, directed to where she actually *was* sitting. If she couldn't respond adequately in that time frame, she didn't deserve to live, let alone carry a badge.

Satisfied, she went back to her chair, folded the bathrobe over the front of her body armor, sat down, and resumed surveillance on her laptop.

* * * * *

The inflatable slid alongside a pair of small jetboats moored two hundred feet downstream from Boothe's condo, and bumped to a stop against the floating walkway jutting into the river. One of the three occupants jumped out and secured the craft to a cleat on the slender dock while the other two quickly disrobed. Watching them begin to shift into their other forms, Claire felt her breath catch at the speed with which the change occurred.

Beside her, Riona let out a low growl. "Any doubts now, cousin?"

Claire shook her head as the three -- the shifts complete -- walked to the concrete breakwater and headed in their direction, the one still human flanked by the two cats. Interestingly, the guy seemed to be wearing a headset under his temple armor. Claire could hear him speaking softly into the microphone as the trio strode purposefully toward the condo.

They paused at the sidewalk between Boothe's building and the one next door and held a short meeting, their conversation interrupted several times to talk with whoever was on the other end of the headset communications. Finally, after a few apparent instructions, the three separated, the man jogging up the steps toward the front of the condo, and the two cats padding quietly to a point just below the broad deck off the main floor of Boothe's quarters.

Riona and Claire slid noiselessly to the very edge of the roof, their noses practically touching the tile. Below, the cats sat on their haunches on the sidewalk and stared at the lighted great room windows twenty feet above them. Occasionally, an eager tail would flick, or an ear would tilt toward a deck party several units to the south, but otherwise both watchers and watched remained still.

* * * * *

Standing in the deeper darkness beside a hulking Lexus SUV, Liam Sullivan surveyed the front of Boothe Deakins' condo. "All outside windows are barred," he said to Lorcan Cole, who sat waiting in a rental van on the other side of the broad river. "So it'll have to be the front door."

"Blow-down or fiddle?" Cole asked.

"Hard to say. A copper with an easy fiddle seems a bit of unlikely. And a blow-down will alert her."

"She can't lack for confidence, and whoever built those places might have done it on the cheap. If she figures she can stop whoever takes a run at her, she might not have done an upgrade on the locks."

"I'll try the fiddle."

"Wise lad."

* * * * *

From inside the building, Deakins had seen the shadowy form pause by the neighbors' vehicle, and knew the nut was getting close to the cracker. She'd

248

deliberately left the deadbolt off, and the double stainless steel night bars were not in their brackets. Any breaker worth his salt ought to be able to tool his way past the standard lock the builders installed in a couple of minutes or less.

Having spotted the two on the back walkway, she knew there were at least three interlopers. Would have been nice to have a line open to Riona and Claire, but they hadn't been able to come up with a way, so she'd just have to trust Riona's experience.

Movement showed by the Lexus, a ski-masked figure coming steathily up her front walk. She watched as he brought out a selection of picks and went to work on the lock. Faint sounds of small metallic clicks and slitherings came through the door. Smiling to herself, Boothe took firmer grips on the two CZs in her lap, and watched in the mirror.

After a final click, the door began to slowly open and the silenced muzzle of an automatic appeared, the gunman's left hand holding the leading edge of the door.

Boothe forced herself to look down at the magazine covering her weapons until she could see his face and saw his head jerk up in surprise when he spotted her apparently sitting quietly right in front of him.

He put three hissing shots into the center of the mirror. Boothe stood, her pistols up. "*Freeze*, asshole!"

With no hesitation, the gunman spun toward her true location and fired three more rounds. The third made it through the impact damage of the first two and bounced her back half-a-step.

Unhurt, Boothe fired twice around the protective panel, one slug catching her opponent in his left thigh, knocking him down to one knee.

"You focking bitch!" he yelled, scuttling to his right as he got off two more rounds, both hitting the *Augard-V*.

Boothe kicked the heavy panel out of her way, fired once more, sending the gunman tumbling across the kitchen floor. He rolled around the central island and returned fire as Boothe dove behind a metal-reinforced great room chair.

* * * * *

The instant the two cats on the riverside walkway heard the sound of shots, they sprang up onto the wide deck, clearing the steel railing by a good foot. Riona went off the roof in a single smooth motion. Claire followed, plunging down on top of the female half of the pair, knocking her smaller foe sideways into the windows fronting the deck.

The cat rebounded from the glass without breaking it, right into Claire's swiping claws, which slammed her squalling into an aluminum table. Peripherally aware of Riona having backed her own opponent into a far corner of the deck, Claire pursued her weight and reach advantage, knocking the table aside and smashing her adversary into the railing uprights.

The smaller cat hooked a foreleg under the railing and pulled herself off the edge of the deck, disappearing into the darkness below.

After a quick glance at Riona, who fiercely shook the lifeless body of her enemy by its neck, Claire leapt down to the barkdust-covered bank and set off after her fleeing prey.

* * * * *

Hearing the screaming catfight and furniture crashing beyond the curtains and windows, Liam

250

realized that it had been a trap. His intent had been for him to open the rear doors and let the cats finish her. Now his only way out was the way he'd come in, and he had to incapacitate or kill the cop to make freedom. Her focking chair must be made of solid kevlar, and only the pots and pans inside the island he hid behind were keeping him from being shot up worse than he was already.

The cop began firing again, and Liam huddled against the thin wood, waiting for the inevitable final pain. But it didn't come. Then he heard the window onto the deck disintegrate in a tinkling cascade, followed by the 'tick-tick' of extended claws on the tiled floor.

And Riona Phelan's husky voice. "Live or die, me boyo. Which will it be?"

* * * * *

Sprinting hard, her long cheetah's body extended, Claire rapidly overhauled her recent foe. Without pausing at the tied-up inflatable, the smaller catwoman sped down the concrete river walkway at over fifty miles per hour, Claire practically on her heels. But the walkway ended, protruding north like a giant finger toward Tom McCall Waterfront Park and surrounded by water. The connecting floating bridge had yet to be funded and built, and now Claire's antagonist was trapped.

Claire slid to a halt, ten feet from the panting, bleeding cat. "Give up?" she asked, grinning.

The woman looked around desperately. "I can't swim."

"Give up?" Claire repeated.

"I've killed no one."

"Then maybe you'll get off easily."

"The Phelans will kill *me*."

"Give me your word that you won't try to escape, and I'll talk them around."

"And *your* word?"

"My word. Leave the fur. I'll escort you back."

* * * * *

Liam Sullivan lay on his stomach on the cool kitchen tile, his hands clasped behind his neck. Riona Phelan stood on his back while Boothe snapped cuffs on his wrists.

"You're not safe yet," he grated.

"Nor you," Riona replied, flexing her claws against the base of his neck. "*I* would kill you for what was done to my friend. Lieutenant Deakins is far kinder."

"Fock you both."

Riona chuckled, and swatted his head, leaving bloody gouges on his scalp. "A far-fetched fantasy, lad."

"No shit," Deakins said, speaking into her cell phone. "Yeah, Deakins here. Got a clean-up on aisle seven."

FIFTY-THREE

Benny Lu faced a baker's dozen of his faithful employees seated in lotus positions on a line of *tatami* mats illuminated by the Saturday morning sun. His words echoed in the silent *dojo*. "We shall aid the Phelan's enemies in the recovery of the Mormon Document."

"At the *Dental School*?" asked Donovan Tran. Lu considered Doctor Tran to be a fine operator, capable of doing exquisite restorations, but also perhaps too much inclined to inquire.

"Yes. This evening. After sunset." Lu paused, and his gaze included them all. "You are proficient in the use of hang-gliders, I understand."

"Yes," they chorused.

"Good. You will launch from the Veteran's Hospital Sky Bridge, glide down to the roof of the Dental School, enter the school, link up with the other seekers, and provide security while they locate the document."

"Where might the document be?" Not Tran this time, but Bertram Why Chang, a gifted orthodontist.

"Doctor Gregorson gave me to understand it will be in the Dean's office, in the walk-in safe."

"Ah," the group replied with murmurs of distress, and another of them spoke up. "The office windows are covered with steel louvres at night. The system is automatic."

"No matter," Lu said. "Entry can be made from the floor below. Our allies will come into the building through the fifth floor tunnel, deal with security, and join you."

"Where will *you* be?"

"With Miz Kwong. She will be taken off the sedatives late this afternoon. I want to be -- *must* be -- at her bedside when she awakens, in mid-evening."

This time, no questions followed his words.

* * * * *

"For its age, this place is an electronic marvel," the police technician told Deakins and Wismer.

"Built in 1955," Wismer replied. He turned to Dean Dorfman. "Isn't that correct, sir?"

"Yes," the Dean said, nodding, lips pursed as he watched someone not directly connected to the school run through the facility's security cameras and motion detectors. "But it's been upgraded continually. The Alumni Association has funded the Dental School very generously."

"When did they add your private elevator up to the penthouse?" Deakins asked.

Now the man looked slightly embarrassed. "Two years ago, about a year after I became Dean."

"And no one knows about it?"

The Dean smiled, looking momentarily younger than his mid-fifties, if not as young as the wild frat boy he'd been over a quarter-century earlier. "It's hardly a secret. All the Department Heads have keys. Sometimes after a hard day in the classrooms or clinics, we have a bull session in the lounge. A few of us."

"All very professional, no doubt."

"Of course." Now he began to look really tickled.

"Solving the problems of the dental community."

"Precisely."

Wismer interrupted her mini-interrogation. "Boothe, maybe you could avoid irritating people key to our op here."

Unimpressed, his partner grinned. "Just curious, Ronald. I don't know much about the dental profession."

254

"Where did you attend university, Lieutenant Deakins?" asked the Dean.

"Before Police Academy? Oregon State."

"A pity. You would have had more fun in Eugene."

"Everyone does," remarked the technician, looking up from the multiple screens in front of him and grinning. "John Landis was right."

"If we could steer away from the Ducks/Beavers thing, folks," Wismer began.

"I was only thinking how the Lieutenant would look in a toga," Dorfman replied.

"Just don't go there, sir," Wismer suggested. "It would *not* be wise. The whole cop thing is a kind of dress-up for her, anyway."

The Dean nodded knowingly. "One can only hope you are correct, Mister Wismer." He sighed, smiling almost paternally at Deakins. "An old man can dream."

Boothe grinned at her partner. "Plenty of places to carry weapons under a toga."

Wismer just shook his head.

* * * * *

"You said you were staying over at Boothe's last night to spend time with your cousin," Paul said, trying to keep from yelling. "That *sounded* harmless enough. Chips and dip and a few beers while watching *Thelma and Louise*, or *The Long Kiss Goodnight*,' I figured. The calm before tonight's storm. *Now* I find out that Boothe shot somebody up, Riona killed another guy, and you -- *You*! -- got into a knock-down-and- drag-out with one of your own kind."

Claire finished the second of three toaster biscuits slathered in butter and honey. "I should point out, before you go any more ballistic, that I'm in one piece and am sitting peacefully in your pleasant, sunny

255

kitchen. It is a very nice late morning here." She bit into the third biscuit, regarding him with both warning and patience.

Paul took a deep breath before speaking. "Your cousin is a revenge-driven maniac, Boothe Deakins is a very aggressive natural killer, and you are a proven risk-taker. Why in God's name did I think the three of you would take a night off?"

"No shit. Pretty stupid, if you ask me."

He was not getting through to her, Paul realized. "Don't blow me off on this, Claire. You took a helluva chance. There will be *no* wedding if you get yourself iced."

"Granted, but I probably saved Eileen Devaney's life. After she killed her guy, Riona would've run Eileen down and finished her off."

"Really?"

"Oh, yeah. Riona has pretty much the one answer for the current situation. Repeat as necessary."

Paul gave up, folded his arms on the tabletop and gazed at Claire in a combination of concern and unfeigned adoration. "Okay, I'll shut up. Not going to win this one, anyway."

"News flash, Bucko. You're not going to win *any* of them."

"While you're alive."

"Right."

"You have honey on your chin."

"No surprise there."

"I could lick it off."

She nodded slowly. "Could. Could maybe use your tongue elsewhere, too."

He laughed. "Where did you have in mind?"
"Lemme think about it. You got any more of these biscuits?"

"Sure." He stood and went to the breadbox, fished out the biscuits, then turned to face her, holding

256

the colorful little bag tightly to keep his hands from shaking. "I don't want to lose you, Claire."

"I'll try not to get lost."

"We'll be together tonight, at least." As he spoke, Paul gently pried apart one biscuit and dropped the separated halves in the toaster.

"Maybe we'll both get lost," Claire mused as she wiped the honey off her chin with a forefinger, sucking it clean.

"Spare me your fatalism. I don't need to be out-Irished."
"We go into the school at six?"

"Off the Casey Eye Institute lot into the basement level. I've got a key."

"Boothe and Ron are up there now. With the Dean, the more fit Department heads, and Riona and her grandfather. We'll pick up my uncle on our way."

"And Janos and Gregorson will be there, but not Lu?"

"No. Riona and her grandfather think he may have been compromised by Cole. Besides, Riona says April Kwong's docs will take her off sedatives late this afternoon, and Lu will definitely want to be there when she wakes up."

"How's she doing? Riona's been over there a lot."
"Riona says her bruises are beginning to fade, and most of the facial swelling is down."

"Poor woman, beaten to shit." He turned to the toaster as the biscuit popped up.

"She's pretty damned tough. She got herself together enough to free Riona. Otherwise they'd both be dead."

Paul began to butter the biscuit, shaking his head. "Still."

"We'll get 'em. There're only nine left."

"And how much plastic explosive?" He handed her the biscuit halves, started another one.

"Boothe's big worry," Claire replied, regarding him playfully around the disappearing half-biscuit. "How's your tongue, lover?"

Paul smiled at her. "Sinuous. You'll see."

* * * * *

"How goes it, More?" Cathal Ramsey asked the woman seated at the kitchen table. The smell of gun oil permeated the air, and the table was covered with assorted pistols and cleaning aids.

"Ah, well enough." Without looking up, she continued running a brush down the barrel of a small revolver. "Not the quality we get at home, but decidedly cheaper and more readily available." She indicated a small .38 with the tip of the brush. "Only one completely useless. With a little work, the rest will function for the necessary time. Oh, and here's a cute one." She picked up another .38. "Take a look."

He examined the weapon. "The number's been filed off."

"Better than that. Look closer, lad."

"Dear God! It's a *copy*. Made from a casting of a gun..."

"...with the number filed off. Clever sods, these yanks."

Ramsey surveyed the rows of cleansed weapons, shaking his head. "Bloody Saturday night specials."

"Well, we've plenty of ammunition, anyway. You can just walk into a store here and buy what you will."

"It's a wonderful place."

"Wonderful for folks like us. Almost as good as the Middle East."

"Splendid people, the Arabs."

"If they only spoke English."

258

"Aye, but one can't have everything. Money talks for you, there. That's why we have automatic weapons and C-7."

More made a sour face. "Lorcan and his explosives."

"Only on the main doors tonight. In case we're slow on their security and the coppers come while we're inside."

"Only nine of us left, too. Pity it's gotten so personal."

Ramsey pulled up a chair and sat down, an expression of concern covering his long, dark features. "At the end, More, my dear, for the Irish, it always comes down to that. Particularly for *our* kind of Irish. Those like Lorcan Cole and Liam Sullivan will strive for revenge even whilst they're being lowered into the sod. I re-conned the school yesterday, and foxed the fifth floor entrance alarm. I'll open doors tonight, pop the safe, and hope all's fine, but after that, well, I'm away. Get some papers, go to work as a bouncer in an Irish theme bar."

"Take me with, Cathal."

"I'd hoped you'd ask."

"I have, and I mean it. I've enough of this."

His smile deepened. He took her hands in his. "Good, then."

FIFTY-FOUR

Emmett McManus' rowhouse was situated on a quiet dead-end street a few blocks off the Sunset Highway in Sylvan. Paul had been prepared for Claire's uncle, but, to his surprise, *three* figures stood on the sloping driveway.

Claire began to laugh. "*Look* at them!" Claire's uncle and the tall woman standing beside him both wore green scrubs. The third person wore black warmups in what Paul suspected were size XXXL.

"Uh, yeah," Paul replied, slowing his Honda CRV and turning into the driveway, "but who are the other two with your uncle?"

"His friend Mai Killian and that wildlife guy, Haggen."

"That whoppin' *big* wildlife guy." He set the emergency brake and turned off the engine, remembering that he'd seen Haggen on local and national television when Duncan had been killed. "Why are they here?"

"Unc'll tell us."

They climbed out of the Honda, and Claire hugged her uncle.

"Pop the back, will you, Paul?" Emmett McManus asked, hoisting a pair of long black dufflebags. Paul reached back inside the car and flipped the rear hatch release.

When the bags were stowed, Claire's uncle introduced Paul to his companions. "This is Paul Tiernan, my niece's fiance'. Paul, meet Mai Killian and Odward Haggen."

"Don't look so perplexed, Paul," Mai said, chuckling as she shook his hand. "We're here to help."

"Mai works with the Oregon Board of Dentistry," McManus explained helpfully.

Paul managed to keep from jumping, but they all noticed his surprise.

"You can't lose your license to practice for killing someone in self-defense, Doctor Tiernan," Mai assured him, laughing, but what Paul saw in the depths of her leaf-green eyes worried him a great deal more than either her words or the thought of facing people who could become killer beasts.

Haggen looked a lot bigger in person than on television. Twenty years ago, he'd started three seasons in the line at Oregon State, and even now looked fit enough to step onto the field. "I'm just along for the ride, Paul," he rumbled cheerfully, his voice making James Earl Jones sound like a tenor.

On their way to the school, after the tunnel on the Sunset, Haggen leaned forward from the middle seat and said, "Just drop me off at the Carnival Restaurant, if you would, Paul, at the bottom of Terwilliger. I'm going to grab a couple of burgers and one of their milkshakes before going up to the school."

"Okay," Paul replied, puzzled. "But how are you going to get *in* the school?"

The huge biologist chuckled again. "Oh, I'm not actually going to be *inside* the school. I get to roam around outside and keep an eye on things." He rubbed his blocky hands together. "Much more fun, to my way of thinking."

"I'll be outside, too," Mai put in. "By the Activity Building, just uphill from the parking structure."

Paul decided not to pursue the subject of who was going to be where. Haggen's deepset eyes were only slightly less daunting than Mai Killian's. He glanced at Claire, who seemed totally relaxed, and wondered how in hell he'd gotten himself in this situation. Love, he supposed, wishing he could predict the outcome at the school. Maybe love would find a way. He smiled at the thought.

261

"What?" Claire asked.

"Never mind," Paul replied as he exited the freeway and headed up toward the school and the post-grad clinic.

*   *   *   *   *

"I never envisioned something of this magnitude," Hyrum Gregorson said, looking nervously around the post-graduate clinic floor at the twenty-or-so people preparing for their night's duties within the Dental School.

"You shouldn't be surprised," Konstantine Janos replied, covering a folding table with a long, white beach towel. "The dental community in Oregon has a history of sticking up for itself. Four of your doctors and one of their wives have been murdered, Hyrum. They tried to kill Howard Pick. They tried to blow up one of my people." The tall, dark Greek hefted three fiberglass weapons cases onto the table, and opened one of them with nimble, clinic-trained fingers.

Gregorson involuntarily sucked in a breath. "What in the Lord's name is that?"

"You told me once you did some skeet as a kid."

"Yes, but that was many years ago."

"Well, this is a Pancor Jackhammer Mark 3-A3 automatic shotgun," Janos replied. "An oral surgeon buddy of mine down in Round Rock, Texas has a part ownership of the company. This is third or fourth generation in development, but the first real production model." He hefted the bulky, futuristic weapon. "A ten-shot cassette, fires at a rate of four shots per second." He smiled at Gregorson, displaying perfectly-white, even teeth. "You hit 'em, they won't stick around this mortal plane. Hit 'em twice, parts of 'em'll be hard to find."

Gregorson swallowed, gulping. "I haven't fired even a *normal* shotgun in years."

262

"You lost some good people, Hyrum. Here's your chance."

The owner of Soyze Dental Associates thought for a moment, then licked his lips. An inner resolve seemed to click into place. "Yes, I suppose it is." He took the weapon from Janos and cradled it in his hands, sensed its power and deadliness. "How does it operate, exactly? And how many cassettes do you have?"

* * * * *

The bore of the pistol pointing at Paul's head from inside the post-grad clinic looked big enough to swallow a golf ball. He managed to tear his gaze away from the weapon long enough to recognize the BDU-wearing person holding it.

"Mister *Fenstermacher*?" he croaked.

"Sorry, Doc," the compact Vietnam veteran replied, smiling thinly as he holstered the automatic. "I never take chances. Nice filling last month, by the way."

"What are *you* doing here?"

Fenstermacher indicated Claire's uncle. "Major McManus and I are in the same reserve unit."

McManus chuckled. "And, Sergeant, you should also mention that you served in Vietnam with Doctor Janos."

"That, too. *Lieutenant* Janos then."

"Staff Sergeant Fenstermacher agreed to organize the school's ordnance and brief our defense forces."

"Four hours this afternoon with the faculty geezers on the firing range in the sub-basement," the sergeant replied, nodding sharply. "Used up a ton of Arwen training rounds."

Paul managed to regain enough composure to introduce Fenstermacher to Claire, then the three filed

263

into the post-graduate Clinic, leaving the sergeant to his door-keeping duties.

"That was the lost filling guy?" Claire whispered to Paul.

"Yeah."

"He looks tougher than hell. I can't imagine him getting all torn up whenever he pops a filling."

"Me, neither," Paul admitted, still seeing the pistol in his mind's eye. What next? he wondered. The *Pope* with ill-fitting dentures? And a bazooka?

Within the Postgraduate Clinic, chairs and units had been pushed aside to the limits of their umbilicals to clear a large central area. Folding cafeteria tables were arrayed at the far end of the big room, covered with rows of what Claire thought were riot-control weapons and a matching number of filled ammunition belts.

She recognized ten or so younger department heads checking the weaponry. Her boss and Hyrum Gregorson stood near the left wall, talking with six tall, black-clad women and a slightly shorter guy dressed in BDUs similar to Fenstermacher's. These must be the Mormon Danites Boothe had mentioned. Claire wondered which four had been in the ultralights that saved their asses on the freeway. Not that it mattered. They all looked chillingly competent, the guy as grim as Sergeant Fenstermacher.

"Those are the strippers?" Paul asked.

Claire laughed. "Keep your voice down, dear. They might come over and kick you in my privates."

"Don't you mean *my* privates?"

"I figure I've got controlling interest at this point in our relationship. For sure in August."

Paul shook his head and grinned. "Love is more involved than I imagined."

From behind him, Claire's uncle spoke up. "You may not yet know the half of it, Paul."

* * * * *

At seven o'clock, when Paul and Claire had met everyone, Boothe and Ron appeared from the security center with the Dean, and Sergeant Fenstermacher stepped in front of the weapon-bedecked tables and addressed the group.

"Okay, folks, we don't think anything bad's going to happen until it's good and dark, but if you'll listen up for a few minutes, more of us might be among the hale and hearty when all's said and done."

In the following silence, the Vietnam veteran motioned to the uniformed Mormon, who came forward to stand beside him. "You've probably all met Sergeant Klaghorn by now. Despite the fact that the Sergeant did his hitch in a water-borne part of our military, he could kick the butt of most everyone here. Mine for certain. He'll be with Doctor Janos and Doctor Gregorson. Should any of us get into a real firefight, they're gonna put it out. The rest of you will get your assignments after we've had supper and viewed the Powerpoint presentation the Dean and the Police Department have put together. In the meantime, I want to go through the re-loading procedure for the Arwen 37S weapons we'll be using tonight. Most of the faculty used these during the anti-Mercury demonstrations in the early Nineties, so there shouldn't be any real problems with familiarity. Just pretend that whoever you're facing is some low-wattage, drooling, nutcase yahoo." Laughter rippled through the crowd at his last words.

Fenstermacher continued talking as he loaded and unloaded one of the weapons with 'reduced-energy baton rounds.' Claire knew she'd be in the fur tonight, so only paid scant attention, letting her mind drift back to the television images of the demonstrators massed in front of the Dental School ten years earlier. She and Paul were still down at Oregon State then, but she

265

remembered patients walking nervously between lines of shouting, sign-waving protesters. One of the Portland stations had compared pictures of the anti-Mercury forces with those taken in front of various abortion facilities, and discovered considerable membership commonality.

The big difference, of course, was when a few of the people in front of the school had taken a notion to come inside the big front doors, the faculty had responded more dramatically than any medical staff would have. The mob, poised to storm into the reception area and the clinic floor, retreated in chaos when their leaders sprinted howling out of the building in a cloud of rubber bullets.

It wouldn't be that easy tonight.

FIFTY-FIVE

Winston Nagumo crawled slowly up the articulated fiberglass ramp to the roof of the skybridge between the Veterans' Hospital and the Medical School. Ahead of him, safely on the roof, Dwight Kumangai rose to his feet and began unfolding and assembling his black hang-glider. While he waited, Doctor Nagumo glanced in the direction of the Dental School, lower and to the east, thinking that its flat roof looked less than large in the dim illumination of the rising half-moon. The Dean's penthouse office resembled a steel-walled fortress, and the only lights in the building were a vertical line of windows demarcating the stairwell.

Several of their number were already on the roof, however, tying down their gliders, in case a later need developed to escape by air down the canyon into the sprawling city lights below. Nagumo couldn't imagine soaring over I-5 to the safety of Johns' Landing, but they'd all studied nocturnal air currents between the river and the West Hills, and he was confident the task could indeed be accomplished.

As he patiently waited, he silently prayed that they would not disappoint Doctor Lu, and that Miz Kwong would awaken to good health and renewed spirits.

* * * * *

On the densely-wooded hillside opposite the Dental School, Robbie Munoz and Janiece Carlton sat inside a camouflaged hide and watched the Considerate Care staffers slip down through the cooling night air to the top of the eight-storey building.

"Oh, shit!" Munoz said, nearly dropping his binoculars. "One of 'em missed the roof. He's hangin' on the edge."

"Five bucks says he doesn't make it," Carlton replied, studying the stocky man's flailing legs through her own night eyes. The hang glider prevented her from having a clear view of his hands.

"Okay, two of 'em got him. They're hauling him up."

"There comes another big guy. Whoa! He took all three of 'em off their feet."

"This is kinda fun."

Carlton regarded Munoz with deep disdain. "Jesus, Robbie! Get serious! The Loots didn't expect this. Get on the horn and tell Deakins we got at least a dozen little Ninja dudes hip-hoppin' around over her head."

Munoz punched a single number on their comm-unit. "Okay, okay, but two of those guys definitely weren't *little*."

"Whatever." Her grin flashed white in the darkness. "And tell her you look stupid in your camo face-paint."

"I'm genetically-disadvantaged, unlike you."

Carlton snorted. "You the palest Hispanic I *ever* saw."

Raising his right forefinger to his lips, her partner informed their superior of the new development. Then the two resumed their surveillance of the rooftop gathering. Neither noticed the lean, black-clad form of Mai Killian climbing swiftly up the fire escape on the darkened west face of the school, at the bare edge of their view of the building.

* * * * *

Cathal Ramsey's efforts on the lock at the entrance to the fifth floor of the Dental School were finally rewarded with a cascading series of clicks. He carefully opened the doors and looked down the long hallway before bowing and gesturing theatrically.

"You're a bloody great genius, Cathal," Lorcan Cole enthused, clapping the taller man on the back. Cole wore standard physician's garb: Black oxfords, dark pants, blue shirt and a rather drab tie, with a white clinic jacket finishing his disguise. He stepped through the doorway, followed by the two Flannery cousins pushing a cleaning cart filled with plastic explosive charges and assorted weaponry. "Stay by the door," he told Ramsey, then glanced at his watch. "Our Asian allies should be on the roof by now, down to here in a few. Radio the others. Tell 'em to come in by ones and twos. Have them change in the loos."

Ramsey watched their leader enter the darkened lecture hall to their left, the Flannerys right behind with their lethally-laden cart. He sighed. More O'Rourke should be here shortly. His job was done when the safe in the Dean's office swung open, then he and More could disappear across the clinic floor roof and into the forested hillside above the school. He cracked his knuckles, and thought of his hopeful future working in some jolly pub, with time for he and More to course in Oregon's mighty forests. A wonderful dream, if their luck swung good.

* * * * *

At precisely thirteen minutes after ten, April Kwong's eyes opened. Benny Lu's chin had fallen nearly to his chest from fatigue after five hours of bedside vigil, but he still caught the tiny flicker of her eyelids and looked up with renewed hope.

"Hi, boss," she said, blinking slowly. Her brown eyes seemed perfectly clear as she looked around the room. "Riona been here?"

269

An involuntary hiss escaped the Considerate Care owner. "Do not mention that woman's name! She is the reason you are in this room, in this bed!"

April stared at him, her eyes widening even further. "Yeah, instead of being croaked, takin' the dirt nap. Riona saved my life. Hers, too, probably."

Lu felt his heart stutter. "*What?*"

"This little Irish prick, Lorcan Cole, wanted the Book of Mormon pages. He had his buddy Patrick work both of us over -- me first -- to force Riona to give him the stuff. When Patrick was finished, and we were left alone, I managed to cut Riona loose. She killed Patrick, then called the cops." Her eyes narrowed to slits and her fists clenched. "I hope she's found Cole and finished the little bastard."

Gulping and swallowing, completely thunderstruck, Lu could scarcely form words. "Lorcan Cole!" he said, at last. As he spoke the name, he realized the horrible perfidy of the man, how Cole had tricked him, and how Lu had stupidly sent his loyal staffers to aid in evildoing.

"What's wrong, boss?"

Lu felt his face redden in shame. He looked down at his hands, folded between his knees. "I sent our martial artists to help Cole recover the document. Somehow it is at the Dental School."

"You're not makin' sense."

"No," Lu agreed, "but I am *seeing* sense." He reached quickly into his sport jacket pocket, brought out his cell phone, tapped in a number, and listened intently for nearly a minute. Then he closed the phone, and his shoulders sagged. "No answer. They are at the School."

"Can you stop them?"

"I can try." He stood, gave April a short bow. "I am happy that you are somewhat recovered, less happy that you have revealed my idiotic folly. I may have imperiled our co-workers needlessly."

"You bring the big Mercedes?"

"Yes."

"Go git 'em, Doc! Show 'em how an Asian dentist can motor!"

Lu ran from the room.

* * * * *

Officer Don Lawrence, astride his BMW 1100 RT-P police motorcycle, couldn't believe his eyes. A hundred yards ahead of him, a black Mercedes turbo diesel driven by a wiry Asian man had just entered the westbound I-84 freeway in a four-wheel drift, rear tires smoking. Lawrence twisted his right wrist and sped up, simultaneously cuing the helmet mike connecting him to his dispatcher. "Got me an improbable," he said, describing the circumstances as he closed on the heavy vehicle enough to read the rear plate.

"What you have, Officer," replied the dispatcher, after a thirty-second search, "is one Doctor Benjamin Lu, who, according to the flag on his name in my computer, may be heading to the Dental School. You are requested to provide an escort."

"Come again?" Lawrence asked, looking down at his speedo, which had peaked just over eighty.

The dispatcher repeated her message, adding, "Flag was placed by Captain Elch. We'll pull somebody off patrol in east county to cover you. Any problem?"

"No," the patrolman answered, signing off. He overtook Lu's Mercedes and gave the driver a nod and a thumbs-up before pulling ahead of the vehicle and turning on his light.

After a moment's hesitation, Lu seemed to understand. The two rapidly threaded their way through the late evening traffic toward Marquam Hill and the Dental School.

FIFTY-SIX

While the rest kitted up on the fifth floor, Jimmy Burke quietly waited by the eighth floor access to the Dental School roof for the appearance of the Asian martial arts group. Burke wore body armor over his street clothes, cradled a silenced AK-47 in his workingman's hands, and took some comfort in the brace of grenades coupled to his web belt. He would've preferred to be in the fur, but the fur held some disadvantages inside buildings, so here he was, itching for action, and little chance for it.

He'd heard creakings from the narrow stairwell which led to the roof, so the sudden opening of the stairwell door and the peering face of the first young, black-clad Asian fellow didn't alarm him. He smiled reassuringly. "Well, you're here, then."

"Yes," the shorter man acknowledged. Then they all silently filed out into the corridor. Two of them were surprisingly large, stocky, muscular.

"I count twelve," Jimmy said. "Is that correct?"

"No, thirteen," the man replied, turning and surveying the group. He frowned, finding only the twelve. "I'll go back up and check."

Shaking his head, Burke motioned him aside with the barrel of the AK. "No, let me. In case something's gone amiss."

Jimmy took the steps slowly, one at a time, his rifle up and ready. He came out inside a small roofed enclosure housing the elevators' external mechanisms. A heavy metal door onto the roof stood in front of him. He opened it carefully, noted that its lock had been punched, and stepped out into the night air.

He was surrounded by tied-down hang gliders. There was no movement, no sign of anyone on the moonlit tar. Without moving his feet, he surveyed the metal shutters covering the external windows of the

Dean's penthouse office, situated to his left. Still no one. Taking a deep breath, he moved cautiously to his right around the outside of the elevator building, nearly stumbling over a prone body rolled against the wall. He'd found the missing ninja. Without looking down, Jimmy prodded the man, was rewarded with muffled grunts. He crouched beside the dark form, and his searching left hand found duct tape, confirming his first suspicions. Someone else was up here.

Abandoning the ninja for the moment, Jimmy backed away from the door and the bound man, retreating across the roof to gain full visibility of most of it while still being able to see the roof access. He knew what had happened was only a warning. No one would deliberately give themselves away for any other reason. The roof was interdicted, no longer safe.

He examined the entire area without finding anyone, and briefly entertained the idea that the Asians had bound one of their own for some reason. Yet they were clearly distressed when the man was missed, so he ruled that out, plus there were thirteen hang gliders. No one had flown away with one. He untaped the grunting ninja and roughly hustled the grateful man -- who'd not seen his assailant -- off the roof to rejoin his fellows. Jimmy couldn't help looking over his shoulder all the way down the stairs, and decided he would stand vigil at their base until Cathal had popped the Dean's safe.

* * * * *

"They're up there now," Boothe Deakins told those assembled in the post grad clinic. "We want them to get *in* the safe, actually *have* the document in their hot little hands, to establish intent. We've got cams in the Dean's office, the back stairwell, and one on each floor, just inside the entry off the main stairs." She grinned. "The moment they have the manuscript

273

and act like they're ready to leave, we need to be in place."

Dean Dorfman raised his hand. "What about Doctor Lu's people? Many of them graduated from the school."

"Well, obviously we don't want to injure them, unless they resist." She glanced over at Carly Meadows and the other Danites, who looked ready for a fight. "But it's an option. Subduing or discouraging them is desirable. We should *not* fire on them with live ordnance. They're the innocents in all this."

* * * * *

Connor Flannery and his cousin Tommy -- the latter in the fur -- crept down the rear stairwell to the first floor, and found Cathal Ramsey had been right, the stairs stopped there. Two additional levels lay beneath them, and any security monitoring station might well be on one of those. Still, the first floor, with its view through the main doors and with windows full length of the building would be a logical choice.

They walked uneasily down the aisle through the semi-darkness of the Oral Surgery department, their noses wrinkled at the disinfectant odor. When they were twenty feet from the double doors at the hall's end, the doors swung open, and three figures in black full riot gear stepped through. The two on the outside carried combat shotguns pointed at Connor and Tommy.

"Drop down or die," the shorter one in the middle said. Connor had been in this situation before. He dropped to his knees, let the AK fall away, done. But Tommy sprang snarling at the trio, caught in his shifted mindset. "No-o-o!" Connor screamed, leaning forward, trying to stop his cousin.

Not quickly enough. Two blasts from the tallest of the trio lifted Tommy from mid-air and smashed him into the wall. He slid limply to the floor, leaving blood and brains smeared over the wall's white surface.

Connor stared open-mouthed and unbelieving at his cousin's twitching corpse, until Tommy's killer prodded the side of his head with the barrel of the shotgun. Connor turned his head and looked into brown eyes set in features filled with such pain he nearly winced away.

"As God is my witness, I cannot tell you how much I regret doing that," said the man, his voice shaking. "Or how much I want to kill *you* this very instant."

The other shotgun-wielder, not quite as tall and darker, put a calming hand on his comrade's shoulder. "C'mon, Hyrum. Let the cops have 'im. We need to get up to the fifth floor, cover that door."

"Deakins is on her way," the third man said. He wore a helmet headset, its microphone in front of his mouth.

The double doors behind the three swung wide again, and a blonde woman in riot gear strode into the hallway, accompanied by a similarly-dressed man. Cuffs dangled from one of her hands.

"Thanks, gentlemen," she said, stepping around Conner and snapping cuffs on his unresisting wrists.

Connor looked up, meeting her grey gaze. "You're the copper."

She nodded, her grin not quite as triumphant as he expected. "Right. And you're the prisoner."

"I've killed no one," Conner told her, his head drooping. He could smell his cousin's loosened sphincters.

The blonde grabbed his chin with her right hand, forced him to look at her. "I have personally investigated every messy homicide you assholes have dropped in our path, and I'm no nearer now to having a decent motive than I did at the first one. You got anything to say before we read you your rights and toss you in the wagon?"

Connor forced a smile. "Not without a lawyer."

"Fine," she replied. The two cops dragged him to his feet. "Good hunting, guys," she called over her shoulder to the departing trio as her partner began reciting the Miranda.

* * * * *

It had taken less than three minutes for Cathal Ramsey to open the door at the bottom of the short stairs leading up to the Dean's office. Leaving Jimmy Burke to guard the roof entrance, the six remaining Irish and all thirteen ninjas trooped up into the spacious penthouse office.

Lorcan Cole whistled as he surveyed the interior of the room. "Bloody Hugh Hefner!"

"A loftier level of taste, I think," Ramsey said. "No nudes whatsoever. That's a very high-end entertainment center. The newest In Focus projector." He pointed to a brass and chrome door next to a well-supplied wet bar on the far wall. "And there's the safe. I'll get right to it." He picked up his bag of tools and instruments and started toward the safe. More O'Rourke followed.

Cole watched the pair narrowly. *Nothing good going there, but something*, he thought. *Might want to deal with that later.* He turned to the assembled Asians. "You lads go down the back stairwell. Two of you each on the seventh, sixth, fourth, third, and second floors. The other three on the first floor with the Flannerys." The thirteen nodded as one, and trotted obediently from the room. Cole turned to the three unassigned Irish. "You lot on the fifth floor. One on each stairwell entrance. One in the hallway to the Medical School. We'll go out the same way we come in."

276

When they'd left, he watched as Ramsey methodically attached sensors to the front of the big safe, handing the readout instruments to O'Rourke. Nothing to do but wait, now, Cole realized, walking around the Dean's desk and taking a seat in the big leather chair.

Focking palatial, he thought, leaning back, clasping his hands behind his head and resting his feet on the polished oak surface.

* * * * *

Every sense on high alert, the six Danite women swiftly climbed the main stairs to their assigned floors. Each of them wore knives strapped to their ribcages and Glock 19's holstered on their waists.

"There's two of them down," Carly Meadows said quietly as they paused on the fourth floor landing. "Twenty left."

The Coolidge twins grinned, eager as always. "We get the seventh Floor?"

Carly nodded. "Jeannie and I'll have the sixth. Marianne and Norah on the fourth. Levi and the shotgunners on five. Stay on this side of the door on each floor. Use your periscopes to see through the little windows. Any sign of automatic weapons or explosives, don't go in."

"Unless we have to," Norah Young replied, and Marianne Packer nodded grim agreement.

"Right," Carly agreed. "Take care. See 'ya."

The twins started up the stairs to the upper floors, the soles of their rockclimbers silent on the smooth concrete steps. Carly and Jeannie kept right behind, ready to fulfill a lifetime of training.

* * * * *

277

On the back stairwell, on the fourth floor landing, Levi Klaghorn lifted his right hand and stopped. "Somebody coming down," he told Janos and Gregorson, then opened the door behind them and stepped into the darkened hallway beyond. He motioned to a door to their left. "Closet," he said. The three men stepped inside and closed the door. They listened to the herd of ninja dentists scrambling down the stairs, heard at least two remain on their level.

* * * * *

Don Lawrence pulled up to the curb in front of the Dental School, pushed down his sidestand with one foot, dismounted and walked back to Doctor Lu's Mercedes, which had stopped behind the BMW.

Lu had lowered the driver's side window. "Looks quiet enough," the motorcycle officer observed to the compact Asian. Lu had a semi-wild look in his eyes. "Is there a good reason to expect otherwise?" Lawrence asked, wondering what the deal was.

"We need to get into the school," Lu replied calmly. He cranked the steering wheel to his right.

Lawrence smiled. "You got a key?"

"I'm sitting in it," the head of Considerate Care said, licking his lips speculatively as he popped his gas pedal and wrenched the steering wheel a few more degrees to the right. The big automobile began to climb the curb.

"Hey, no!" Lawrence started to protest.

"Sorry," Lu answered. The window slid closed.

Lawrence pounded on the car's roof. "You can't *do* this!" His words were lost in diesel roar.

The Mercedes trundled over the low curb, then began to quickly pick up speed as the heavy car rocketed toward the building's front entrance.

Open-mouthed, Lawrence watched the Mercedes crash through the sets of double doors like shit through

278

a goose. Steel door frames pretzeled over its roof as the car disappeared into the building in a cloud of glass shards and diesel smoke.

Lawrence ran for his radio.

* * * * *

"Dear sweet baby Jesus!" Janiece Carlton exclaimed, as the Mercedes vanished from their view.

"Well, I won't have to tell the lieutenants," Robbie Munoz said. Fifty yards away, the motorcycle officer yelled into his radio, his left arm waving.

"Hope they record that call," Carlton said, grinning.

"We better get down there."

"Right."

The two officers pulled aside the camouflage tarps and scrambled downslope as fast as possible.

* * * * *

The Mercedes came to rest with its nose indenting the outer wall of the Records Department. A few patient charts fluttered over the partition and settled on the car's hood.

Benny Lu climbed out and discovered more guns than he'd seen outside of a war movie pointed his direction, some of them in the hands of Dental School faculty. The Dean himself stood twenty feet away, regarding Lu in total amazement.

Not about to be deterred, Lu raised his hands and said, "My people are in the building with a man named Lorcan Cole. They are innocent! He must be stopped."

A tall blonde woman dressed in some kind of S.W.A.T. clothing approached him, grinning. "We know, Doctor Lu. The problem is being dealt with as we speak. Our people will not fire on yours. Get some armor on, and we'll let you talk them out."

279

* * * * *

Donovan Tran and two other Considerate Care staffers had just passed the crumpled corpse of a large cat when they heard the roar of a heavy car smashing through the front of the building, tires screeching. They rounded the corner from Oral Surgery at a dead run and saw Doctor Lu with his hands in the air, surrounded by weaponry.

Without pausing to assess the situation, they sprinted full tilt at the nearest members of the group threatening Doctor Lu and launched their counterattack.

Tran leapt screaming from the floor in a perfect flat trajectory, his extended right foot centered on the slowly-turning blonde woman with an automatic rifle slung from her right shoulder. To his astonishment, she slipped aside, and he missed, barely brushing a shirt sleeve. He compensated, spun, landed crouched beside Doctor Lu, and stepped in front of the older man. "Do not harm him!" Tran scarcely noticed one of his companions rolling on the floor with the Chairman of the Anatomy Department while the other struggled in the clutches of Doctors Coogan and Jackson.

In the following two heartbeats of silence, Doctor Lu placed both hands on his employee's shoulders and said, "It is all right, Doctor Tran. I am fine. We must alert the rest of your compatriots. Cole lied, you see."

* * * * *

"There's two of 'em," Lorna Coolidge told her sister. "They're unarmed."

"Let's go."

"They're *big* guys."

"So? Let's grind some hind." Grinning, they opened the door.

The Ha brothers were halfway down the dimly-lit seventh floor hallway when the door at the main stairwell opened.

"Women," Justin grunted in surprise, seeing tall females dressed in martial arts garb.

"No worries, my brother," Dustin replied, flexing his thick shoulders. "We shall stomp them most severely."

"Indeed." Justin cracked his knuckles, eager to make up for his humiliation on the roof with the hang-glider. The two burly oral surgeons raised their arms to attack position, and advanced toward the women.

The first few seconds went well enough. Both women seemed inclined to evade, brushing off attempts at contact, doubtless fearful of their opponents' size and strength. Then Justin swung his right leg in a swift, powerful arc to end the duel, and found himself inexplicably slammed sideways into the hallway wall, his leg nearly wrenched from its socket.

As he rebounded from the white cinderblock, something struck his neck with horrendous force, driving him to his knees. A second blow followed. The world went dark.

When he recovered consciousness, Justin found himself shackled, with his hands cuffed behind his back, lying on the floor, his brother snoring beside him, similarly restricted. The two women had disappeared.

His head sagged to the floor. This was not good.

The ponderous door to the vault swung open easily on its tall hinges. Cathal Ramsey stepped aside, his features still professionally composed, and Lorcan Cole entered the vault. Uninterested in Cole, More O'Rourke watched Ramsey. She found his expression compelling. Shared heritage made most of their kind dark and rather brooding, but Cathal's thoughtful mind and considerate nature always showed on his face.

Others, like Lorcan Cole, were aggressive and inclined to cruel excess and thoughtless revenge. Liam Sullivan, dead or languishing in gaol, was an easy match for Cole on those traits, and the four who'd died out on the big motorway had been the same. All as Irish as the bogs and fens of their native land. The Fenian Men, the IRA, Sinn Fein, the Real IRA, regardless of their time in history, all were similar.

"And here 'tis," Cole said, picking up a small stainless steel box sitting on a shelf directly opposite the vault entry. He held up the box, clearly labeled 'Mormon Manuscript' in black lettering, and More had to laugh.

"Lorcan, that seems a bit obvious," she said.

"True enough." Grinning, he walked out of the vault, placed the box on the Dean's desk, removed a key taped to the lid and unlocked the box. The three of them peered inside at the plastic-wrapped parcel.

The ink on the top sheet had faded to a medium brown, but to More's eyes, it looked genuine. She glanced up at Cathal, who gave her a little smile and shook his head very slightly, once.

Cole shut the lid, relocked it, and dropped the key into a trouser pocket. He stepped away and brought a silenced pistol from underneath his right lapel, pointing it at them. "Into the vault, then, the both of you. I'm leaving here alone. I've seen you're not to be trusted."

"What!" Cathal exclaimed.

"Don't be a fool!" More added.

"Move." Cole pointed with the pistol, short, chopping motions.

As Cathal stepped into the vault, Cole pushed More away and shoved the big door shut behind Ramsey, spinning the locking shafts into place.

Then he shot More twice in her stomach.

As she folded to the floor in agony, she heard him speak as though from a great distance.

"Shift and heal if you can, my dear. Then perhaps you can claw through the door and save your man before he suffocates." He chuckled to himself as he walked away, carrying the box, leaving More crumpled and bleeding on the carpet.

* * * * *

Carly Meadows, Jeannie Simmons, and the Coolidge twins stood on the landing between the sixth and fifth floor and listened to the ongoing battle taking place on the fifth. The four had dealt with the ninjas on the upper floors, and had started down to aid their comrades on four.

Even through the heavy steel door of Five, the hissing rattle of silenced assault weapons was almost completely drowned out by the booming of the shotguns.

"I hope Levi's all right," Jeannie said, hugging herself nervously.

"I can hear his M4," Carly replied, smiling thinly. "It sounds different from the AKs."

As she finished speaking, the door to five opened enough to let a man wearing body armor over street clothes fall sideways through the opening.

Seconds later, the four Danites had his weapon and were covering him with their own. They looked down the hallway to see Klaghorn limping in their direction, followed by Gregorson and Janos. Two bodies lay midway down the corridor in pools of blood.

"How bad?" Carly asked Klaghorn as he got nearer.

"A big nick," he answered, grimacing. "I won't be sprinting for a while." He gestured back down the hall. "If two of you would see to those gentlemen, I'll bandage up and the three of us'll head for the upper levels."

"Sure," Carly said, nodding to Janos and Gregorson. The latter, she noticed, had recognized her. He was blushing.

* * * * *

"I don't know if you heard the noise or not," Jimmy Burke said, "but all hell's broken loose down below. I heard shotguns."

"Then we'll go up," Cole replied, the Mormon document box tucked securely under his arm.

"Remember, there's someone on the roof."

"Down the back stairs, then."

"That might be dicey."

"Let's try. You've got the grenades."

The two exited the eighth floor down the back stairwell, moving stealthily. As Burke stepped around the railing between the sixth and fifth floors, someone fired a shotgun three times from the open door on five, nearly cutting the man in half.

As Burke's body fell backward, Cole grabbed the grenades from his belt. He pulled the pin on one and lobbed it down toward the shotgun-wielder, then ducked.

When the grenade had detonated and the ricochets stopped, Cole peeked over the concrete rail. The door to five was closed. He sprinted down the stairs.

When he hit the fourth floor, Cole threw his remaining grenade up the stairwell, waited for the explosion, then continued racing toward the first floor and the outside door adjacent to the parking structure.

Reaching the outside door, he paused to let his breathing return to normal. There were no sounds of pursuit. He opened the door and strolled calmly down the walkway, took the two steps up to the deserted lot.

Thirty feet across the lot, nearly to the lower level of the parking structure, Cole heard the sound of heavy rolling footfalls close behind him on the asphalt. He turned, instantly drew his pistol again, and saw it swatted away by a gigantic paw with four-inch claws.

The creature loomed over him on its hind legs, tall and dark and immensely broad. He saw the opposite paw coming, could not avoid it. It struck the left side of his head, clubbing him into the ground and unconsciousness.

* * * * *

The door to the Dean's hidden private elevator hissed open. Surrounded by Claire's family, all in the fur, Paul entered the Dean's office. While Boothe had assured them the office appeared deserted on the cam, Paul kept the Pancor Jackhammer pointed into the room.

"I smell blood," Magnus Phelan said from behind Paul.

"Nobody here, though," Paul replied.

"The safe's open," Claire said, and Riona went to the vault and examined it, sniffing audibly.

"Two of our kind were in here," she said. "One was Cole. A third left blood on the carpet."

"Let me check the stairs down to the eighth floor," Claire's uncle suggested.

"No need," said a voice from the doorway. Mai Killian stepped into the room. "I watched from the

285

roof. Cole got all the way to the ground level in the melee, but was, shall we say, *accosted*. And everything else is mopped up."

* * * * *

More O'Rourke gathered herself and sprang to the hillside off the end of the roof over the first floor clinics. She landed beside Ramsey, straightened, and began brushing off her clothes. "I'm a mess."

"Well, since you watched me open the safe closely enough to remember the combination, I'll not complain." He indicated the forest. "Best we be off now."

"Indeed." The two trotted away upslope, to freedom.

FIFTY-SEVEN

Lorcan Cole came back to himself and discovered he was strapped into a dental chair. He fought against the restraints on his waist, arms, and legs, to no avail. It only made his head ache even more. He looked around the brightly-lit room, saw the Phelans watching avidly along with several others he didn't recognize.

A blonde woman in black stepped to his side, smiled down at him. "Hello, Mister Cole."

"You're the bitch cop."

"Yes, indeedy," she acknowledged. "And this is Doctor Kent Dorfman, Dean of the school. The Doctor is going to give you some options."

Cole looked to his right, saw a smiling, stocky man holding a dental drill.

"Have you ever seen the movie 'Marathon Man,' Mister Cole?"

"Fock you. I know my rights."

The man's smile turned cold. "I'm sure you do. In the movie, the tooth used to torture Dustin Hoffman was tooth number eight." The thing in his hand whined ominously, and the Dean regarded it fondly. "The evildoers did not have the benefit of *this*, however."

He held the instrument in front of Cole's face. "This is an Encore Air Orbit handpiece, Mister Cole. Manufactured in the late Sixties, practically an antique now, but it is the most powerful handpiece ever built. Four hundred thousand revolutions per minute under full power. It goes through tooth structure like a hot knife through butter." In his hand, as it revved, the thing seemed to buck. It howled like a banshee, and the Dean looked inordinately pleased.

Cole pushed his head back against the headrest. "Get it away!"

Instead, the Dean brought it closer. He had to raise his voice to be heard over the instrument's scream. "You have only to confess, Mister Cole." Then he shrugged. "But, then again, perhaps you'll be lucky, and pass out from the pain."

The handpiece was nearly in Cole's mouth now. The Dean's smile widened as he leaned over the bound man.

"Do you feel *lucky*, Mister Cole?"

Terrified, Cole tried to pull away from the howling thing, and failed again. His resistance crumbled. "I'll talk," he gasped.

EPILOGUE:

The eastern sky was beginning to lighten as Paul and Claire arrived back at Claire's condo. Exhausted, they shucked their soiled clothing and showered together.

Seated on her bed, Paul watched Claire blow-dry her hair. "There's just one thing I don't understand," he said, as she turned off the dryer and laid it on the counter.

She came and sat beside him, took his hands in hers. "What's that, lover?"

"When we got back to your uncle's, and Professor Haggen climbed out of the car, his sweat pants were on backward. The waist cord hung down over his butt. I know it wasn't that way when we dropped him off at the restaurant." He shook his head. "I don't get it. What the hell was he *doing* out there?"

Claire laughed, shoving him onto his back and kissing him soundly. "Better not to ask, I think."

* * * * *

The sounds of hospital breakfast carts woke April Kwong just as the Sunday morning world outside her windows began to brighten. Still a little disconnected from seventy-two hours of sedatives, she turned her head toward the door.

"Hello," Riona said nervously from her seat beside the bed, regarding April with anxious eyes.

April smiled, reached out and took Riona's right hand in her left. "Thanks for savin' my life."

Riona shook her head, anguish on her dark features. "*I* placed you in harm's way. I *had* to rescue you, and you and the scissors made that possible."

"So we're even."

"Never completely, I'm afraid."

289

"Hey, I'm only a little sore now, and they said the staples on my right shoulder'll be off soon."

A shudder seemed to engulf Riona's slim body. "Please do not be brave on my account. You suffered terribly."

"Did you get Cole?"

"Not personally, but he is in custody, along with several of his surviving followers." Riona's voice began to break slightly with her last words. Tears welled in her eyes. "Can you forgive me?"

Choking back a sob, heedless of her own tears, April reached for her friend. "Easily," she said. "So easily."

* * * * *

A pair of jail guards led Lorcan Cole into a visitor's room, his ankles shackled but his hands free. When he saw who sat on the other side of the clear plastic partition, Cole tried to retreat from the room, but the guards grasped his upper arms and propelled him forward.

Immaculately groomed and wearing a suit, Magnus Phelan sat watching, his smooth features composed. When the guards had sat Cole down and retreated to stand near the door, he smiled and spoke. "They presume I am some sort of lawyer."

"You're old. You'll not be there when I'm free," Cole snarled. He understood the purpose of this visit, the calling-out, the establishment of eventual revenge. He had not expected the Phelans to defer to the police. Once they did, he *had* expected this visit, just not so soon.

The old man's smile thinned. "Do not be too certain, Mister Cole. And, if not myself, Riona will look after you when the time comes, I assure you. Twenty years, forty years, no matter. It will still happen. You will be free. We will be ready."

290

"I have friends."

"Fewer than formerly. Many of your acolytes died in your recent misadventure. Those who remain may not have cause to love you. Word spreads, you realize." He leaned forward. "Riona is *quite* skilled," he said softly, his dark gaze kindling. "As you know, we *all* understand *fast*. Riona understands *slow*."

* * * * *

The uproar in the Day Room brought Karl Elch out of his office more from curiosity than anything else. Whistling and cat-calling didn't indicate any sort of altercation, and the Day Room wasn't the quietest of places most times. At least, he reflected, Chief Albright was out for the morning. Noise always made the Old Man jumpy. It was not PC.

What he saw in the middle of the room made him doubly glad the chief was gone.

Detective Lieutenant Boothe Deakins stood quietly, her long arms at her sides, wearing what Elch thought was called a 'belly-shirt' and low-rider jeans, her taut midriff bare.

Her partner and everyone else in the room began to clap.

Elch didn't want to know the cause of whatever this was. He turned without saying a word, went back to his office, and closed the door.

He had noticed, however, that her belly-button was an 'inny.'

* * * * *

Benny Lu had been in the Salt Lake City airport a number of times, but had never realized how large it was. After a considerable walk, he, Magnus Phelan, and Hyrum Gregorson were met just past the Security Check by four clean-cut young gentlemen whose dark clothing and polite demeanor plainly bespoke officialdom.

Brief introductions and briefer smiles followed, and the trio were led swiftly out to a black Buick waiting by the Arrivals level. Three more similar-looking men stood by the vehicle and an identical one parked behind it, their expressions brightening as they caught sight of the metal briefcase carried by Doctor Gregorson. Their fame, or rather that of what they carried, had preceded them, Lu decided.

"Where are we going?" he asked Magnus Phelan.

"I believe we have a date with destiny, Doctor," the older man replied, chuckling as they were ushered into one of the big cars. "Isn't that correct, Doctor Gregorson?"

Gregorson had mostly lost the haunted look he'd worn immediately following the battle in the Dental School. A slow smile crossed his plain features. "Yes," he said quietly. "I believe we do."

* * * * *

A week later, Carly Meadows and Boothe Deakins sat quietly on a shaded bench in the Pioneer Cemetery in Manti, Utah. The Manti Temple, dedicated by Brigham Young in 1888, sat on a rise in the distance, bathed in afternoon sunlight.

"This was...interesting," Boothe said. She'd taken some time off after the case was closed, and had joined Carly and the Coolidge twins for a trip to Manti. They'd spent the morning at the Family History Center, the Coolidges pointing out pictures and records of Boothe's ancestors. Used to her family being free-thinking and free-wheeling pot growers, Boothe had been amazed to find staid, proper Mormons in her background.

292

"Wasn't it?" Carly replied, laughing. "And you want to look sharp now."

Boothe glanced up from her study of the closely-mown grass in front of the bench. A tall, dark woman wearing running shoes, jeans, and a white T-shirt walked down the gravel path toward them, her hands in her pockets, whistling.

She stopped in front of Carly. "It went well, didn't it?" Her eyes were an impossible leaf-green.

Carly laughed. "You *could* have let us know you were there, Eldest."

"I thought you'd do better without me hovering."

"You might have been right."

The dark woman held out her right hand to Deakins. "I trained Miz Meadows as a younger warrior, Lieutenant. My name is Mai Killian."

* * * * *

The Oregon Zoo had requested dental personnel for 'Teeth and Claws Week,' and Paul, Claire, and Riona Phelan had volunteered to meet the public and answer questions about animal dentition. Paul had convinced Zoo management that he was a skilled ventriloquist, so the two women were in their shifted forms, chatting with zoo-goers, mainly children with their parents. This was their third day at the Zoo, and Paul stayed close to preserve the illusion, but was still amazed that kids felt almost no hesitation in petting the two cats, or even tentatively touching long fangs.

After an hour or so, the crowds thinned slightly, and Paul noticed four middle-aged men in aloha shirts, baseball caps, and shorts standing near a refreshment stand. He cautioned Claire and Riona to use their best judgment and not frighten anyone, then strolled over to the quartet.

"Is this an official visit, Sir?" he asked the Dean, who stood closest, holding a well-licked vanilla ice cream cone.

"Not exactly."

"Did you come to volunteer?"

"No, Doctors Lu, Janos, and Gregorson suggested we visit and see how well you and Doctor McManus represented the profession."

Paul shook hands all around. "And so far..?"

"Everything seems fine. I must say that I knew some of our graduates were quite wild, but not to this extent."

Paul shrugged. "It was news to me, too."

"Also, I'd like to invite you and your intended to the ground-breaking for the new Dental School next Wednesday."

"Really? Down by Johns Landing? Thanks."

"Governor Stratton will be there, doing the honors. And Senators Smith and Blutarski."

"We'll be glad to," Paul said. "Provided, of course, that I live until then."

Dorfman looked puzzled. "Why is that?"

Paul lowered his voice. "*The Oregonian* was here on the first day we were. Some local stringers must have put the word out about Claire and Riona. I haven't told them yet..."

The four dentists clustered closer around him, trying to hear better. "Yes..?" they asked in near-unison.

Paul glanced over at Claire with affection, and smiled. "Both Colbert *and* Jimmy Fallon called."

The Dean put his arm around Paul's shoulders, and smiled paternally. "My advice, young man, is to hold out for Jimmy Kimmel."

ACKNOWLEDGEMENTS:

WORDS: John H. Quiner, Sr. Mary Thaddeus SJM, Michael Contris, Steve Perry, Keith Tittle, and the Lucky Lab Rats Writers' Group.

FAITHFUL READER: Sandra Hazard

PROFESSIONAL HELP AT THE ORAL LEVEL: Richard M. Adams, Erwin T. Bender, Robert Bruckner, John L Deveny, Henry Cline Fixott, Arthur E. Fry, John Paul Jerabak, Robert L. Lang, Arnol R. Neely, Clarence O. Pruitt, Barnadette A. Skully, Evelyn M. Strange, Louis G. Terkla, and William B. Wescott.

SPECIAL CREDIT: Dean Jack Clinton, who made the final shoot-out possible.

MORE THAN SPECIAL CREDIT: David Keller DMD, who did the final check on the Mormon elements. I passed.

DESPOILERS OF THE PLANET: Don Christie, John George, Jack 'Spider' Hoey, 'Dirty Dave' Longtin, Tom Schmid, and Tom Zinser.

For those of you who enjoyed the famous University of Oregon documentary, 'Animal House,' the Dental School Dean is Kent Dorfman, 'Flounder' in the film, Eric 'Otter' Stratton is the Governor of Oregon, and 'Bluto' Blutarski is a Senator. It only seemed right.

As always, all errors and omissions are totally the responsibility of the aged author. This book is a work of mostly fiction, and any resemblance to anyone living, dead, half-dead, or distressingly amoral is probably not intentional, except when it is. And to Al

Chambers, one of the nicest guys in my graduating class, I apologize for killing you, Al. Honest.